The

CHRISTMAS
DRESS

CHRISTMAS
DRESS

A Novel

COURTNEY
COLE

WILLIAM MORROW
An Imprint of HarperCollinsPublishers

THE CHRISTMAS DRESS. Copyright © 2021 by Courtney Cole. All rights reserved. Printed in the United States of America. No part of this book may be used or reproduced in any manner whatsoever without written permission except in the case of brief quotations embodied in critical articles and reviews. For information, address HarperCollins Publishers, 195 Broadway, New York, NY 10007.

HarperCollins books may be purchased for educational, business, or sales promotional use. For information, please email the Special Markets Department at SPsales@harpercollins.com.

FIRST EDITION

Designed by Diahann Sturge
Falling snow © Ravindra37/Shutterstock
Dress with mannequin © debra hughes/Shutterstock
Window frame © Sakarin Sawasdinaka/Shutterstock
Christmas garland © Kostenyukova Nataliya/Shutterstock

Library of Congress Cataloging-in-Publication Data has been applied for.

ISBN 978-0-06-309985-2

21 22 23 24 25   LSC   10 9 8 7 6 5 4 3 2 1

To my editor, Tessa.
I'm gonna make you love Christmas.

The
CHRISTMAS
DRESS

CHAPTER ONE

*Y*ou can't leave me," my best friend whispers into the phone, her voice urgent and filled with abject terror. In the background, I hear Lillianna Cox, the world's worst boss, having one of her legendary temper tantrums.

"Yikes. That's at least one good thing about this whole situation. I'll never have to hear *that* again."

It's not the answer Cassie wants to hear.

"Meghan Ann Julliard. Get right back onto that plane and fly back to New York. I can't do this alone. I heard she's making us work late on Christmas Eve, and anyone who doesn't show up to her party on New Year's is getting written up. Then—"

She cuts off, and the phone goes dead. I can only imagine that Lillianna caught her on the phone. Personal calls are prohibited at Stitch, and since it's the top fashion magazine at the moment, everyone will put up with any rule and the world's worst boss to work there. I personally tried for four years to get on staff . . . and a scant six months later, here I am. *Leaving it behind.*

So, as I sit on the El and watch Chicago's skyscape blur past, I don't see the cheerful holiday lights, the festive trees, or the winter wonderland that others might.

I see my hopes and dreams swirling into a storm drain along with the muddy street slush.

I lean my forehead on the window, the chill leaching into my skin and my breath fogging up the glass.

I'd worked so hard to end up getting screamed at by Lillianna. Fetching her coffee, running her errands, staying up late at night writing fluffy fashion reviews, dealing with temperamental models . . . all menial things with the ultimate goal of making connections so that I can start my own fashion house someday.

It took an instant, *a split second*, for my dad's heart to stop beating and my whole world to change. I miss him. And I miss my life in New York. I miss having my own dreams. Even the bright red holiday coffee cup in my hand doesn't lift my spirits.

The train lurches to a stop, and I yank the handle of my suitcase up. Sadly, as I do, I also smash the jaunty red cup into my chest, where the lid comes off and coffee spills like a giant brown bloodstain all over my favorite winter-white coat.

You've got to be kidding me.

I have no time to mourn or the doors will close, so I tumble out onto the street, my oversize bag in tow.

Standing at the corner of Park and Westwood, I assess the damage and take a deep breath.

My coat is probably ruined.

My life is probably ruined.

Am I missing anything?

I step on the curb and notice my white wedge boot, spattered with mud.

My boots are ruined, too.

Perfect.

I square my shoulders and stand on the sidewalk, the cold wind blowing my hair, and stare up at the faded sign on the building in front of me, the building my father poured his heart and soul into for over forty years.

PARKVIEW WEST.

I haven't been here in years. It holds so many sad memories for my family, memories I don't like to think of. Because of that, my dad had visited me in NYC twice a year for the past four years. He hadn't made me come here. He loved me *that* much.

With a sigh, I lug my suitcase through the heavy double doors.

The lobby is just as I remember it. Faded, like the rest of this place. Faded beige furniture, faded fake flowers, and even the Christmas tree in the corner has a few lights out. The lobby's ceiling is domed and grand, but this building, while a remnant of Chicago's glory days, is like a beautiful woman fading with age.

It's apropos considering most of the tenants who live here. I inwardly cringe. Although it's true, and most of the tenants *are* elderly, that was a mean thing to think.

I set my bag down and hear the crackling sound of a record playing. Bing Crosby.

"Hello?" a thin voice calls from the back. "I'll be right out. I just need to reach this . . . Oh, no."

There's a staggeringly loud crash, and I rush around the counter.

An elderly lady with purple hair (bright purple, not geriatric purple) is sprawled on top of smashed boxes, rubbing her hip.

"That's gonna leave a mark," she mutters. Then she looks up at me with cloudy yet stern eyes. "You shouldn't be back here. It's against the rules."

I hold out my hand and help her up. "It's okay. I won't tell the boss."

"Well, you can't. He died last month. I'm afraid I'm all you've got. Can I help you?"

Her red glasses are askew, and it takes all I've got to not reach over and straighten them for her.

"Are you sure you're okay?" I ask her, my hand still on her elbow.

"I'm fine." She lifts her chin. "I'm only helping out until the new owner gets here. She was supposed to be here last week, but something more important came up, I guess." She eyes me. "You here to visit someone? You've got to be on the list, or I can't let you in."

Her purple curls are stiff from hair spray.

I pause because I've just been insulted by someone wearing red-and-purple pants.

"I'm Meghan Julliard. The new owner." I hold out my hand. "And you must be . . ."

"Sylvie Reinhart," she prompts sternly. She doesn't even react to the fact that she had just insulted me. "I've been keeping this place running while you took your sweet time getting here."

She stares down her nose at me, even though she's four ten, at best. Her shirt reads I'M NOT SHORT, I'M JUST A TALL ELF.

"What took you so long? We needed you."

I stammer. "I've had things to wrap up. A person can't just drop everything and move. I had to find someone to sublet my lease, I had to turn in notice at my job, I had to . . . Oh my gosh. Why am I apologizing? I'm here now."

"But you don't want to be," Sylvie says knowingly, crossing her small arms across her chest.

"Does that matter?"

"Not to me," she decides. "It's all yours now. Your father's lifework." She digs in her pocket and hands me a key. "This unlocks the middle desk drawer. The passwords to everything are written on a list in there."

She starts to walk out.

"Sylvie?" I call.

She pauses, but doesn't turn around. "No. I'm not available to train you. You should've been here last week. I've got Christmas shopping to do now."

"You've got toilet paper on your shoe," I tell her weakly.

She glances down to see the long stream of paper trailing behind her, then clears her throat as she dislodges it. She walks indignantly away, leaving it on the floor.

I take a deep breath and look at the back office.

It has my father written all over it.

The clock hanging over the door is ten minutes behind. The old office chair at the desk has rips in the brown leather. The files are bulging and unorganized, stuffed into an open desk drawer, and there are overflowing boxes on shelves over my head. If I close my eyes, I can almost see him hunched at the desk, haphazardly balancing the stacks of paperwork and his ever-present cup of black coffee.

"I miss you, Dad," I whisper, my shoulders sagging. I sit at the desk, and the old chair groans, which is insulting, considering I can still shop in the juniors section. I reach over and lift the arm of the record player off the old vinyl, and when Bing stops singing, I lower my head to the desk.

This is how I stay for a few minutes, until someone clears his throat in the doorway.

I lift my head and find a well-dressed older gentleman watching me. He's waiting patiently, and lord knows how long he's been standing there. He's even wearing a bow tie and *is that a pocket watch?*

"Can I help you?" I ask, getting to my feet.

"You must be Meg," he says warmly, sticking out his hand.

"I am."

"I'm Tom Rutherford from 104. Your dad talked about you constantly, young lady. I feel as if I already know you."

I smile. "I hope he didn't bore you too much."

He shakes his head. "Of course not. He kept me entertained with your escapades in New York City. Did you ever find the snow boot you lost on the subway?"

I silently mourn that monogrammed boot for a second before I shake my head. It had been a Christmas edition last year, and I'll never be able to get a replacement.

"Sadly, no. But it served me right and taught me a lesson."

He waits.

"Never drink four Cosmopolitans after work with the girls."

Tom smiles. "Wise advice, Ms. Julliard."

"Please call me Meg," I tell him.

"Thank you, Meg," he answers. "I don't want to bombard you on your first day here, but I have an issue. My hot water still isn't working. Sylvie told me last week she'd called for repair, but, and I'm sure you'll discover this, Sylvie sometimes forgets, and I'm not sure if she ever called. Would you mind checking?"

"Of course!" I scramble for a notepad. "You're in 104?"

He nods. "It's at the back corner of the courtyard."

"Prime real estate," I remark as I write his name and condo number down. He grins.

"I was on a waiting list for two years for that one," he answers. "Mrs. Bertram lived a *long* time. May she rest in peace." He crosses himself.

"May she rest in peace," I echo, although I didn't know her. "How long has Sylvie had to fill in for me, Mr. Rutherford?"

"Tom, please," he says. I nod. "Did she tell you she was filling in? She was always trying to help your father, whether he asked for it or not. Between you and me, her 'help' usually causes more work in the long run, but she means well."

"So she helped my dad out when he was still alive?"

"Yes. If there's anything you need to know about anyone, you can ask Sylvie. She keeps her ear to the ground."

"She isn't my biggest fan right now," I admit to him. He smiles gently.

"Her bark is worse than her bite. She doesn't have any family, and your dad was all she had. She is very protective."

"He was my dad," I answer slowly. "There's no need to be protective with me."

"She's something else." Tom shrugs. "You'll see."

"Well, thank you," I tell him. "I appreciate the heads-up. And I'll get a plumber up to you ASAP."

"Thanks, Meg." He winks at me, but not in a creepy way. "It's nice to finally meet you."

"Likewise."

He backs out of my doorway, leaving a cloud of Old Spice behind, and I actually find the scent comforting. It, too, reminds me of my father.

My eyes tear up, even though I wasn't expecting to get emotional this early in the day. I haven't even been up to his ... er, *my* ... apartment yet.

"Oh, and, Meg?" Tom's voice calls from the lobby. I poke my head out. "The elevator is still broken. No one is in a wheelchair currently, but you never know when that might change. So it should be fixed, too."

Tom disappears down the ground-floor hall. Even though I haven't been here since I left for college when I was eighteen, I know from memory that this building has six floors. My apartment is on the top floor. With no elevator.

My sister and I used to run up and down these stairs just for fun, but that was back when we were ten and twelve. A lot has changed since then. For starters, I no longer exercise for fun.

I eye my large suitcase, then eye the stairs. They are original wood with a faded green runner, and they seem to go on and on and on.

This day just gets better and better.

I'M OUT OF breath when I reach Dad's condo.

I lean on my bag while I fumble with the keys, and finally, when the key turns in the lock, I fall through the door, literally tripping over my suitcase.

The stillness in the apartment hits me first.

It's the kind of quiet that you can *hear*.

I scan the room, which is exactly the way my dad left it on the day he died over a month ago.

A cup of coffee, half drunk, is on the end table. A newspaper is open there too. A dish towel is draped over the sink. Pictures of my sister and me from when we were young adorn the walls.

A photo of my mom is on the mantel. And his little Christmas decoration box, filled with handmade ornaments from my childhood, is open in the corner. That means he'd been planning on decorating right after Thanksgiving.

I swallow hard.

He must've been feeling lonely. I should've come home for Thanksgiving, but Lillianna bullied everyone into working, and I hadn't stood up to her. I hadn't known my dad was going to die, but it's still guilt I'm going to carry.

I followed his wishes in his will. I had him cremated and then interred with my mother in their grave, with no fuss and no funeral. I'd done it all from New York, because funerals are for the living, and I didn't want to see my father's urn lowered into the ground.

Now, however, I'm second-guessing that.

My dad was a man who deserved a funeral.

And everyone who knew him deserved to pay their respects and get some closure.

But I can't focus on the past. I'm here now.

Out of old habit, I head for my old bedroom, but once outside the door, I pause. I know what's inside. A shrine to my sister, and I can't face that today. So instead, I change it up.

I busy myself unpacking, clearing out a drawer in my father's bedroom, which is now mine. I carefully keep his things as they were. I don't know when I'll able to move them. Mentally, I make a note of the things I'll change when I can . . . the paint color, from blue to white. The curtains, from drapes to sheers. New throw rugs. New cushions.

But not today.

Today, I'll just spend this time accepting the fact that I'm here, and everyone in my family is dead, and I'm all alone.

And calling repairmen, of course.

I don't know a lot about condominiums, but surely having an inoperable elevator is breaking some sort of code. I search online for a repairman to call.

"The first I can get there is next week," the guy tells me.

I call another.

"My schedule is full. The holidays, ya know."

"But Christmas isn't for three weeks. Can't you work us in?"

"No, I'm sorry. It'll be after the first of the year."

I hear the same thing four more times.

With a sigh, I give up for now, before I stab myself with the nearest sharp object, deciding to shower and wash the airplane germs off instead. I turn on the water, grab some clean clothes, and look forward to letting my tense muscles relax in the steam.

Only . . . there's no steam.

I check the faucet, and yes, it's turned all the way to the left.

Still no steam.

The water is ice cold.

"This is not what I need today," I say with a groan.

I pull my fuzzy robe on and stomp down the six flights of

stairs, back to the office so I can look up Sylvie's phone number. She answers on the first ring.

"Sylvie, I'm sorry to bother you. I know you're Christmas shopping. But did you happen to call the plumber?"

"Of course, I did." There's a pause. "I think."

I take a breath. "Well, maybe I can call them and check. What company is it?"

"We don't use a company." She's impatient, and I can hear Christmas carols in the background. "We use a handyman. He does all the buildings on this block."

"Okay," I answer, as patiently as I can. "Do you know his name?"

"Of course I do," she snaps. "It's Logan Scott and his phone number is on the list of passwords in the drawer. As I told you."

She hangs up on me. I know for a fact that she didn't mention anyone's phone number being on the list, but I'm not going to bring that up. That is not the hill I want to die on today. Instead, I dig the list out of the drawer, and sure enough. The phone number is there.

I call it immediately.

It goes to voice mail, so I leave a detailed message. *Please help. We have no hot water, the elevator is broken, I'm not sure what else is wrong, everyone is busy since it's Christmas, and if Sylvie already called you, why hasn't this been fixed?*

Or something to that effect.

I also may have sounded impatient.

I get grumpy when I'm cold and haven't eaten, and also when I'm wearing a robe in public. Why hadn't I put clothes on to come down here? I'm the owner of this building now, I've got to act like it.

Suddenly, the weight of what I'm doing settles onto me, like an anchor at the bottom of the sea. I've got sixty tenants depending on me to keep this huge building running. *Me.* Someone who forgot to pay her water bill last month. This isn't going to end well.

There's no way I can do this. This is going to be a fiery train wreck. I don't know the first thing about running a building. *I'm going to fail.*

I shook my head. No. That was Drake's voice. Not mine. Failing was exactly what my ex-boyfriend expected. And the reason I'd broken up with him last week.

To be honest, I don't think I ever really loved Drake Dillard. Not in the *love* love sort of way that everyone else seems to have, and that was the ultimate problem.

I want a romance like my parents had, one that spanned decades, one where they believed in each other no matter what. They supported each other. Is that so much to ask?

Drake was wrong. I don't need him. I can do this. I have to. I just need to start asking myself, *What would my dad do?*

I eye the boxes lining the shelves above me. If I go through them, maybe I can find out. With a sigh, I put my phone back in my pocket and climb a ladder, pulling the lid off the closest box.

I'm not going to think about Drake or doubt myself another single minute today.

I've got other things to do.

UNFORTUNATELY, I'M DOING those things, standing on the third-highest step of the ladder, when the office door opens.

Also, unfortunately, the ladder is directly in front of the door, so it knocks over, and I fall flailing and very ungracefully into a pair of very strong arms.

Those arms are attached to a man with the bluest eyes I've ever seen.

"You must be Meg," he says gruffly, his voice a combination of smooth caramel and a smoky jazz bar, filtered through a perfect mouth, while he still holds me in his arms, tucked next to a warm, solid chest. "Do you realize you're not wearing clothes?"

He sets me on my feet, and I scramble to regain my wits, cinching the belt of my robe even more tightly closed.

"Yes, I'm aware. Are you a tenant?" I ask, not sure if I'm hoping he is, or isn't.

He laughs. "No. I'm a bit younger than your target demographic, I'm afraid. I'm Logan. Your handyman."

Only now do I notice the toolbelt on his slim hips. *Oh my gosh, Meghan, what is wrong with you?*

"Uh. Um. Hi! I'm sorry if I was . . . terse . . . on the phone. It's my first day, and it seems like everything is broken."

"Don't worry," he says soothingly. "It's not broken. You've got a boiler that's on its last legs, but your dad and I have managed to help it limp along for a couple years now. We can make it last a few months longer. And the elevator is probably just a blown breaker again."

"Again?" I'm weak in the knees now, although I don't know if it's this beautiful, capable man in front of me, or the news that everything isn't broken.

"Oh, yeah. It'll need to be replaced, too. But we're limping along."

"We seem to do a lot of limping," I point out. He smiles.

"Yeah. Your dad was very forgiving with some of your tenants' rent. Social Security isn't what it used to be, and some of them . . . Well, things are tight for them. He doesn't say anything when they pay late."

"That sounds like him," I say wryly. He smiles again.

"I've heard a lot about you," he tells me. "And from what I remember, I doubt you'll be okay with cold showers. Let me look at that first, then I'll take care of the elevator. I'll be back in a little bit."

He disappears from the office before I can ask what my dad has told him.

That guy is my handyman.

Those blue eyes, that smile, that left-cheek dimple.

Suddenly, Parkview West doesn't seem quite as bad as it did before.

CHAPTER TWO

*A*s I wait for Logan, I look down and remember that I look like a crazy person in my fuzzy pink robe and bare feet. Not to mention, I'm cold because this building is outrageously drafty.

I dart toward the stairs so I can throw something else on.

It's amazing to me how the third step on the staircase still creaks after all these years. Jo and I used to jump over it so we could sneak up on our dad when he was working late.

The painting of Dunnottar Castle in Scotland hangs just over the step, like it has for decades. Jo and I used to pretend we lived there, that these very steps led to the stone tower that overlooked the sea. Sometimes, we pretended this landing was the tower, and we were princesses stuck inside.

It wasn't until after Jo died that I stopped pretending, and climbing this staircase has never been the same since.

It's when I step onto the fourth-floor landing (the one with the painting of Edinburgh Castle, because my dad was obsessed with Scottish history) that I pause to catch my breath. As I do, a woman steps out from her condo.

She's tall and slender, with snow-white hair elegantly coiffed into a French roll. She's wearing a fig-colored pencil dress with pearl buttons fastened up the front, and a slim gold watch on one wrist. She smells like Chanel No. 5.

"You must be Ms. Julliard," she says softly, one perfectly manicured eyebrow lifted. I pull my robe closed again self-consciously.

"Yes, I am." I turn and offer my hand. She shakes it with just the right amount of firmness.

"I'm Ellie Wade. It's lovely to meet you. I do hope you'll like it here. Can I trouble you for just a moment? My hot water is out."

I let out a long sigh.

"It seems everyone's must be. I have the handyman here, and he's fixing it as we speak."

She smiles, and it lights up her face. For a moment, she looks twenty years younger.

"Lovely!" She's about to shut the door when she pauses. "Would you like a cup of tea, dear? I'd love to get to know you better."

There's an air of dignified loneliness about her, and I truly feel bad for declining.

"I wish I could, Ms. Wade—"

"Call me Ellie," she interrupts.

"Ellie," I amend. "But I need to throw some clothes on so I can follow up with the handyman. I'd love a rain check, though."

"Well, I wasn't going to say anything about your choice of attire, but you're right. Clothing might be best." She smiles. "And our dear, dear Mr. Scott. You'll like him. Everyone does. He does a lot of work for your father pro bono, you know."

I stare at her. "He does?"

She nods. "He's such a good boy."

"Apparently." Although that boy looks like he's thirty or so. "I'm going to go let him know that your hot water is affected as well. I'll follow up with you later, Ellie."

I make record time sprinting up the remaining stairs, pulling on a pair of jeans and a sweater, and then running back down. I jump over the creaky step for old times' sake.

I'm landing the dismount when Logan rounds the corner. His eyes widen. I bow dramatically.

"I'd give myself a nine out of ten," I announce.

His eyes crinkle at the corners as he grins.

"Eight and a half. You barely stuck that landing."

"Humph." I dramatically turn up my nose, and he laughs.

"Ellie Wade says her hot water is out, too. Will whatever you did fix the entire building?"

Logan nods. "For now. But you should know, what I was saying earlier is still true. There are a lot of things wearing out in this old building, and at some point in the not-too-distant future, they'll need to be fixed."

"That sounds expensive," I say. He nods.

"Very."

"Well, that's a problem for another day," I decide. "Is the elevator fixable?"

"Already done."

"It seems like this old building should be put out of its misery," I say offhandedly. Logan's head snaps up.

"Some of these tenants have lived here for a decade or more," he answers. "They have no family, and nowhere else to go except a nursing home or assisted living. Please don't do that."

I stare at him, at the worry creasing his brow. "You care about them," I observe.

"You will, too," he answers. "Once you get to know them."

"Everyone so far has been very welcoming."

"Your dad was very good to them," Logan tells me. "I hope you will be, too. This place is all they have."

"I hear you donate your time to the cause."

He smiles slightly. "I do. I charged Jerry—I mean, your dad—half price for repairs. And when his budget didn't allow that, I let it slide until he could pay me. It's the least I can do."

"You have to make a living, too," I point out. "Giving your services away for free doesn't seem very profitable. It's not very good business to get involved in your client's personal affairs."

He shrugs. "I live alone. I don't have many expenses. I'm fine. Besides, sometimes, when you care about your clients, you can't help but get involved."

He lives alone. Did he point that out on purpose?

"Well," he continues. "I should get going. Do you have my

cell number in case you need to reach me? You called my office number before."

"Sylvie probably has it."

"Oh, she does." He chuckles. "But good luck getting it. She protects that thing like a rooster guarding a henhouse. Here, let me add you."

I hand him my phone, and he plugs in his number. "It really was nice meeting you," he says as he hands it back.

"You, as well."

He opens the front doors, and snow blows in.

"Stay warm!" he calls as he walks away (and here's some real talk: he looks *really* good walking away).

I feel a bit flushed right this second, and I know it doesn't have a thing to do with the weather.

Today, I just need a hot shower now that the water heater is fixed.

I'm walking back up the stairs when my eye catches Ellie Wade's door on the fourth floor.

It has a festive wreath with red holly and a bow hanging on it, which doesn't reflect the quiet sadness I felt when I spoke with her. There's something that draws me toward it.

On a whim, I pause, catch my breath, and decide my shower can wait for a few more minutes. I knock lightly.

Ellie opens the door a scant moment later, a dark green dress in her hands.

"Ms. Julliard!" she exclaims, with a broad grin. "You came for your rain check! Come in, come in."

"Meg, please," I tell her. She swings the door open wide, and I enter the quiet apartment.

Unlike her front door, the apartment isn't decorated for the holidays, which surprises me. Instead, there are several organized stacks of various items, some on her sofa, and some on the coffee table.

"Please excuse the mess," she says, even though it's as neat as a pin. "I'm sorting through some of my things. Come in. I'll make you that tea. Here, have a seat."

Ellie discards the dress on the end of the sofa, and I sit next to it.

While she's gone, I gaze around.

Photos of her and a young woman hang on the walls and sit on the mantel. There's a striking resemblance between the woman and Ellie. They have the same strong nose, the same sparkling eyes.

"Your daughter?" I ask when she returns with a tea tray.

"Oh, yes. My Betsy. She lives in London now. She has a great big job that keeps her away from me. But I'm so very proud of her."

She is. It exudes from every pore.

Ellie pours me a cup of tea, and as I reach to take it, I knock the dress off the couch, and it pools onto the floor.

After I situate my tea on the end table, I bend to retrieve it and am instantly interested in the quality of the workmanship.

"This is an amazing piece!" I say as I examine it. The fabric is thick, yet stretchy, and I can imagine that it molds perfectly to a woman's figure. The forest green has a slight sheen from the embedded gold glitter, and it's clearly a high-end party dress. "It reminds me of something Grace Kelly or Jackie O would've worn." I hold it up to my body, and the soft, thick fabric calls to me, almost as though it wants me to put it on.

"Oh, yes," Ellie says, glancing at it. She takes a sip of tea. "It's beautiful, to be sure. Isn't it odd how the loveliest things can hold such beautiful and awful memories at the same time?"

I pause, the dress hanging in my fingers, and look at Ellie. She's staring at it absently, like she's no longer here.

"I'm sorry?" I don't know what else to say. I've never been good in awkward situations. Once, I laughed during a funeral. I can't explain it.

"I wore that on the best and worst day of my life," she says, blinking. "Life can be such a paradox, my dear. Seeing you hold it up like that . . . watching it move . . . it's almost like the first time I put it on myself. I was there for a moment, wrapped in my memories. I'm sorry. You can put it on the discard pile." She gestures to the pile in front of me, but I hesitate.

"It's so lovely, Ellie. Surely you could pass it to your daughter. They don't make clothing like this anymore. I should know—I work . . . er, *worked*, in fashion."

"Did you?" She's interested in that and takes another sip of tea.

"Yes. I've always wanted to work in the field. I got a degree in fashion design, and I was working as an entry-level assistant in

New York for a fashion magazine. It's been a dream to have my own line. I used to alter my sister's clothes for her, back when she was . . ."

My voice trails off, and Ellie watches me.

"Back when she was sick?" she asks gently. I'm surprised by the lump in my throat that still forms when I talk about Jo after all these years. "Your dad told me about her. She was such a beautiful girl."

"She was," I agree. "I altered her clothes back when she was sick. My parents couldn't afford to keep buying her new ones as she lost weight. The radiation made the weight just fall off her."

"You were so young to be sewing back then," Ellie says, and there is admiration in her voice. "I'm impressed."

I shrug. "It's natural to me, I guess. My mom used to say I was born making my own paper dolls so I could design their outfits." Ellie laughs, a light, tinkling sound.

"Why, then, are you here?" she asks. Her gaze is soft, but her question is direct. I can tell that she's truly interested. She's not just making small talk. She genuinely seems to care.

"I'm the only one left in my family," I finally say. "I had to come back and take over for my dad."

"He wouldn't want you giving up your dreams," she chides. "He was very proud of you."

"He's the one who left me this building," I answer. "So he must've wanted me to be here."

"You could always sell it," she suggests.

"I can't. Chicago real estate being what it is, I can't count on someone else to not simply knock it down and replace it with a high-rise or something. As Logan reminded me earlier, so many of you depend on this as your home."

"Well, I'm personally not depending on it," she answers, pouring more tea into my cup. "I'm moving to a retirement community at the end of the month."

I flinch. "Oh, no. Is it because of the elevator? Because I can promise you . . . I'll make sure it doesn't stay broken again."

She smiles, and there is sadness in her eyes.

"No, dear. It's not that. My daughter worries too much about me. This old building, while it is lovely, is a bit drafty, and it's hard to get to and from the street when I go out. A retirement village has scheduled outings, their own shuttle, and structured activities with people my age so I can make friends. Or so Betsy tells me."

She's tolerant of her daughter.

"So you're sorting through your things, to downsize for your move?" I guess.

"Yes. I've accumulated more than I thought over the years. I've lived here at Parkview West for ten years."

So she moved here when I was twenty. How had I never noticed her? *Because I wasn't paying attention. That's how.*

"Well, I'll be sad to see you go," I announce. "It would be nice to have a friend here."

She looks at me reassuringly. "You'll have friends, dear. More than you can count. Everyone here has been waiting for you."

"I hope they enjoy being underwhelmed," I answer wryly. She laughs.

"You're funny. I like that."

I smile with her. "I use humor to hide my awkward personality," I tell her. She laughs again.

"You're a delight."

I lay the dress back out on the arm of the sofa and marvel at the way the elegant boat neck lies just perfectly.

"You said you wore it on the best and worst moment of your life?" I glance back at her, and she looks away. "It seems that it's attached to strong memories for you."

"Have you ever loved someone so completely that you thought you couldn't *breathe* without them?" she asks.

I think of Drake, and I shake my head. "No."

"Never?"

"Not ever."

"Well, you've got plenty of time," she decides. "I wore this dress when I was about your age, actually."

"I'd love to hear about it," I say hopefully. The dress catches the light from the flames of the fireplace, and it shimmers. It sounds silly, but just looking at it makes me a little bit happier somehow, like the possibilities in life are endless. "I know we just met, but a dress like this has a story that needs to be told."

Ellie hesitates. "I'm not sure you want to hear it on the very first day we've met. It's not a fairy tale."

"Life isn't a fairy tale," I tell her simply. "But sometimes, it's still beautiful."

"That's very true, sweet girl," she answers. "Some parts are incredibly beautiful." She sighs. "I'll make you a deal. If you promise me you'll wear the dress this year, I'll tell you the story. She deserves another night out."

"I wish I could promise that," I tell her. "I really want to hear the story, but I don't have anywhere to go. I don't know anyone here, remember?"

She thinks on that. "Okay. Let's just say this . . . I'll tell you the story if you promise that you'll wear the dress if an occasion arises." She waits for my answer.

I feel safe enough in agreeing, because my social life in this city is nonexistent. And there's something telling me that I need to hear the story.

"If you're sure you want to hear it, I'd better make more tea."

She smiles, then disappears into the kitchen, and I check my phone.

Nothing from Drake, thank goodness.

Two missed calls and four texts from Cassie.

Come back.

Save me.

> I'm going to kill you.

> Answer your phone.

I shake my head and answer her.

> You're fine. You've got this. I'll call you tonight.

I set my phone down just as Ellie returns with a fresh pot. She pours us each a cup, then settles back into her seat.

"Frankie was the love of my life," she says softly, looking into the fire. The flames make her face look soft, her eyes like gold. "He took my breath away. That walk of his! So confident. His shoulders were so wide, just like his smile." She holds a hand to her heart, as if to still its fluttering. I marvel at that, at a love that can still rattle a heart decades later.

"You're lucky to have found that," I offer.

She shrugs, but nods. "I know. I met him on Navy Pier. Lord, he was handsome. Jet black hair, bright blue eyes. I wish you could see him." She pauses, and I know she's back on the day she met him.

"He had the broadest shoulders and slimmest hips you've ever seen. I was having a sack lunch, and I couldn't keep my eyes off him. He was juggling with his food—his orange, his wrapped sandwich, and his Yoo-hoo. He was showing off, trying to make everyone laugh. But then he missed his sandwich, and it ended up in the lake. You should've seen the look on his face!" She sighs, and I know she can see it clearly in her head. She presses one hand to her heart again and stares into the distance. "I ended up doing the gentlemanly thing and shared my sandwich with him. It took off from there."

"I love this story," I tell her. "It's swoonworthy, Ellie!"

Her cheeks flush. "He always made me swoon," she confirms. "He courted me for months. We couldn't stop thinking about each other. Even though we were as different as we could be. He was from a more sophisticated family, while my family was quiet and rather poor. Normally, two people such as us would never have wound up together. But it seemed like Fate had a hand in it, you know? We wanted to take full advantage."

"That sounds like Romeo and Juliet!" She shakes her head.

"They didn't have a very good ending, dear," she reminds me. "But then, neither did Frankie and I."

"What happened?" I ask, almost afraid. *Did he die?*

Clouds descend on Ellie's face, and I regret asking.

"I wish I could convey to you how perfect we were for each other," she says. "We were so different, yet we fit together so perfectly. He had a way about him that just made me want to open up and share everything. He made me laugh, he hid notes under my porch mat . . . It was an ideal life. Until it wasn't."

I suck in a breath, waiting to hear.

"Christmas Eve was coming up, and his mother, Francesca, was hosting a huge party—the first she'd hosted since Frankie's father died. She was a socialite, and little by little, even though

I came from a poor family, I think I finally won her over. At least, I *thought* so."

"Uh-oh," I murmur. Ellie nods.

"Never underestimate the mother of a son," she says. "That's a good lesson for you, dear."

"What happened?" I ask again.

"He was going to propose to me at that party," Ellie answers simply. "I knew it. He'd hinted, and I saved up all the money I'd earned to buy this dress at a secondhand shop. The first time I saw it, I knew it was for me. It just felt . . . *right*. I asked the shop owner to set it aside for me while I saved, and she was so kind. She hid it behind the counter for me. It took me two months to save enough. I didn't have enough money to buy jewelry to match, but I didn't care. I was so happy that I thought I'd burst."

She sips her tea, and her perfectly painted nails tremble ever so slightly.

"You don't have to tell me about it," I assure her. "Really. I don't want to make you upset."

"It feels nice telling you," she answers. "It makes it real. Sometimes, I fear it was all a dream. That he was too perfect to ever have existed at all."

"He was real," I tell her. "I can see how much you loved him." I reach over and grasp her hand. She smiles.

"I did. I really did. That's why losing him was so difficult." She takes a deep breath. "Francesca was a perfectionist in every way. She knew that Frankie was going to propose and since all her friends would be there, she wanted it to be perfect. She insisted that I wear her sapphire and diamond necklace and earring set. They'd been the last gift that her husband had given her before he died."

"This can't end well," I mutter, cringing.

"No, it did not," she confirms. "It started off perfectly, though. The party was beautiful . . . filled with candles and music and the most delicious food. Frankie and I danced and danced. I looked beautiful in this dress. I knew it, and Frankie couldn't keep his eyes off me." She preens for a second, and it's not hard to imagine how beautiful she'd been. She's still a handsome woman, even now.

"Frankie dropped to one knee a few minutes before midnight, right in the middle of the room. We'd been dancing so much our cheeks were flushed, and I thought I'd die from happiness. Everyone was watching, and he snapped open a box that held the most beautiful ruby ring, surrounded by sparkling diamonds. I was happier than I'd ever been in my young life. And then . . . I heard the most god-awful scream."

I almost want to plug my ears. I don't want to hear the next part. But at the same time, I'm glued to her every word.

"It was Francesca. One of her earrings had come out of my ear during the night. It was very valuable, keep in mind, both monetarily and emotionally, because her late husband had given them to her. She was inconsolable. We hunted high and low, but we couldn't find it. As the evening progressed without any sign of it, she became convinced that I'd stolen it. I was poor, remember. She said the most horrible things to me that night. Frankie couldn't talk her out of the notion, and in the end, she insisted that he end things with me because she could no longer trust me."

Ellie's face is twisted in pain now, and I squeeze her hand.

"Surely no one believed you would steal from them," I say gently. "Surely not Frankie."

"It didn't matter what he believed," she says limply. "Since his father was dead, he was the man of the house, something Francesca was very serious about. She insisted that they leave the party. I'll never forget the way he looked at me over his shoulder as they walked away. So sad, so helpless, and perhaps, just a little bit of uncertainty. I don't think he was entirely sure if I'd done it or not. It broke my heart."

"I can't even imagine," I breathe. "And everyone at the party was watching?"

Ellie nods sadly. "Oh, yes. I ran out, and I couldn't bear the humiliation. I packed a bag that very night and left for my aunt's in Indiana. I stayed with her for several years while I finished college."

"Did Frankie try to contact you?"

"He didn't know where I was, dear. I didn't tell a soul. I couldn't bear to hear him officially say it was over. So I ran."

"I don't blame you," I tell her firmly. "I would've done the same thing."

"But don't you see?" she asks, turning to look into my eyes. "I don't know what would've happened. I wasn't brave enough to find out. Instead, I eventually married someone else, someone who I loved, but it was never quite the same. We had a beautiful daughter, and our life was perfectly lovely. But I'll never know what could've been."

"That's . . . tragic," I finally say honestly.

"I know."

And now I know why this gentle woman permeates an air of sadness. Hers is a life unfinished. A life that *could've been*.

Lord, I never want that for myself.

"I'm sorry, Ellie." I don't know what else to say.

She shakes her head, as if to shake the melancholy away. "Don't be," she says. "I have a beautiful daughter, and my late husband was a good man."

"But he wasn't Frankie."

"No, he was not." She reaches for my empty cup. "I'm sorry if I've made you sad on your very first day here. Don't fret for me, sweet. I'm just fine."

She stands up. "Now, don't forget your end of the bargain. You must wear the dress if a situation arises. I promise you, it'll fit. It's magic that way."

She winks, and I smile, humoring her.

"Okay. I won't forget. But how about you hang on to it until then? Then if I don't use it, you can give it to your daughter."

"I don't know if it feels right giving it to Betsy, considering that it was meant for someone other than her father," Ellie says, and that makes sense.

"Okay," I finally say. "I'll take it. If you're sure."

"I'm a hundred percent certain. That dress gave me a beautiful evening . . . right up until it wasn't. It can do the same for you . . . without the heartache, I pray."

She smiles and walks me to the door, with the dress draped over my arm.

"I'll see you again soon, Meg," she promises.

Ellie closes the door behind her, and the sadness of the story seems to close off with her, because as I walk up to my condo, I feel lighter and lighter, happier than I've been all day. I hang the dress on a hanger and leave it on the outside of my closet door. Looking at it makes me happy, even though I know I won't be wearing it anytime soon.

Something about it reminds me of the Roaring Twenties, the swing bands of the forties, and the glamour of the fifties all at once, as strange as that seems. Like the dress has chameleon tendencies and can fit anyone, at any time, any place.

I curl up on the couch and call Cassie to talk her off the ledge I'm sure she's standing on. At Stitch, there's always a crisis, and always a ledge. And for the first time, I'm sort of glad I'm not the one standing on it.

CHAPTER THREE

The magic of the dress has worn off by the next morning.

As the building owner, I'm apparently always on call. I can't just ignore the persistent knocking on my door at five A.M. and hope it goes away. I know this because I tried, and the knocking only got louder.

I open the door and find a man and his little dog in front of me. When he sees me, his head snaps back, and for a minute, I'm offended. But then I remember that I slathered on an overnight hydration mask before I went to bed. My face is a lovely shade of tomato right now.

"You must be Meg," he says hurriedly, regaining his composure. "I'm Ed Plume, from apartment 308. I was just out walking Tootsie, and I heard water in the basement again while I was waiting for her to do her business."

I stare at him, not registering what he's trying to say or why it's me he's telling.

He stares back, not sure why I'm not springing into action.

"Another pipe has burst," he says, as though explaining to a toddler. "You need to come right away before the basement floods."

This spurs me into movement.

I grab a robe and join him in the elevator. As we travel down, I rub at my eyes and stare at my feet. Once again, I hadn't put on slippers.

"Does this happen a lot?" I ask Ed.

He shrugs. "Twice in the past year, give or take. The plumbing needs to be replaced here, I believe."

Along with everything else.

"Do you always walk your dog so early?" I ask him. I bend to scratch Tootsie's ears, but she emits a small growl. With her thinning gray facial hair, she looks like a grumpy little troll. I back away.

"I do. I rarely sleep anyway."

"I'm rather partial to it myself," I mutter. He grins.

"Sorry 'bout this, then."

He doesn't sound very sorry, to be honest, and his eyes *do* twinkle merrily.

"Say, I've never seen anything like that before." Ed motions to my mask. "Why do you want it on your face?"

"It's to keep me young," I say simply.

"Age comes to us all," he answers. "But it won't be chasing your heels for a while yet, young lady."

He gets off on the third floor, and I continue to the basement alone.

As I open the door to the boiler room, I am appalled.

Water rushes from a copper pipe. I don't know a lot about this, but I'm almost positive that copper pipes are not a good thing.

An inch of water covers the floor.

I screech a little when my bare toes hit the cold, but I persevere, and splash my way across the icy floor to the broken pipe. I hadn't thought to bring anything, not my phone, not my towels, not *anything*, and I silently lament my thoughtlessness.

I pull off my robe and wrap it around the water flow, my lack of experience showing. It soaks the robe within two minutes.

I'm standing there helplessly, wondering what to do when Sylvie appears, perfectly dressed.

"Oh, dear," she mumbles, eyeing the situation, the flood, the gushing water, my nightgown, and my sleep mask. "Thank goodness I called Mr. Scott."

She also carries a stack of old towels.

Bless her.

"You called Logan at five in the morning?" I ask. She gives me side-eye.

"Should I have waited until this evening, after the entire

floor has flooded?" I flinch. She notices, but doesn't relent. "Ms. Julliard, these things must be dealt with swiftly and firmly. Mr. Scott knows that. He's a professional."

The way she says that makes it clear that she knows I *am not*.

Sylvie forages around on the other side of the basement, and in a minute, the water gush stops.

She reemerges, wiping off her small hands.

"The main water valve needed to be turned off," she says. "Until the break is repaired. I'll go back to the office so that when tenants start calling about the lack of water, I can explain. There are towels to start cleaning up the mess, and there is a Shop-Vac in the corner."

She leaves me alone, and I assess the area.

It's dark, it's wet, it's creepy. The machinery moans and groans, the cold air from outside somehow finds its way in here, and the *smell*. It smells like old musty shadows.

The last thing I want to do before I have coffee is mop a dirty cement floor in a place where monsters could lurk.

"This is so not in my wheelhouse," I mutter.

"Good thing it's in mine," Logan says enthusiastically, coming down the stairs. His toolbelt jingles in an impossibly cheerful way. He glances at me warily, and I remember the face mask and my thin nightgown.

Dang. It.

I act as normally as I can.

"You work with monsters?"

"Monsters?" He arches an eyebrow.

"I was just thinking about how this basement seems like it could hide lots of monsters."

"I don't know about monsters," he says, setting down his toolbox. "But I do know it's rumored to have a walled-up passage that used to be a secret exit. This building was an illegal bar in the twenties. Did you know that?"

"A speakeasy. I vaguely remember hearing that when I was a child," I answer. "I grew up here, you know."

"I know."

He squats down and assesses the damage.

"All these copper pipes need to be changed out," he tells me. "They're very old, and corroded. You might want to be careful of your hair. It could turn your highlights blue."

My hand instantly flutters to my hair. Are my highlights so obvious?

"Thanks for the heads-up," I reply self-consciously. "How can we fix the problem today? Is there a patch, or . . . ?"

"I'll replace this section of pipe. And then we can keep li–"

"Limping along," I interrupt.

"Exactly."

"I think I need to sit down with my dad's accountant and figure out exactly where we are financially."

"Don't quote me on this," Logan says as he fiddles with the pipe. "But I think your dad kept his own books."

"Please be wrong," I beg.

He grimaces. "I don't think I am."

My shoulders slump. He glances at me, and his eyes are very blue, and very kind.

"You don't need to worry about paying me right away," he offers. "So you can take that off your list of worries."

"You've got bills to pay, too," I tell him. "I'll figure something out. In the meantime, and before anything else, I've got to have coffee. This pipe didn't even have the decency to burst at a humane hour."

Logan throws his head back and laughs.

"Should I bring you a cup?" I ask.

He shakes his head. "Let me get this fixed, and then I'll be up." He pauses. "Oh, and, Meg? I think you might've had an allergic reaction to something."

He stares at me in concern, and it takes me a minute to again remember my tomato-red face mask.

Oh, my lord.

I tell him what it is, and he shakes his head in amusement, and he'll never look at me the same again, I'm sure.

I trudge up the stairs, and to my apartment, where I fix a cup of coffee, wash my face, and get dressed, in that order. I sip the liquid gold while I brush my hair and pull it into a messy bun on top of my head, then find my favorite gray cardigan, the one that almost hits my knees and has pockets. *Everything is better with pockets.*

I wipe my counters, and I realize that I'm procrastinating. I don't want to go to the office where I know Sylvie is. Just the thought of her stern eyes sends a shiver up my spine.

Sighing, I know that I can't put it off. I'm the owner here. If she can't get along with me, then she doesn't need to work here.

In fact, *does* she work here?

There's only one way to find out, so I square my shoulders and head downstairs.

SYLVIE IS SITTING at my father's desk and examining a pile of papers.

I sit in the chair next to her and fiddle with my cup.

"Um, Sylvie," I begin. She glances up impatiently.

"Yes?"

"I have what might seem like a silly question." She waits, and it's apparent that she expects silly questions from me.

"Do you work here?" I ask quickly. "I mean, like, on the payroll?"

She seems taken aback. "I . . . I mean . . . technically, not on the payroll. But your father appreciated my help, and that was all the payment I needed."

"I sure don't want to impose on you," I tell her. "It's not fair to ask someone to work and not pay them. And from what I understand, I can't afford to hire anyone."

She stares me in the eye.

"Are you firing me?" she asks slowly, and I swear, she's looking into my soul.

"Of course not." I shake my head. "I just don't want to take advantage of you."

"You're firing me," she says stiffly, standing up to her full height of under five feet. I'd never before realized how intimidating that small stature could be. "I know where I'm not wanted."

She marches out before I can think of something to say.

I'm clearly still not fully caffeinated.

Logan ambles in a few minutes later. "What did you do to Sylvie?" he asks.

I tell him, and he cringes.

"You'll want to fix that," he advises. "She might not seem like it, but she's very sensitive."

"But my dad wasn't paying her," I say. "That's not fair. She's supposed to be retired."

"Some people need to feel needed," he says simply. "Your dad always made her feel very important. She has an interesting life story. You should ask her sometime."

I nod, feeling sheepish. "I didn't mean to hurt her feelings."

"I know."

Something about this man makes me self-conscious.

"You're pretty," Logan says bluntly. I startle, and he grins, pointing to my coffee cup. I relax. Oh, yes. My favorite cup. It says GIVE ME COFFEE AND TELL ME I'M PRETTY.

"The perfect way to a woman's heart," I say. "Add some tacos and I'm yours."

I instantly feel awkward. *Why did I say that??* To anyone else, fine. But to Logan? He's so . . . so . . . gracious, handsome, generous. What is wrong with me?

"I'll remember that," he says easily, with a smile. "Anyway. Your pipe is fixed, madame. I wet vacced the water up, and put the wet towels in the hampers downstairs, along with what looks to be . . . your robe. You're set for the day. Although, you should know, one of the things Sylvie did was wash the miscellaneous laundry for the building. So . . ."

"I'll need to do it now," I finish for him.

He nods, and I picture the loads of dripping wet towels and my precious Chanel plush robe, waiting to be washed.

"I'll have to fix this," I say.

Logan smiles. "Good luck. When Sylvie gets miffed, it lasts for a while. She was already agitated with you."

"I know. Do you know why?"

He looks uncomfortable and shifts. "Um. She hasn't directly said. That's something you'll need to take up with her."

He knows. He just doesn't want to say.

"Okay. I'll do that."

"Good. Anyway. I hope you have a good day. If you need me, just text or call."

"Thank you, Logan."

He grins one more time, and I again notice the dimple in his left cheek. He disappears out the door, and I inhale the manly smell he left behind, like snow, and pine, and wood.

When I'm finished daydreaming about him being a handsome woodsman, I turn to my dad's computer, determined to find his accounting.

LOGAN WAS CORRECT. My dad kept his own books, but luckily, he kept excellent records, and everything is rather straightforward in the software program.

Unfortunately, the straightforward program tells me what I already suspected.

We're broke.

We have nothing in the bank. We barely stay in the black with the tenants' lease payments every month, because there are always pricey monthly repairs. This building, it seems, is crumbling down around our ears.

I walk out into the lobby and turn in a circle, assessing it with impartial eyes, looking past the faded first impression.

The wood is elaborately carved, the domed ceiling is unique, and I know there is original tile beneath the thinning carpet. The building has quite a few beautiful elements, and they certainly don't make them like this anymore, a building with handcrafted touches. Nowadays, they're thrown up as quickly as possible, and each one is like the next.

Parkview West has character. I'll give it that.

And history. *It was a speakeasy.* I wish I could remember the stories my dad used to tell, but memories of Jo's illness eclipse everything else in my mind from back then.

"If this building has historical significance, maybe . . ." I spin around again and eye the heavy front doors with original leaded glass. "Maybe there are grants to apply for. Historical societies, maybe?"

"Do you always talk to yourself, young lady?"

Joe Riordan emerges from the hall. I feel my face light up like a Christmas tree.

"Joe!" I rush to him and hug him tight, this trim white-haired man I've known since I was ten. He's thinner now and walks with a cane, but he's still the same, and he still wears his customary tweed newsboy hat. "How are you?"

"I can't complain. It wouldn't do any good!" He laughs, and as always, it's a sound that makes me laugh, too. There's something about Joe that just makes a person feel good. His familiarity makes me feel comfortable. He's one of the only people left in the world who know my history, my story. It's nice.

"I'm so sorry about your dad, Meggie," he tells me now, his brown eyes somber. "He was a good man, and he lived a good life. He's at peace now. I hope you feel that."

"No more struggles for him," I agree.

But mine are just beginning.

Changing the subject, I ask hopefully, "Do you remember any of the stories my dad used to tell about this place being a speakeasy?" Joe doesn't disappoint. His eyes light up.

"Of course, I do. You surely remember how much I love history."

"I do," I assure him. "You're the reason I passed world history my senior year in high school." He chuckles, pleased by this.

"Well, I do enjoy it. I actually have some old newspaper stories highlighting local speakeasies, and this place was included. Would that help you?"

"Oh my gosh, YES."

I grab him into a bear hug, and he beams.

"Well, then. I'll just go dig them out. Feel free to stop by later today and I'll have them ready for you."

"You're the best, Joe. The *very best*."

He grins again before he takes his leave, and for just a minute, I let myself enjoy the feeling of being a genius.

Because surely this idea has merit.

Surely this idea can save this building.

CHAPTER FOUR

$\mathcal{I}$n general, you won't get federal grants for property that isn't a nonprofit," the nasally woman on the other end of the phone tells me. "You can, however, apply for federal tax grants that can assist you in the next tax year."

Oh, man. I need help right now, and more than just a tax easement. I think of the clacking boilers, the breaking pipes, the rickety elevator.

"There's nothing else?" I ask, my voice thin, as I lean back in my father's chair. It had taken me thirty minutes just to find the correct phone number to call, and then another twenty minutes of waiting on hold.

"Well," she says. "Sometimes there are funds available at the local level to help preserve local history. It will take elbow grease on your part to research it, find them, and apply. You'll

need to provide proof of your property's historical significance, of course."

Okay. That's something.

"Thank you," I tell her sincerely. "You've been a great help."

I hang up and glance at the overstuffed boxes. Maybe my
dad's hoarder tendencies will come in handy, after all. There's
got to be information in there somewhere that will help.

FOUR HOURS LATER, as I sit in the middle of the floor, surrounded by empty cartons, stacks of old taxes, and fluttering
papers, I have to admit defeat.

There's not a single thing in a single one of these boxes that
can help with anything.

Someone should've told my dad that you only need to save
taxes for seven years. All this, every last thing, can be shredded.

My shoulders ache and my back screams at me. I arch it,
stretching, and watch my phone light up.

Glancing down, I find a text from Cass.

Drake called me last night. He really misses you.

Horror fills me up, and I snatch up my phone.

He does not. He misses the idea of me.

Who does he think he IS calling you???

There are instantly three bubbles. She's answering.

He says he took you for granted, and that he feels horrible.

He sounded rough, Meg.

Good, I answer. He DID take me for granted. And he was con-descending, and pompous, and how did I tolerate that for so long??

He has a beautiful face, Cass reminds me.

She has a point. He wasn't hard to look at.

He's rich, she goes on.

Not relevant, I answer. He thinks money is the be-all, end-all.

It makes things easier, she texts.

Whose side are you on?

She sends back a crying-laughing emoji.

Always yours, she assures me. I was just helping you with your pros and cons list.

I already made that a month ago. He came up wayyyyy short on pros. Which is why I broke up with him. Don't let him push your buttons.

I won't, she promises. Oh no. Dragon is coming. Gotta go.

I picture Lillianna storming across the newsroom at Stitch and reflexively cringe.

"She can't hurt you anymore," I mutter to myself, like a mantra. "She can't hurt you anymore."

To an outsider, our fear of the Dragon might seem overinflated or exaggerated. But in real life, it's something Lillianna purposely cultivates with an X-Acto knife. She knows exactly what she's doing, and she's an expert at it. There's not a single person in the entire industry who hasn't felt her wrath at some point or another.

Objectively, I have to admire her for taking the industry in hand like that.

Personally, I hate that the mere mention of her name raises my blood pressure by twenty points and causes a cold sweat.

"She can't hurt you anymore," I mutter one last time for good measure, still trying to convince myself. "She's across the country."

That's a thought that does, in fact, make me feel better.

She's across the country.

I take a cleansing breath. I've got different problems now. Beginning with these mounds of papers. This level of messiness almost gives me hives.

I pile as much as I can into the biggest boxes, and I'm tugging them through the lobby when Sylvie steps out of the elevator.

She glances my way, then full-on stares.

"What are you doing?" she asks, her eyes wide.

"My father has a lot of old papers that we no longer need," I tell her. "I want to shred this."

"Your father kept that stuff for a reason," Sylvie says.

"And that reason is . . . ?"

She looks flustered. "I don't know. Tax reasons, I suppose."

"We don't need records this old. They will just collect mice and dust."

She's flabbergasted and appears a bit like a rattled hen.

"Meghan, I must speak up on your father's behalf. He wouldn't want you to just throw away his things."

I level a gaze at her. "Sylvie, you don't need to speak up for him *to me*. I'm his daughter."

"You rarely acted like it."

She lifts her chin and walks out the front doors, leaving me staring after her.

What in the world?

I called my father every Sunday. We spoke for at least an hour, and he texted me regularly. But of course, there's no way Sylvie could know those personal things. She wasn't family. She was someone who helped him around the office.

Dang. I should've asked her where the large paper shredder is.

OF COURSE DAD put it in the basement. He never used it and wanted it out of the way. It's not even plugged in.

I drag it over to an outlet, plug it in, and spend the next hour shredding boxes of paper. While I hunch over the shredder, feeding paper by paper into it, I gaze around. The basement walls are brick, and clearly original. I think about what Logan said . . . about the rumors of having passageways bricked up down here.

It's a fascinating thought.

There's so much room down here, lord only knows what it contains.

By the time I feed the last bit of paper into the machine, I feel pretty accomplished. I even break down the cardboard boxes and stack them against the wall.

I'm congratulating myself for my productivity and sense of order as I march back up the stairs, completely and totally proud of myself.

Right up until the door won't open.

I try again, more forcefully.

Oh, no. *OhnoOhnoOhno.* It's locked.

It locked behind me.

I beat on the door, holler, and rattle the doorknob.

But no one comes. My phone is sitting on my desk upstairs, of no help to me now.

With flushed cheeks, I woefully sink to the steps.

I'm not normally claustrophobic, but being in a locked creepy basement makes my heart pound. The water dripping nearby adds to the spooky ambience. It's chilly down here, and damp, and that just makes it all worse.

My foot taps nervously on the step, and my hands get sweaty. Somewhere, down a darkened corridor, I swear I hear a shuffling noise. My imagination, of course, goes to the worst possible place.

Serial killer? Zombie? Vampire?

"Hello?" I call. No one answers, and the noise stops. My heart pounds, and I get up and rattle the door again.

"Someone! Can anyone hear me?" I yell, pounding on the door.

Miraculously, it opens.

Ellie's stunned face pokes in.

"Meg?" she asks. "What in the world are you doing down here? You must be freezing."

I was so panicked; I hadn't even noticed that I'm covered in goose bumps from the cold.

"The door locked behind me," I tell her. "How did you hear me?"

"I was coming down to my storage unit," she says. "And thank goodness. I wouldn't have heard you otherwise."

"There are storage units down here?" I ask dumbly.

She nods. "Yes. We can pay extra for a storage room. I need to sort through mine." She eyes me. "But Meg. The door doesn't lock from that side. It just gets stuck. You have to open it with a bit of oomph."

I stare at her. "I wasn't locked in?"

She shakes her head. "No. But I'm sure it was frightening to think you were."

"I've never felt claustrophobic before," I tell her. "But it's creepy down here."

Ellie starts walking down the steps, her slender hand gliding along the railing. "It's the energy," she says knowingly. "This place has quite a history, or so I'm told. It was an illegal bar during Prohibition."

I freeze and look at her.

"Have you heard any of the stories?" I ask her, a bit breath-lessly. Because that would be too good to be true.

"A few." She nods. "It's said that this was the favorite bar of Johnny Torrio."

She waits for a reaction, but I can't give her one. "I don't know who that is," I admit.

"Johnny Torrio was Al Capone's boss."

I inhale sharply. "What?"

"Oh, yes. Like I said, these walls have seen some things, I'm sure."

No wonder the hair was raised up on my neck a few min-utes ago.

Ellie continues down the steps, as though she didn't just de-liver earth-shattering news to me. I stare after her, then scuttle behind like the White Rabbit following Alice.

"Do you know any specifics?" I ask, matching her step for step as she heads for her storage room down the darkened hall.

"Sweet girl, this basement needs its lighting fixed," she says, as she tries to turn on the lights, to no avail. "My storage unit works, but the hall lights don't."

"I'll add it to the list," I promise. I ask again, "Do you remem-ber any specifics?"

She scrunches her face, trying to remember. "I believe it was called the Red Alibi, if I remember correctly. Your father told me when I was touring this place as I moved in."

"Did he tell you anything else?"

She shakes her head. "No. I don't believe so. Only that it was a pretty lively place back then."

"The Red Alibi," I murmur. "That sounds colorful."

"In more ways than one." Ellie nods. "Think of the era. I'm sure some very colorful things happened here. Meg, would you be a dear and help me carry a few things up to my apartment?"

"Of course," I answer. She opens the door to her unit, and inside, her things are neatly stacked in labeled boxes. She scans them and finds the three she's looking for.

Photos.

Jewelry.

Christmas decor.

"You stored jewelry down here?" I ask her, scanning the dusty room.

"Where else would I put it?" she asks, unconcerned. "Can you carry one, and I'll carry one? I can come back down for the third."

"I can carry two," I assure her.

I reach my arms out and take the two large boxes, making sure she gets the photos, which I assume is the lightest. I follow her up the stairs, trying to be prepared to catch her if she stumbles. She never does; her steps are steady and true.

"Ellie, are you going to decorate your apartment?" I ask at the top. I'm a bit out of breath, but she doesn't seem to be. "I thought you were boxing everything up."

She shakes her head. "No, dear. I brought this up for you.

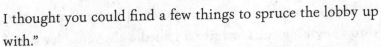

I thought you could find a few things to spruce the lobby up with."

She smiles sweetly, and I can't help but smile back. "That is so sweet of you," I gush. "When I first arrived, all I could focus on was how faded everything looks."

"It just needs some love and elbow grease," she says, as we walk toward the elevator.

"And a lot of money," I mutter as we step inside.

She lifts an eyebrow.

"The Parkview needs *a lot* of repairs," I tell her. "It's over-whelming. I'm not sure what I'm going to do."

The old elevator lurches upward, and Ellie scrunches her face again as she thinks.

"Hmm. There's got to be something we can do," she says aloud. "Some way to raise money. Let's think."

"I've been doing nothing else," I answer. "I was thinking that if I could prove this place has historical significance, we could maybe get grants from historical societies to help renovate it."

Her face lights up. "That's brilliant, Meghan!"

"Maybe, but I have to prove it." My shoulders slump. "There wasn't anything in my father's stuff . . . just old bills and taxes. That's what I was shredding in the basement. There was noth-ing helpful."

"Did you check his storage unit?" Ellie asks.

"He had one, too?"

She nods. "He mentioned it once, that it was near overflow-ing."

"That sounds about right," I mutter. "The man could never throw anything out. I imagine it's filled with even older taxes."

"Never assume anything, dear," Ellie chides kindly. "That's something I've learned in my seventy-four years of life."

"Good point," I agree. "I'm sorry. I really don't mean to be negative. Truly."

She smiles again. "It's okay. Sometimes, it's hard to see hope in the middle of turmoil. But trust me, it usually comes out in the end. You just have to look for it."

"Has that happened for you?" I ask her.

"Oh, yes. Many times." She pushes the hold-open button. "When my Betsy was a baby, she was ill, and we thought we'd lose her. But she lived, and thrived. It was a miracle."

Her face falls a bit though, as we step out, and I feel certain she's thinking of Frankie.

"And in love?" I ask softly.

"I married a good man. We didn't have a passionate love affair, but he made me feel safe, and secure, and he loved me. That's not something I can bring myself to regret."

"As well you shouldn't," I agree. "Some people look their entire lives to feel that way."

"And some people, like your parents, were lucky enough to have found it *all*," she says. "They were so fortunate."

"They had their share of sorrow, though," I answer, thinking of my sister.

"That is true," she agrees. "Life hands out such hard knocks sometimes, and all too often to the very best people."

We carry the boxes down the hall to her apartment, and I help her stack them in the living room.

"I'll go through those today," she says. "And I'll bring you any Christmas decorations that would fit well."

"You are so kind," I tell her. "Thank you."

She walks me to the door, and as I open it, she speaks.

"You know, I did just think of something else that might be helpful."

I turn, hopeful.

"Your dad always said that the main room of the speakeasy was bricked up along with the escape hall."

"That makes sense," I reply. "Logan thought he heard that the old exit passageways were bricked up, too."

"There's something else . . ." Ellie says thoughtfully.

I wait.

"Your dad said, and don't quote me on this, but he said that it's rumored that Ernest Hemingway himself carved his name into the wooden bar top."

I stare at her. "Ernest Hemingway. *The* Ernest Hemingway came to the speakeasy that used to be this house?"

"And Al Capone, and Johnny Torrio," she reminds me. "I think, dear, that you just got your *historical significance.*"

I feel like fainting. In fact, for a brief second, my vision pixelates. I steady myself on the doorjamb.

"Yes," I say weakly. "I think we have."

CHAPTER FIVE

$\mathscr{S}$o are you wanting to open it back up as a bar?" Cassie asks. I pace across my living room again, my phone held to my ear.

"No, I don't think so. But I could have the speakeasy restored, and we could give tours," I say, thinking out loud. "For extra money."

"Or you could open a bar," she suggests, for what I'm sure is selfish reasons. Cassie does love a good bar. And a good male bartender.

"I have a condo full of elderly tenants trying to live out their golden years," I tell her. "Having a bar in the basement wouldn't please them, I'm sure."

"So? Relocate them."

"Oh my gosh. They aren't rescue animals, Cass. This is their home." Sometimes, my best friend's cavalier attitude is frustrating. She's so no-nonsense that she almost crosses the line into heartlessness. *Almost.*

"That's true. Well, first, you have to get in there and verify that you have Hem's signature. After that, you've got to figure out who can help. You know . . ."

Her voice trails off.

"What?"

"I know who could help. Someone who is a wizard at raising capital."

She pauses, and her meaning hits me.

"No. I am absolutely not asking Drake. Next idea."

"Just think about it, Meg," she says. "He's really good at financial stuff."

"Cassie, we broke up. Get that through your head. I don't want his help. Not in any way, shape, or form. Okay?"

She sighs. "Sometimes, you can be so stubborn."

"*Okay?*" I push her to agree.

"Fine. Okay."

"I swear. You should just date him yourself," I tell her. "You love everything about him so much."

"I think that's against girl code," she says wryly, but she doesn't protest as much as I thought she would.

"Oh my gosh, would you really want to? I was just joking."

She's quiet for a minute. "He's handsome. Rich. Ambitious. What's not to like, besides the fact that he's your ex?"

I think about that for a minute. About Cassie's no-nonsense

attitude. "Well, you have thicker skin than me. So maybe he wouldn't crush your dreams. You have my blessing," I announce. "Just don't ever bring him around me."

"So you won't be the maid of honor at our wedding?"

"Chickens, line up over here," I call out dramatically. "Cassie needs to count you before you're hatched."

She laughs, and I laugh, and I really miss her.

"I wish you were here to have a cup of hot cocoa with tonight," I tell her. "I miss you."

"I miss you, too. But you're going to do fine there. I'll come visit as soon as the Dragon gives me vacation time."

"Sooooo, never?"

She guffaws again, and we hang up.

I stare around the apartment, and the reality of the fact that I'm all alone hits me yet again. It's definitely not that I want Drake back, or even someone like him, but the idea of him and Cassie together makes me feel lonely. It must be the same way most of the tenants here feel. Most of them don't have anyone in their lives, either.

They must be just as lonely as I am.

An idea begins to form.

It would be crazy . . . I don't have time to organize a Christmas party for them. Christmas is just three weeks away.

However, I could do it with help.

I'm a *genius*.

I could ask Sylvie to help, thus soothing her ruffled feathers.

I am beyond a genius.

EXCEPT THAT SHE DECLINES.

"I'm not at your beck and call," she tells me moodily, after I traipse downstairs and knock on her door. She answers wearing a light-up, battery-operated Christmas tree sweatshirt and Rudolph earrings. "You'll have to find someone else."

"But Sylvie," I say, "you're the one who knows this building and all the tenants best. How can I throw a party without your help? Especially in this time frame?"

"You should've arrived on time," she admonishes me yet again. "Then maybe we'd have time. As it is, we don't. Do you think you invented the idea of a Christmas party? We've always had one. This year, however, you weren't here to approve it, so it's not happening. None of the tenants will have a fun party to look forward to. Merry Christmas."

She closes her door in my incredulous face.

Okay. We're back to three birds with one stone.

I honestly wasn't expecting this.

Like Logan said, Sylvie is someone who needs to be needed. That's obvious. Only, I told her she was needed, and it didn't work.

I pick up my phone and text him.

> You were wrong. Sylvie doesn't want anything to do with me.

He answers immediately.

Take her a cupcake from the shop down the street. It works every time.

A minute passes.

Red velvet. It's her favorite.

I smile.

Do you know this from personal experience?

Again he answers right away, something that Drake never, ever did.

There was an incident once involving me not locking the lobby bathroom door, and her catching me with my pants down.

He sends an immediate second text. Yes, literally. I send back several crying-laughing emojis.

I know, I know. I seem perfect, but everyone makes mistakes. ☺

I roll my eyes, but I'm still laughing. I can't help but picture little Sylvie, toe-to-toe with tall Logan, and I can literally see her not budging an inch, lecturing him about privacy, and how bathroom locks operate. Then I envision Logan slinking back with a cupcake in hand. I giggle out loud.

Okay, fine. If he can grovel after something like that, I can, too.

I throw my coat on and head down to the cupcake shop. I get there right before they close, which I'm sure doesn't endear me much to the clerks working the counter.

It also limits the selection.

I scan the glass display case.

"Do you have red velvet?" I ask the girl in the elf cap.

The bells on her cap ring as she shakes her head. "We did this morning. But now, all we have left for today is what is here. You can come back in the morning if you need red velvet. It's been really popular because it's red. You know, with Christmas."

"That makes sense," I agree. "I'll take that strawberry one instead, please. I think that should work. It's almost red."

It's a dream confection, rich strawberry with spun sugar frosting, and mini gingerbread men on top for the holiday.

The cashier boxes it up in a pretty little pink box, and I feel really confident as I head back to the Parkview.

My only regret is that I didn't think to get one for myself.

I take it back to the front desk, grab some paper, and write *I appreciate you, Sylvie*, with a heart. Then I leave it in front of her door. I ring her doorbell and dash down the hall.

From around the corner, I watch her peer out and pick up the box. I smile.

Mission accomplished.

She'll be putty in my hands now.

Except that as I head back down the hall, I hear her door open again. I perk up, thinking she might've come out to see me.

I go straight back, round the corner, and instead of Sylvie, I see the box back where I'd left it.

Puzzled, I go get it.

The cupcake is still inside.

It didn't pass muster.

With a sigh, I snatch the box, take the elevator back to my apartment, and listen to it groan and creak the entire ride to the top floor. It actually makes me nervous to be the only one inside. I certainly don't need to be trapped again today. Once was enough.

Luckily, it comes to an uneventful stop on my floor. I step out, knowing full well that one of these days I won't be so lucky. This elevator *will* break again someday soon.

I've got to sort this out.

But not tonight. Tonight, I change into pajamas, drop onto my couch, and eat the cupcake with my hands like an animal.

When I text Logan, I leave sugary fingerprints on my phone.

You were wrong. Gift = Rejected.

He answers back with a crying-laughing emoji.

Dangg. That's gotta hurt.

I tap out a reply, while licking my fingers. Why, yes. Thanks for pointing it out.

I add, You give terrible advice, btw.

Now, now, he answers. Don't blame me. You're the one who got on her bad side.

I need a new plan, I tell him. A new and improved plan.

Hmmmm, he replies. Let's call it Operation Sylvie.

I giggle aloud. Very clever! No one will guess what we're talking about.

Stealth is my middle name, he answers. I picture him grinning, the one dimple on his cheek popping, and my stomach actually flutters.

Lord help.

I don't need this right now. I don't need a distraction, even if it is a swoonworthy, handsome distraction. I just got out of a relationship. I don't need another. What I need is a miracle. To fix this money pit that I've inherited.

I prop my feet up on the coffee table and notice that it's the same oak table that we've always had, for as long as I can remember. It has the old rings from back when I always forgot to use coasters. My mom used to get so annoyed. I smile with the memory.

The couch is old, too. We've had it since I was in high school. My father wasn't one for extravagance, and the day he bought this, he'd grumbled about the cost. I remember the delivery guys had to carry it up all the flights of stairs because it wouldn't fit in the elevator. They weren't happy, and my dad was stingy. So my mom had tipped them quietly and heftily, while my dad wasn't looking.

I smile again.

All my memories from here aren't bad. I just need to sift through them and find the ones that make me smile.

I stand up, stretch, and realize that I'm still too amped to sleep. I dig in my bag for my favorite vanilla bodywash and use it to make a bubble bath.

The water isn't as hot as I'd like, but I make do, vowing to ask Logan to turn up the temperature tomorrow. I find Josh Groban's Christmas album on my phone and turn it on, adjusting the volume to play softly. If anything can help me get in the mood for Christmas, it's Josh.

I slip into the water, use a folded-up washcloth to steam my eyes, and rest my head against the tiles.

Josh croons "O Holy Night," and I lie in the water, trying to soak every last trouble I have away.

While he sings "I'll Be Home for Christmas," I shave my legs.

I dry off, shivering, while he sings "Silent Night."

I stand at the balcony, looking out at snow-covered Chicago while he sings "Little Drummer Boy." I keep my phone in my pocket, and Josh is my only company. Below me, yellowed lights flicker in other homes, and I picture all the mothers and fathers getting ready for Christmas, wrapping gifts, telling stories of Santa.

My own father used to say we had to not only leave out cookies and milk for Santa, but we also had to leave out carrots and water for the reindeer.

The reindeer need their strength to fly all around the world, he'd tell Jo and me. We swallowed it hook, line, and sinker. Every year, we'd set out a big bowl of water and an entire plate of carrots, right here where I'm standing. Jo and I always imagined all the reindeer crowding around the plate, filling up their bellies.

I smile at the memory and use my foot to clear off a little spot of snow. Maybe I'll try to remember to do it this year. Just for old time's sake . . . for Jo.

I listen to the words of "Little Drummer Boy." For the first time, I consider the fact that Mary was a young mother, probably sleep deprived, and a young kid had come, playing his drums for baby Jesus.

I wonder if Mary had secretly cringed. *Jesus just went down for his nap. Don't wake him.*

But because she was a saint, she probably smiled gently, and said, "Go ahead. Play your drums. I can always put him back down for a nap later."

Oh my gosh, Meg. You're being ridiculous. I am, and I know why. I'm stalling because I don't want to sleep in my parents' bed.

When I do, it will mean, once and for all, that they aren't here to sleep in it themselves.

And heaven knows I'm not going to sleep in my old bed. It's in the bedroom that Jo and I used to share, and that's not a place I'm ready to visit just yet. After Jo died, I slept on the couch until I left for college. I thought maybe I should try to overcome my fears and sleep in my old bed, but my dad had always said I didn't have to. It caused me night terrors, and he'd understood.

You'll come to terms with this in your own time, Meggie, he'd told me one night, after pressing a kiss to my forehead.

The problem was . . . I never really did. My dad had to visit me in New York, because this place triggered my nightmares.

But here I am. Back. And so far, as long as I sleep in my dad's bedroom, I seem to be fine.

Or fine enough.

I step inside, slide the balcony door closed, and lock it.

I turn down the covers and stare at my father's bed.

I grab my sleep mask and climb in.

I turn off the lamp, pull the mask down over my eyes, and settle into the fact that this bed is mine now.

This building is mine.

This life is mine.

CHAPTER SIX

$\mathscr{I}$ wake up leisurely. Glancing at the clock, I see it's almost ten A.M.

I stretch, sit up, and pad out of bed to the kitchen to make coffee.

The problem is, I don't have any cream or sugar.

So I get dressed and carry my cup downstairs.

When I enter the lobby, Sylvie is sitting in a wingback chair in front of the dark fireplace.

"In the winter, your dad was always downstairs by seven," she tells me sternly. "He turned on the fireplace and had coffee made for anyone who wanted to grab a cup."

"We have a Keurig," I answer. "It's coffee on demand."

"Not everyone likes that or wants to figure out how to run the machine. Your dad always made a pot and put it in a carafe."

Sylvie's expression is severe, as though I had committed a cardinal sin.

I stare at her and walk to the fireplace. I turn the key to power the gas on and light the flame.

"There," I tell her. "It's lit."

She and I both know she could've done that and had probably done it a thousand times in the past. But she smiles tightly now.

"Thank you."

"You're welcome."

I head to the kitchenette, brew coffee, pour it in a carafe, and take it to the coffee station.

"And coffee is on."

"Oh, I don't want any," she says. "I had mine in my apartment at a normal hour. It's practically afternoon now." She stays in the chair, and I wonder if she plans on watching me all day. Her green sweatshirt says DEAR SANTA, I CAN EXPLAIN.

If she has an explanation, I'd love to hear it.

I leave her in the lobby and collapse at my dad's desk.

I text Cassie.

I think I might've met Dragon Lady's match.

Cassie answers a few minutes later. Are you currently knee-deep in a toy store, hunting for a toy that has been sold out for months that she can give to a distant friend's daughter, and if you don't find it, she says she'll fire you?

Um, no, I answer.

Then you haven't met her match.

Yikes. I definitely don't miss that. Some days, I'd go home with hives because of Lillianna.

You're the boss, Cassie adds. Act like it.

Wow, tough love. I don't love that. I send a laughing emoji. Besides, I tried that, and it backfired. It's why I'm hiding in the office right now.

I'll have to talk to you later—I'm currently running the risk of rabid Christmas shopping moms tearing my limbs off, she replies.

I laugh softly. Tis the season!

I lay my phone down and look around. I need to do something that makes me look professional. Like I know what I'm doing.

I pull out a notepad and start listing things that I know need fixing.

When I'm finished with that, I set it aside, and start a new list.

TO DO, I write in block letters at the top.

1. DO RESEARCH ON HISTORICAL SOCIETIES.
2. DO RESEARCH ON THE RED ALIBI. SEE IF IT'S REAL.
3. DECORATE THE LOBBY WITH ELLIE'S DECOR.

I pause on that one and leave number four blank. I take my list to the lobby and glance around to see if Ellie had brought the box down.

"What are you looking for?" Sylvie asks.

"Why are you asking? Would you even help me find it?" I ask, more snidely than I meant to. Her head snaps back.

"I didn't mean that," I add quickly. Sylvie's eyes narrow.

"I was looking to see if Ellie had brought down her Christmas decorations. She said she would give us a box for the lobby."

"The lobby is already decorated." Sylvie sniffs. "I did it myself. Because you weren't—"

"Yes, because I wasn't here." I sigh. "I get it."

Sylvie stares at me, then at my list.

"You should add 'order supplies' to that list," she tells me. "We're out of sugar, dish soap for the kitchenette, paper towels, and Post-it notes."

I'm writing all that down, when the lights suddenly go out.

I look up, confused.

"Also, you can add *pay electric bill*," Sylvie says calmly.

My eyes widen, and I stare at her.

"Is that why you're waiting out here? You knew the electricity was scheduled to be turned off? Why didn't you tell me?"

"You didn't ask," she answers, not unkindly. "If you'd been here, you would've seen the late notice come in the mail. But you didn't consider it important enough to get here, or to figure out a plan to manage the building in the interim. You simply thought it would magically take care of itself."

I blink. "I didn't mean to," I tell her. "I had just been told that my father died, and that he didn't want a funeral, and that I was essentially an orphan. I wasn't thinking clearly. I'm sorry."

"Don't play the sympathy card, dear," she answers. "It's not flattering. Yes, I knew the electricity was going to be turned off. Yes, I was waiting down here to watch it happen. I wanted to use this as a lesson for you. You've got responsibilities now. You can't just blow them off."

She gets up and walks into the office.

Stunned, I follow her. She's on the phone already with the electric company. She pays the bill over the phone, including the $100 reconnection fee.

"So you'll be out within the hour?" she asks. "We have a building filled with elderly tenants, so the sooner the better. You can see on our history that we've never been late before. We're under new management, and we're experiencing some growing pains. That's all. I thank you for your patience."

She hangs up and turns to me. "They'll be out in half an hour."

She walks away.

The tenants begin arriving immediately, coming to ask about the power outage.

"I'm so sorry," I tell each of them. "It'll be back on momentarily. Please help yourself to some hot coffee in the lobby."

I light some candles on the mantel, and in combination with the fire (which thankfully is gas, so it didn't go out) it looks festive.

A group of tenants stay seated in the lobby, so I carry around the carafe, and fill their cups. They chat, and overall, everyone is extremely patient.

I learn some new names and faces. Ellen George, Bob Rickhart. Virginia Jones. Maeve Richardson.

They're all kind. They're all patient.

Twenty-six minutes later, the power comes on.

"Now that I captured your attention," I call out, "let me just wish you all a Merry Christmas. I'm happy to be here. I won't forget to pay the electric bill ever again."

They disperse back to their rooms, and I text Logan, telling him all about it.

Harsh! I've never seen her quite that angry.

Thanks for that, I reply. Do you have anything helpful to say?

Hmmm. Keep her away from the knives, he answers.

I search through all the mail in the office, attempting to find any other bills. They all seem to be late, but not dangerously so.

I pay them from my personal bank account, which wasn't hefty to begin with.

I also run out to the grocery store and replace the empty supplies. I have no idea where I'm supposed to order them from, but I'll figure that out another day.

Today is a day for putting out fires.

APPARENTLY, LITERALLY.

Because Jay Mallack comes into the office at 5:37 P.M., and tells me that the dryer downstairs is smoking.

"I'm so sorry," he tells me as we take the elevator down. "It's industrial-size, so I was washing my comforter. Jerry always let me, because it's too big for my apartment-size washer."

"I'm sure it's not your fault," I assure him. I march over to the dryer and unplug it.

A haze of electrical smoke surrounds us, and I stay surprisingly calm.

"I'll have to get a new one," I tell him. I open the dryer door and take out his comforter, which is thankfully mostly dry. I hand it to him with a calm, very calm, smile.

"Here you go," I tell him sweetly. "I'll get this dryer replaced as soon as possible."

"At your leisure," he says cheerfully, as we ride the groaning elevator back to the lobby. "I think you've got more pressing matters." Meaning the vehicle that currently holds our lives suspended with its old, squeaking cables.

He steps out and heads upstairs, leaving the scent of peppermint gum behind, and I walk calmly, so calmly, up to my apartment.

I close the door calmly.

I walk to the bedroom calmly.

I collapse face-first on the bed calmly.

Then, and only then, do I let loose the most bloodcurdling scream I've ever heard, into the safety of my pillows. I beat my hands and feet against the bed as I wail, allowing every single emotion I've had over the past couple of days to escape and finally be heard.

When I'm finished, my voice is hoarse, and I lay still.

I lay quietly until walls darken with night, and lights from the city create shadows on the ceiling.

I stare mindlessly upward, willing my mind to be numb, to no longer freak out, to simply be calm.

For that, I quickly decide, I need wine.

A nice red to coordinate with the holidays would be nice.

I set about digging through my father's cabinets and come up empty-handed.

How can someone not have wine?

I know, I absolutely know, there must be some somewhere.

I head downstairs to the kitchenette, taking the stairs two at a time. I'm rumbling around the kitchen cabinets, looking behind every jar and canister, when I hear a soft exclamation from the doorway.

I glance over to find Ellie, her hand pressed to her chest.

"I'm sorry," she says. "I wasn't expecting anyone down here at this hour."

I check my watch. It's midnight.

"I didn't mean to startle you," I tell her. "I'm on the hunt for wine."

She smiles broadly. "I doubt you'll find any. But what you will find, and what I'm here looking for, is your father's Glenlivet."

My head snaps back. "You drink scotch?"

"Not usually," she admits, coming into the kitchen. "My late husband did. I think it tastes like lighter fluid, no matter the vintage. But tonight, my soul needs settling."

She opens a cabinet door and finds two glasses.

Then she disappears out into the hall, and I find her scavenging in my father's desk, coming up with a bottle.

"It's in the second drawer on the left, at the back," she tells me. "For your future reference."

I eye the old bottle, covered in dust. "I'm not sure I like scotch."

"Oh, you won't," she says cheerfully. "But it'll get the job done. Let's sit in front of the fire, shall we?"

We turn the fireplace on, and the flames lap invitingly. I curl up in one velveteen wingback chair, and Ellie crosses her legs in the other. She pours amber liquid into two glasses and hands me one. I sniff at it, and my nose wrinkles instinctively.

She smiles. "To doing the job!" She holds up her glass with elegant fingers, and I clink mine against it.

"To holiday cheer!" I toast. "And new friends."

Ellie sips at her liquor, but I can't. The smell makes me shudder. So I hold my breath and knock a gulp back, then another. It lights a fire from my lips to my belly. The warmth isn't unpleasant. *But the taste.* I shudder at the sheer thought of the taste.

"To getting the job done!" I toast with another glass, thinking of everything I'd conquered today.

Ellie laughs lightly.

"Be careful, dear. It's got more kick than wine."

I, however, am confident in my ability to hold my liquor, bolstered by memories of college frat parties and, more recently, nights out with the crew at Stitch. We'd celebrated many, many closely made deadlines with copious amounts of alcohol at the corner bar.

I take a few more fiery gulps.

Then a few more.

The flames from the fire seem warmer now, and I take off my cardigan. Ellie peers at my face.

"Your cheeks are flushed, dear," she says gently. "You should slow down."

I can't feel my nose, so I decide to heed her advice.

For now.

I lean back in my seat.

"You know what the worst thing is about all this, Ellie?" I ask. I cross my feet on the coffee table. She waits. "It's that I didn't even get to see my dad before he died."

I reach for my glass, but Ellie subtly moves it out of my reach. I slump back into the seat.

"Are you worried that he didn't know you loved him?" she asks, her forehead wrinkled. "Because that's not true. He knew, my dear."

"I know. I told him on every phone call. But I didn't come, Ellie. I didn't come here to see him, because the memories here choke me. When I'm here, I feel strangled by all the sad things in our past, and so, I left him here alone."

"He wasn't alone, Meg," she reminds me. "We were all his friends. He was surrounded by people who loved him."

"I do appreciate that," I tell her genuinely. "That gives me comfort."

"Good. Because it's true. We all loved him. He was a very good soul. And if you give us a chance, we'll love you, too. He told us so much about you. Every accomplishment you made, he celebrated with us. We watch your blog, you know."

"My blog." I say the words woodenly. "I haven't written on it since I left New York."

"I know. Don't you think you should? How will we know what to wear if you don't tell us?" Ellie smiles, but thinking about my blog makes me sad, and it's not just the liquor talking.

"I had something to say then," I tell her. "Now, I'm not around fashion, I'm not around fashion shows, I don't have access to emerging trends. I'm nobody here, Ellie."

"Oh, Meg," she clucks. "That isn't true at all. You have an eye that is all your own. You don't need to be at Stitch to use it."

"I was using that blog to help build a platform for myself," I admit. "I wanted to become known as an expert, so that one day, when I can have my own line, people won't doubt my skill."

"You can still do it, darling," she says, and she sips at her scotch again. She drinks like such a lady.

"It's kinda hard to do from here," I answer, and my shoulders slump.

"Meg, you know what I've always believed? Put on some good lipstick, and get things done."

"That sounds vaguely Elizabeth Taylor-ish," I tell her. She smiles.

"She was a determined woman," she answers approvingly.

"She had, like, a hundred husbands," I reply, rolling my eyes.

"Do you think men are a weakness?" Ellie asks. She sips again at her scotch. "Because they aren't, my love."

"They want you to give up your own dreams and follow them," I grumble.

"The right ones don't," Ellie says stoutly. "Was that what your ex-fiancé was like?"

"We weren't engaged," I tell her quickly. "We were just dating. But yes. That was *exactly* what he was like. Drake is very ambitious, but single-minded with his own interests. He really needs someone who only wants to support him, and not have a huge need for her own career. He wants a stay-at-home soccer mom wife to take care of."

Ellie considers that.

"Well, from the sounds of it, he's not a bad person, he just wasn't the one for you," she offers.

"My best friend certainly doesn't think he's bad," I tell her. "She wants to date him."

"Oh, my," Ellie breathes. "That seems unconventional."

"I know. When I left, he texted me that I'd be back. He basically said I needed him and couldn't survive on my own. And she still wants him after that."

"Hmm. Well, I guess she's not as strong as you."

"I don't know about that." Even though I'm surprised at my best friend, she's still my best friend, after all. "She just . . . I don't know. Maybe she's tired of the rat race. It's hard to get ahead in that world."

"Only the strong survive," Ellie says pointedly.

I shrug. "Maybe. Let's call her."

I'm drunk now, there is no doubt.

"Honey, it's one A.M."

"Ish okay," I slur. "She's called me in the middle of the night plenty of times. This one time, she was stuck in a cab and got claustrophobic."

I'm rambling. I dial Cassie's number in order to video call.

She answers on the first ring. "This better be important," she mumbles, without opening her eyes. "I had to work late for Dragon Lady. I just got home an hour ago."

I nod. "It's very important. Ellie wants to know if Drake is a bad guy."

"No, I didn't want you to call her," Ellie protests gently. Cassie props herself on an elbow, her dark hair tumbling over her shoulder.

"What did you drink?" She sighs.

Ellie holds up the scotch bottle. Cassie sighs again.

"Why?" she asks simply.

"Dunno," I announce.

"Meg, I call that Glen-leave-it-alone for a reason."

Ellie apologizes profusely to Cassie. "I'm so sorry. We'll let you go. Meg is struggling with life decisions tonight, and as her best friend, her first thought was to call you, I think."

Cassie sits up. "Are you struggling with the fact that you left Drake?" she asks, wide awake now.

"No," I answer definitively. "You can still have him."

She looks visibly relieved to me.

"Why are you wondering if he's a good person?" she asks, confused now.

"I asked her, and she didn't think she was unbiased enough to answer," Ellie interjects. "It's okay. We're terribly sorry for waking you."

"Drake isn't a bad guy," Cassie tells her. "He's driven, and he can seem cutthroat to some, but that's just his business side."

"He's only got a business side," I say as I lose my balance and fall into the side of the chair, face-first.

"That's not true," Cassie says. "He's ambitious, and he works a lot. But do you remember the time he set up the dinner for you in Central Park? Or the time he booked the helicopter for you?"

I blink. "His assistant did those things."

"At *his* direction," Cassie answers.

"Those seem like sweet gestures," Ellie says, looking at me.

They do. When you look at them that way.

"Maybe I just didn't see him the way I should've," I offer. "He just wasn't the one."

"And that's okay," Ellie assures me. "It's good that you figured it out."

Cassie starts to say something, but we're interrupted by a very stern voice.

We turn to find Sylvie in the doorway, her hair in curlers and wearing a fuzzy robe.

"Do you ladies realize what time it is?" she says, her voice like steel. I'm sheepish.

"I'm sorry, Sylvie," I tell her.

"Your boyfriend issues aren't the problem of everyone in this building trying to sleep," she snaps. I don't bother telling her that I'm not having boyfriend issues. "Please keep it down."

She stomps off, and I look at Ellie.

"Yikes. I'm never going to get on her good side."

"It's not looking good at the moment," she says. "But never say never."

"We've gotta go, Cass," I tell my friend. "I need to drink some water."

"Drink several glasses, then take some aspirin before you go to bed," my best friend advises sagely.

"K." I hang up and try to stand. The room spins. "Oh my gosh. You were right. This stuff has legs."

The idea of the bottle walking around with legs makes me giggle, and Ellie slides her arms beneath mine. "Let's go, dear," she says as she guides me to the elevator.

I laugh the entire way up to the top floor, and Ellie, bless her, never complains.

She sees me into my apartment and looks at me.

"Will you be okay now?"

I nod. "A hundred percent."

She pauses and looks at me again.

"A thousand percent," I amend.

She smiles nervously. "Go to bed, dear," she says before she leaves.

I immediately feel her absence, and the reality of being alone surrounds me yet again. I don't like it, and I pull out my phone.

I start texting people as I crash into bed.

I don't know how long I'm conscious before darkness takes me, and my hand falls to the side, my phone slipping into the sheets.

CHAPTER SEVEN

I wake up with a kink in my neck.

The sun assaults my eyes.

I clamor out of bed, ignore my pounding head, and pull my drapes closed. The darkness is a relief. I catch sight of myself in the mirror, and freeze.

When had I put on Ellie's dress? The last I remember, I had dropped into bed. I must've gotten up at some point.

But even though I don't have any recollection of putting it on, I look good in it. When I'd first seen it, I honestly thought it was going to be too small for me. But it fits me *exactly right*, like it had been made just for me. I turn this way and that, admiring the way it drapes over my hips and hugs me in all the right places. Modest, yet still sexy and elegant.

They don't make things like this anymore.

They don't make things like this anymore. But they *should.*

Inspiration strikes, and I take off the dress, hanging it back on the closet door. I grab my sketchbook and sit in line of sight of the dress. I ignore my pounding head and dry mouth, and I sketch out a design, one founded on this very dress.

Elegant neckline, thick breathable fabric that hides imperfections, draping lines to accentuate the good, sexy, yet classy.

"The world needs more class," I tell the design. I drag my pencil down the curve of a hip, and then pat at my own.

"You look fantastic," I tell my hips.

"Stop talking to yourself," I add.

I set my design aside. For the first time in a long time, I feel comfortable. I feel accomplished, in my element. That's *something*.

I grab my laptop and type out my first post in weeks on my blog, *The Fitting Room Floor*. I decree the benefits of staying classy.

I almost include a picture of the dress, but hold back.

I'm going to keep it to myself for now. I have this idea . . . a kernel of an idea . . . that I need to create an entire line around this one dress.

Maybe I could call it the *Back to Class* line. Or maybe *Back 2 Class*. Eww, no. Maybe the *Timeless* line? I think on that as I carefully step out of the dress, hang it up, and put my robe on.

Gah. All this thinking hurts my poor hungover brain.

A knock on the door interrupts my brainstorming.

Is it Ellie, coming to check on me, or Sylvie, coming to complain to me?

Turns out, it's neither.

Logan stands in front of me, a cup of coffee in his hand. He offers it to me with a grin.

"I figured you'd need this."

I take it, but eye him.

"Um. How did you . . . ?"

"How do I know you tied one on last night?" He grins broadly, an adorable smile that melts my insides. "I gather you haven't looked at your texts this morning, and you have no recollection about last night?"

About last night.

Those are three words that *never* bode well. Ever.

"Oh my gosh. What did I do??" I turn my back on him and race to my phone.

"I wouldn't do that right now," he advises, but of course, I ignore him.

"Oh my gosh," I mumble while I scan through our text thread.

> You're sexy. ☺

> You wear that toolbelt REAL NICE. ☺

> Hey, my plumbing has some issues. Want to come over and clean it out? ☺

"No, no, no, no, no," I gasp, and I throw my phone across the bed, as though getting it away from me will fix the problem.

"I have no idea what got into me. I'm so, so, so sorry. I don't remember doing that AT ALL. I . . . This is humiliating."

Logan leans against the doorjamb, his grin unfaltering.

"To be fair, I *do* wear this toolbelt real nice," he says helpfully.

I drop my head into my hands, unwilling to look at him.

"It's okay," he says soothingly. "Don't worry. I didn't come over and take advantage of you."

I want to die.

"I . . ." I flounder. "I have no words. I tried scotch for the first time, and . . . I'm sorry."

I feel weak in the knees, and not in the good way.

"So that's what drunk texting looks like," he says cheerfully.

"As if you've never seen it before," I mutter.

"I haven't. Not like that."

"Well, then, I'm honored to be your first."

I flush, because I really don't have the right to be salty about this. He's the one who was aggrieved. Of course, it could always have been worse.

"At least I didn't send any inappropriate pictures." I shudder.

His eyes widen. "Oh, yes. That would've been . . . tragic." I roll my eyes and he smiles. "Listen, no harm, no foul. It's okay."

He's standing in my apartment now, all fresh air and sparkling eyes, and I'm last night's cigarette butts and stale whisky. Figuratively speaking, because I don't smoke.

"Did you need something?" I say, trying to be subtle, but

also wanting him to go before he sees the fur growing on my tongue.

"Hmm?" He turns to me. "Oh. I just thought you could use some coffee. Sylvie called and asked me to come refill your salt bags, and so I thought I'd stop and say hi while I was here."

"Wait. Sylvie called you?" I narrow my eyes. "I thought she hated me now."

"She might." He shrugs. "But she doesn't want anyone to slip on the icy sidewalk out front. They could break a hip, you know."

"I didn't even think about salt on the ice," I say limply, sitting on the sofa. "What else have I not thought of?"

Logan sits next to me, patting my shoulder. "Don't worry about it. If you forget something, we'll remind you."

He bends forward, peering at the coffee table. "Hey, did you draw that?" He gestures toward my sketchpad. "That's really good!"

He picks it up to examine it, and I yank it away. "Don't. It's not ready to be seen yet."

"That looked amazing!" He turns to me. "Are you a designer?"

I sigh. "I was. I wanted to be. Now I'm an apartment building owner."

He eyes me. "The two don't have to be mutually exclusive."

"Oh, yeah. I know many, many condo owners who dabble in fashion in Chicago." I'm sarcastic, and now he's the one rolling his eyes.

"Somehow, I have the feeling that you can do anything you put your mind to. And don't hate on Chicago. Oprah built her empire here."

He stands up.

"Thanks for the vote of confidence. But I've got my hands full at the moment."

He shrugs. "Well, it's just something to think about. It's a shame to waste a talent."

"Thank you for the advice," I tell him, ushering him out. "And thank you for delivering the salt. I really appreciate it."

"If you need anything else, just let me know." He winks as I start to close the door, but he wedges his foot in to stop it. "Hey, Meg?"

"Yes?"

"Sylvie told me you're having man trouble. Don't fret about it. Anyone would be lucky to have you."

My eyes widen, and I literally can't think. So I do the only logical thing.

I slam the door in his face, and then lean on it.

He thinks I'm a drunken has-been who has man trouble. How humiliating. If I could die right now, in this spot, I would.

I grab my phone so I can text Cassie and tell her all about it, when I see that I'd already been texting Cassie all night. And she's not the only one.

"Oh no," I mutter, scrolling and scrolling. "Oh, no, no, no." I'd been texting Drake and also Lillianna.

Lillianna. What was I thinking???

You were the worst boss ever.

You have impeccable fashion sense, though.

But still. Why do you have to be so mean?

Everyone calls you the Dragon Lady and trust me, you've earned that title.

On that last one, I also included the purple devil emoji.

Oh my gosh. Oh my gosh. Nooooooooo. She didn't reply, but her read receipts are on, and it clearly shows that she saw the texts.

I just want to die.

And *Drake*.

My missives to him aren't much better.

You know, for such a hot guy, why do you have to be so self-absorbed?

Good boyfriends are supportive.

You weren't. It's so sad.

You could be so much more than you are, you could be a well-rounded individual, if only you thought of other people a little bit more.

He actually did answer that last one.

> Meg, I think you should go to bed.

That's it. That's all he said. Of course, the time stamp on the text was three thirty A.M., so he wasn't wrong. I should've just gone to bed. Ironically, I was the one who wasn't being considerate.

I'm ridiculous. I made myself a laughingstock, and now I don't know how to fix it. Should I pretend it didn't happen? I slowly get ready for the day, pondering my options while I down two bottles of water, and take some aspirin.

I could move to Mexico and leave no forwarding address.

I could text everyone and apologize.

I could pretend it never happened.

I could declare temporary insanity.

I could say someone hacked my phone and pretended to be me.

I mull over these options, and honestly, moving to Mexico doesn't sound so bad. Except I'd have to work on my alcohol tolerance if I'm going to start drinking tequila. Apparently, I've become a lightweight.

Even walking down the stairs as softly as I can hurts my head.

As I pause on Sylvie's floor to rub my temples, I glance toward her apartment.

Be the bigger person. It's not her fault you're hungover.

I square my shoulders and head her way.

She doesn't answer her door.

I knock again.

Still no answer.

"Hey, Sylvie?" I call through the door, wincing from the sound of my own voice. "I just wanted to tell you thank you for ordering the salt. It's something I hadn't thought of. The sidewalk isn't safe without it. So, thank you! Oh, and also, I'm not having man trouble."

I wait for a second, and then with a sigh, I turn around.

Marvin Fairwater is standing in his doorway, across the hall, eating a bowl of cereal as he watches me.

"Sylvie isn't home right now," he tells me. "It's Monday. She always goes to the cemetery on Monday mornings."

"The cemetery?"

"Where your father is buried," he says gently. "And her late husband."

I gulp.

"She goes every Monday?"

"Without fail. She says she likes to start her week the right way."

"I didn't know that," I say weakly.

"Well, from what I've heard, you two started off on the wrong foot. But nothing is irreparable, Ms. Julliard."

"Meg," I tell him. "Please."

"Meg." He smiles. "You're as pretty as your daddy said. I can't imagine why you would be having man trouble."

I blush. "Thank you. And I'm not. Having man trouble."

"That's good." He keeps smiling. "Your daddy was as proud of you as he could be," Marvin adds. I blush again.

He laughs.

"Have a nice week, Meg." He starts to retreat, but pauses. "Oh, and, Meg? The Keurig in the lobby is out of hot cocoa."

He closes his door, and I tap a note into my phone. *Order more hot cocoa pods.*

I make my way down to the lobby, and as I walk through, I find a wooden table next to the fireplace with a carafe sitting on it, and a stack of cups. The hand-lettered sign says: HELP YOURSELF TO A CUP OF HOMEMADE HOT CHOCOLATE. MERRY CHRISTMAS!

Sylvie had put out cocoa until the Keurig pods are ordered.

It's getting harder and harder for me to swallow my guilt.

So you know what? I'm not going to try. I grab my coat from the hook by the door and head out into the snow. I might regret this. In fact, I probably will, but I've got to make things right with her.

WHY DO I live where the air hurts my face?

I rub my hands together and wish I'd brought gloves. And I have to remember to moisturize when I get home. This cold wind will chap the heck out of a face in two minutes flat. I hold my arm out for a cab amid the Christmas lights, which don't look as festive during the day. It's the night, when they're truly magical.

Down the block, a bell ringer stands near a red bucket. While I wait for a cab, I jog down and put a couple bucks in.

"Thank you, miss," he says with a smile. "God bless you."

"And you," I answer back. "Stay warm." He laughs at that, because of course it's impossible.

A cab pulls up and I drop inside of it, ignoring the smell of stale popcorn because at least it's warm.

"Graceland Cemetery," I tell the driver. He nods wordlessly and noses the car onto the snow-packed road. I watch the scenes of Christmas blur past me as we drive to Lincoln Park.

The storefronts are packed with Christmas spirit, with festive sweaters and bells and brightly wrapped packages. I know, however, that all those packages are empty. They're just for show. It seems a perfect analogy for me and my life here. I have no one to buy anything for. Except maybe Cassie. I'll just send her a gift certificate for a massage.

She needs it, I'm sure.

The cabbie pulls up to the gates and I climb out into the cold.

I crunch over the snow into the hallowed ground, and the serenity here is notable. It's hushed, and reverent, and the snow glistens, untouched. The trees that line each row sound almost like wind chimes, as they rustle with their icy branches.

Walking here, even on a cold day like this, makes me feel peaceful. My family deserves a place like this to rest, a serene respite in the middle of a bustling city. It had been expensive, but worth it.

I walk down the path that I know leads to my parents, past

the statue of the boy playing a flute. The pond in front of him is frozen now.

I find their grave quickly.

Gerald and Elaina Julliard.

They lie next to my sister, Josephine.

"Hey guys," I say quietly. "I'm sorry I didn't bring you flowers. I'll come back another day with some."

I kneel and brush the snow from their headstones, just so their names show.

"It's beautiful here," I tell them. "I wish you could see it. The snow is perfect, there are no footsteps. It's like a winter wonderland. Jo, you'd love it."

My sister loved winter. She loved making snowmen, and snowball fights, and Christmas lights. One year, when she'd been too sick to leave the hospital, we'd hung lights all around her room, and my mother had made a snowman out of cotton and four bottles of glue. I still remember looking at it, and thinking it was the saddest snowman I'd ever seen.

But Jo had loved it.

"Sooooooo, I don't know if you know this, but I'm back home. It took a little bit of time to get things wrapped up in New York, but I'm home. And I miss you guys. SO MUCH. It feels nice to be home where you are, but at the same time, it makes me sad, you know? Because everything looks the same as always, except you're not there. And I'm the only one left."

I take a breath and wish with my whole heart that they could hear me.

"I don't know what to do with the apartment building, Dad. I don't want to let you down, but it needs a lot of work, and that will take a lot of money, and I don't have it. I accidentally got the electrical turned off, for Pete's sake. I've upset Sylvie, and she's the one who knows how to do things. I don't have any way to repair everything... You guys, it's a mess. I don't know how I'm going to fix it all."

All of a sudden, tears well up, and I wipe them away.

"I don't want to disappoint you, Dad. And all the residents. They've lived here for so long. What if I run the building into the ground? What will they do?"

I feel the weight of all that responsibility pushing on my shoulders and I can't seem to breathe. I put my hands on my hips, and try to open my airway, so I can suck deep gulps of icy air down.

"You're not alone."

A quiet voice comes from behind me, and I whirl around.

Sylvie stands there in her hot pink stocking cap with a purple pom-pom on top.

"You're not alone," she says again. "I'm here."

"I'm so sorry, Sylvie," I tell her, apologizing in front of my entire family. "I didn't mean to offend you. When I came back, I didn't really want to, and I accidentally took it out on you. I don't want to fail my dad. And I don't want to fail the residents. But I don't know what to do. I just don't."

I'm crying again, and I feel silly, but Sylvie steps up and wraps her small arms around me.

"There, there," she says awkwardly. "It's okay. I'm here now."

"I came here to find you," I sniffle. "But I stopped here first."

"As you should," she agrees. "But now, let's get you out of the cold." She steps back and pulls out her phone. "I'll get us an Uber."

Her tech savvy surprises me, but of course I don't say so. I wouldn't want to offend her again.

She eyes me. "You should really be wearing boots and mittens, Meghan."

"I know. This was a spur-of-the-moment thing, and I wasn't prepared."

She sniffs, but not as snottily as she would have before. Maybe I'm making headway.

We walk to the entrance, and I low-key keep my arm on her elbow to make sure she doesn't slip. She's tiny and mighty, but she *is* still older, and it's icy.

The Uber has arrived when we reach the entrance, and we climb into the warmth. Sylvie turns to me.

"I'll be happy to help you sort things out," she tells me. "I'm not a real employee, but I want Parkview to succeed. I'm sorry I allowed the electricity to be turned off. That wasn't nice of me."

I wounded her with those words, *you're not a real employee*, and I flinch.

"Sylvie, don't apologize. You were right. I should've been here. I'd love to pay you, if you'll accept it."

"You don't have any money, dear," she reminds me. In the rearview mirror, I see the driver's lip twitch.

"I have a little," I tell her. "And hopefully, I'll keep making some. You deserve to be paid for a job well done."

"Well, I don't need the money," she tells me. "In fact, if you pay me, it'll interfere with my Social Security and all that. So your gratitude is payment enough."

"Well, you'll have that in spades," I assure her.

She smiles now, a real grin.

"First, we need to get the office in order," I tell her. Her grin disappears.

"What's wrong with the office?" she asks.

I stutter. "Um. Er. Nothing. I just may have ransacked it hunting for historical records."

I spend the next few minutes telling her of my idea about funding for a historical building, and the speakeasy in the basement.

"Well, you should've led with that," she tells me when I'm finished. "I know all about the Red Alibi. I thought it was fascinating, so I dug up all kinds of information years back. I'll just need to find it."

I'm speechless, and I stare at her.

"Close your mouth, dear," she advises. I close my mouth.

She peers at me.

"Have your boyfriend troubles been keeping you up? You've got bags under your eyes."

"I don't have boyfriend troubles," I say weakly.

She purses her lips. "Well, there's one thing I've learned over the years. Men come, and men go. You'll be fine."

"Seriously, though. I don't have man trouble," I tell her as we climb out of the car. We go inside as she answers, and I hold up my hand.

"Hold that thought."

I pour a cup of coffee, put a lid on it, and duck back out in the cold to take it to the bell ringer down the street.

"Maybe this will help keep you warm," I tell him.

He smiles, which makes my heart smile.

When I go back to the Parkview, Sylvie pretends to not know what just happened, and I pretend to have not seen her outside spying on me.

"Well, you were right," she says as she examines the mess in the office. "First things first. This has to be organized and put away. Then . . . we build our case for the historical society. Should I order us breakfast?"

Her hand is already on the phone.

"I think I love you, Sylvie," I say, as I drop into the chair.

She grins, and I'm pretty sure I'm forgiven.

CHAPTER EIGHT

$\mathcal{B}$y the end of the day, the office is in pristine shape, with everything filed, and everything in its place. Sylvie pretends not to notice that my father's scotch is missing, and for that, I'm grateful. She even managed to hang a slightly ragged string of red foil garland in front of the desk when I wasn't looking.

"You sure made a mess of this office," Sylvie says as she collapses at the desk at five o'clock.

"I know," I admit. "I knew everything had to be reorganized anyway."

Sylvie looks at me sharply. "Was there something wrong with the way it was before?"

"Oh, no," I rush to assure her. "I just wanted to get acquainted with everything. So I wanted to look through all that was here."

Sylvie doesn't look convinced, but doesn't press it. Surely, she remembers the overstuffed boxes on the shelves.

She absently pulls on Rudolph's red pom-pom nose on her sweater. "Now, I just need to remember what I did with that box of research. I was hoping it was here."

I glance at her quickly. "You don't know where it is?"

"I said I *thought* it was here," she says grumpily. "I specifically remember it being on that shelf."

She points, and of course, it's not there.

"Well," I say patiently. "Maybe it's in your storage unit."

"I don't have one," she answers. "Not everyone does, you know."

"Okay. Well. Maybe it's in my father's?"

She ponders that. "It could be, although I don't remember giving it to him."

She's rubbing her temples in what I assume is an attempt to stimulate her memory when my phone vibrates with a text. I pull it out and gasp.

You'll never work in this industry again.

Lillianna's words are as cold as her Dragon Lady heart as she answers my drunken texting finally.

"What is it?" Sylvie asks.

I sigh and set my phone down. "Collateral damage from a night of drunk texting."

She narrows her eyes. "I knew your father's scotch was gone. You know he saves that for special occasions."

I sigh again, and she softens.

"What did you do?" she asks, more gently now.

"I texted my boss in New York. My ex-boss. I told her what a horrible person she is, and she just now answered. She's going to make it impossible for me to ever work in the fashion industry again."

Sylvie ponders that. "Is she a terrible person?"

I nod. "One thousand percent."

"Then you only spoke the truth," she says simply. "I've always found that to be best, even if it's painful."

"You definitely are a matter-of-fact person," I agree. "But sometimes, well, the truth doesn't need to be pointed out unnecessarily. I worked for so long to try and get along with her. To do everything she asked, no matter how punishing or humiliating, and I ruined it all in two minutes' worth of texting."

"Well, it's a good lesson," Sylvie says uncertainly. "But I still say honesty is best."

"You don't understand how hard I worked," I tell her. "Nights, mornings, weekends, holidays."

"Oh, I understand that," she says. "You never came home. Your father celebrated holidays alone."

She's stern again, and I'm sheepish.

"You really drive in the guilt, you know that?"

She shrugs. "I'm honest." I don't see the point in rehashing the benefits of tactfulness with her again.

"I regret, terribly, not coming home more," I tell her. Sylvie fiddles with Rudolph's nose again. At this point, I'm worried it will come off in her hand.

"I overheard what you said in the cemetery," she answers. "But what I don't understand is why you didn't. Your dad was a good man, Meghan. He loved you. And have you ever considered that he felt the same way you did about this place? It reminded him of bad times, too. But it also was home, and he had good memories, as well. He felt a strong obligation to keep it running for everyone who lives here."

"And so do I," I say unnecessarily.

She nods. "Listen, your dad didn't leave this place to you as a punishment. It meant so many different things to him, and I'm sure he wanted you to feel the same way. You don't have to give up your dreams for it. You can have your cake and eat it, too."

"Logan said the same thing," I tell her. "But you don't understand. New York is where I need to be to make anything happen in fashion."

"Says who?" she snorts. "Your dragon lady? The *man*?" She wrinkles up her nose in 1960s-esque disdain. "You don't need *permission*, Meghan Julliard. Take what you want."

I smile at her enthusiasm. "It's just the way it's always been. I don't make the rules, Sylvie."

"Then you can break them," she says confidently. "Listen, you are surrounded by walls that have been breaking the rules since the Roaring Twenties. Prohibition? Not here, lady." She puffs her chest up proudly. "Take that spirit, let it soak into your bones, and channel it into what you need to do. Break the rules, then make your own."

She gets up. "I need to shower. I'll also hunt for that box. In the meantime, sort out your man problem. I think I've seen Logan giving you googly eyes."

"I don't have—" I start to protest, but she's already gone. "Man problems," I mutter to myself.

I'm still muttering to myself as I walk up the stairs. I most certainly don't have man problems. I only had one problem . . . a two-hundred-pound arrogant problem, and I lost that weight the day I broke up with Drake. *Man problems.* I roll my eyes.

As I round the corner by Ellie's, I hear her voice. She seems to be arguing. Not vehemently, not hotly, but gently.

I pause and find that her door is cracked. I'll have to talk to her about that. She can't just leave her door unlocked like that.

"Bets, there is no rush," Ellie says quietly. I can imagine her pacing as she speaks, each footstep quieter than the one before. "I'm perfectly fine here for now. I'm healthy, I'm mobile . . ."

I almost snort. She's more physically fit than many people I know who are half her age. I obviously can't hear her daughter speaking, but from Ellie's tone and her periodic sighs, I'm guessing Betsy doesn't agree.

Finally, Ellie speaks again. "Betsy, I'm fine for now. It's the holidays, and I really wish you could come home to spend them with me. But since you can't, I am going to spend them here, in the home I've known for years surrounded by the people I know. After the holidays, we'll discuss my next steps. I love you. Goodbye."

It's a firm end to the conversation on her part.

I'm proud of her.

I poke my head in her door.

"Ellie?" I call. The door swings open a bit farther, and I see her sitting in front of her fireplace. It's not on, it's black and cold. She sits in front of it, anyway, her shoulders slightly slumped.

"Meg," she says, as warmly as she can muster. "Come in."

"I'm so sorry," I reply as I approach. "Your door was open. You really shouldn't leave it like that, by the way. But I heard you talking to your daughter. Are you okay?"

Ellie sighs and nods, then pats the seat next to her.

Obligingly, I sit and wait for her to speak.

"Betsy feels guilty," Ellie finally says. "Because she moved to London for her career, which I am in favor of. She worked hard to get where she is, and nothing should stand in the way of it. But because she feels guilty for being so far away, she overreacts sometimes. She wants to know that I'm safe."

"You're safe here," I point out.

Ellie nods. "I am. I've only fallen one time over the years, last year, in fact, and that really set her wheels spinning."

"You fell?" I ask. "Here?"

She nods. "On the staircase. I was carrying up a sack of groceries, and I misjudged the step. It wasn't an age thing. It was just me not paying attention. It wasn't a big deal."

"Were you hurt?" I practically hold my breath.

"Not really," Ellie says. "Bumps and bruises. But Betsy started imagining the worst, and now she's worried that I'll fall and break my hip next."

I swallow hard, because the truth is, if Ellie were my mom, I'd worry too.

"She thinks I'm alone here, without activities," Ellie continues. "But what she doesn't realize is that I have friends here. This is my home."

"Surely there's something we can do," I say, feeling rather helpless and wishing there were a real adult here to fix this. Someone adultier than me.

Ellie goes on, "I've already told Bets that I'm not moving to London. That rain—I can't do it at my age. I want to feel the sun on my face in the spring. I like my memories here. She's upset because she thinks I'm choosing memories over actually being with her. And if I refuse to move to London, she at least wants peace of mind that I'm safe."

Guilt twinges in me, rippling through my chest. I'm sure my father felt much the same way about me—in a different way.

"My dad was always worried about me being out in New York alone," I tell her. "He knew it was important to me, but he worried."

"And yet you were perfectly safe," Ellie says, drawing the parallel between herself and me. "You might've been young and healthy, but you were also innocent and naïve. Yet you still survived. I always told him you'd be fine."

"You did?"

She nods with a smile.

"With everything I'd heard about you, I knew you were too feisty to ever quit, or to ever be taken advantage of."

"I don't know about that," I admit. "Dragon Lady—my boss—she took advantage of us all. And we allowed it because we were all so hungry to get ahead. She cost me moments with my dad. Moments I can't get back now. I allowed that."

"Meg, you can't blame yourself for that. You didn't know that they were last moments. We never do," Ellie points out and pats my leg.

"But the worst part is that I still want to get ahead," I admit to her. "I still want to chase my dreams. That makes me a horrible person, and one he would be ashamed of."

"He would not," Ellie says firmly. "He loved your conviction, and your ambition. And I firmly believe you can do anything you set your mind to. You *can*, Meg."

"Well, so can you," I reply. "You're not at the stage yet where you need assisted living, Ellie. You're so fit and healthy. You make whatever choice is right for you. And don't do anything until you're ready. Do you promise?"

She looks at me.

I hold out my pinkie, encouraging her to link hers with mine.

"A pinkie promise?"

I nod solemnly. "My sister and I considered this the most sacred of vows."

Ellie smiles gently. "A covenant that can't be broken?"

"Exactly."

"Okay." She links her pinkie with mine. "*If* you'll promise that you don't give up on your dreams here. On any of them."

I hesitate, but she lifts an eyebrow. "Fair is fair, sweet girl. When the going gets tough, the tough get going."

"I think I've seen that on a gym poster," I say wryly.

She smiles. "Do you promise or not?"

I squeeze her pinkie with mine. "Okay. I promise. You drive a hard bargain."

"Now. How do you intend to get on with your dreams?" she asks as she sits back in her seat.

"You don't waste any time, do you?" I ask. She grins, and although we had talked briefly in the basement about my trying to get some historical society grants, I tell her again about my plan of trying to have Parkview West declared a historical landmark.

"I just have to find the research that Sylvie did years ago, which will save me months of time, and then I have to figure out how to pitch a case to the historical boards."

Ellie grins, angelically now.

"Meg, dear. Have I told you what I did as a profession before I retired?"

Her eyes have a mischievous twinkle and I narrow my own.

"No, you haven't."

"I was an attorney, dear. A quite fine one, if I do say so myself. I can argue a case with the best of them."

I stare at Ellie, at her refined grace and her lovely eyes, and of course she had made something out of herself after her fiancé jilted her. Of course she had.

"When the going gets tough, the tough get going," I say softly.

"That's quite right," she agrees.

"Thank you," I tell her. "I'll find that research, and I'll get it to you to start building the case."

"And I'll start researching the grants myself, and the history of this building, as well. Between the two of us, we'll find something."

Impulsively, I hug her.

"I'm not the huggy type," I say, into her shoulder. "But this is amazing, and I appreciate you."

"I'm not the huggy type, either," she replies, but I don't miss the fact that she wraps her slender arms around my shoulders. She smells like lemons and cinnamon.

"Darling girl," she says, as she pulls away. "Have you bathed today? You smell like dust."

She sneezes for emphasis.

"As a matter of fact, I'm on my way to do just that."

I stand up, and Ellie walks me to the door.

"Everything will work out," she tells me confidently. "Just have faith, Meg."

I smile. "I'll try."

She closes the door behind me, and I practically skip up the rest of the stairs to my apartment.

CHAPTER NINE

I'm toweling off my wet hair when my phone rings, and I pick up to find Cassie on the other end.

"What did you do to her?" she hisses.

I'm disoriented for a minute. "To whom?"

"To Lillianna, *obviously*," Cassie snaps. "She's been on a tirade, and she has absolutely *forbidden* anyone to be in contact with you. We can't help you, give you a reference, or even speak to you. The punishment is getting fired. *What. Did. You. Do?*"

"Oh." My shoulders slump. "She did say that I'd never work in the industry again. I guess she meant it."

"You need to tell me everything, and tell me right now."

"Well, do you remember last night when I was drunk-texting you? You weren't the only one."

Cassie gasps, and I tell her all of it.

"Meg," she says in horror. "I can't even . . ."

"I know," I agree. "Me, either."

"You've slit your own throat," she says limply.

"I know."

"All of that . . . that time *wasted*."

"Hey, now," I speak up. "Maybe not *wasted*. Lillianna isn't the only person in the industry."

Cass is silent.

"I mean, she's important, but she's not the *only one*." My voice is weaker now.

Cassie is still silent.

I groan. "Okay. I totally screwed myself."

"Yes, you did. I'm speechless, Meg. Just . . . speechless."

"That's a relief. I'd hate to hear what you really think," I answer wryly.

"Okay. Well, I can't be caught talking to you. I'm outside right now and my nose is freezing closed. I'll talk to you tonight when I get home. *If* I get home. She's in such a bad mood now that we all have to practically work around the clock. So . . . thanks for that. I love you, babe. But you know how she is."

"I'm sorry," I start to say, but Cass has already hung up.

I don't even have time to be annoyed, because someone starts pounding on my door.

"Meg, come quick."

I recognize Tom Rutherford's voice on the other side of the door, and when I throw it open, he's frazzled on the other side. "Come quick," he repeats, turning and rushing for the elevators.

I rush after him, in my bare feet, almost getting accustomed to being summoned like this. I should really start leaving my slippers by the door.

"What's happening?" I ask as the doors close, and he jams at the first-floor button with his finger.

"When I came back from my walk, there was water pouring in through the ceiling. I don't know what's happening. But if I had to guess, Melody Hansen's plumbing broke. Her bathroom is above mine."

We rush to her door, and Tom pounds on it.

No answer.

"You have the keys, right?" he asks quickly, glancing at me.

"Not with me. They're in the office." I feel like a failure as a building owner.

He listens, and we can both easily hear the sound of moving water inside.

"Get back," he tells me. With a spryness I wouldn't have imagined, he kicks in the door, hitting it at the doorknob. It swings open.

"Melody?" I call, as we rush inside and follow the water sounds.

"Melody!" Tom yells.

There's no answer, and we quickly discover why.

I push open the bathroom door, and she's in the tub, her arms floating on top of the overflowing water, which cascades onto the floor, and through the floorboards.

"Oh my gosh!" I exclaim. Tom and I pull her out, hefting her wet body over the side of the tub, along with several more gallons of water.

"She's breathing," he says. "Call an ambulance!" He pulls a towel from the rack and covers her with it, and as I rush to find her phone, I can't help but note how pale she is. How blue her lips are.

Is this my first tenant death? *I don't want this.*

My blood pulses in my temples as I call 911 and give them our address. I feel like I've disassociated from my body as I hang up.

"They're on their way," I tell Tom. His head is bent over Melody's.

"Her breath smells like fruit," he tells me. "That's a symptom of a blood sugar crash. She's diabetic. She should have a glucometer somewhere. Probably in a little bag. Try to find it."

I feel helpless as I search, but I do find a little zipped black bag next to her recliner. I rifle inside and find the glucometer, test strips, a syringe.

"Found it!" I yell.

"Look and see if there are sugar tablets in there. Or maybe injectable sugar."

I can't believe I'm in this situation. I literally know nothing about diabetes or first aid, and vow to myself to take a class when this is over.

"There's a syringe, but I don't see anything else," I tell him. "No tablets."

"Call Sylvie," he says quickly. "Ask for some glucagon." He's supporting Melody's head, and her short hair is soaking wet.

I dial Sylvie's number, thankful that I somehow remember it.

She answers on the first ring, and I quickly tell her the situation.

She hangs up without answering, but rushes in two minutes later, out of breath.

She loads a syringe with something and hands it to Tom. "I swear, I've told her a hundred times to be careful about her insulin," she mutters. "She always takes it and gets distracted before she eats. Then her sugar crashes."

Tom isn't listening, of course. He's injecting the contents of the syringe into Melody's thigh.

"I really hope you guys know what you're doing," I tell them.

"Of course I do," Sylvie answers. "I'm diabetic, too."

My heart is still racing, and I can't help but wonder . . . am I liable if they somehow make things worse?

This is part of being a condo owner that I don't know. That I didn't bother to find out, because I didn't foresee it happening. How many other things like this are there?

We hear the wail of a siren just as Melody's eyes open.

"What in the world . . . ?" she whispers, looking up at us, and then down at her naked, towel-covered body. "Oh, dear. Did I pass out again?"

"Again?" I ask Sylvie. She nods.

"It happens frequently."

I feel limp as the EMTs come in and bustle around Melody. They help her slip on a robe, and then eventually, they take her out on a stretcher and Sylvie promises to call Melody's son.

I feel silly because I hadn't thought of saying that.

I didn't even know she had a son.

I tell Sylvie that, and she glances at me. "That'll come with time. You aren't just born knowing these things, girl." She looks around. "A more pressing issue is . . . this needs cleaning up."

Tom has turned off the water by now, but beneath us, the floor groans.

"I'm not sure it's safe to be standing in here," Tom says. "I don't know how much damage was done, and that tub itself is heavy."

I nod, and we all leave the apartment.

"I'll call Logan," Sylvie says, bustling back toward the elevator. I look at Tom.

"Thank you so much," I tell him softly. "If it weren't for you, I don't know what would've happened."

"Think nothing of it," he says. But it's a big deal, and I know it.

"I've got to learn about the health issues of everyone here," I say unnecessarily. "I'm sure my dad knew."

"Your dad knew everyone here for a long time," Tom says forgivingly. "You'll get there."

He leaves me alone, and I wander out to the courtyard for some air.

It's bitingly cold, but the undisturbed snow glistens. Somehow, the surrounding building muffles the city noise, and it's quiet here, peaceful.

I brush snow from a bench and sit down, pulling my sweater more tightly closed. A bright color, a blur of movement, catches my eye, and I find a cardinal sitting on the bench across the paths.

It looks at me, its red head tilted.

"Aren't you cold?" I call. It doesn't fly away. It stays, watching me with glittering black eyes.

"They don't migrate," a low voice says from behind me. Ed and his little Yorkie quietly join me on the bench. The cardinal stares at them, but doesn't fly away. "Isn't he a beauty?"

"How do you know it's a he?" I ask, as his little dog, Tootsie, roots into my pockets, hunting for a treat. She's wearing a little pink parka with a fleece-lined hood.

"The pretty ones are males. The females are a very drab brown."

"Of course." I roll my eyes. I think of Drake and how he was immaculately dressed in four-hundred-dollar shoes everywhere he went. "That seems to be the way of it."

Ed smiles. "I sense a little bitterness."

"Oh, no. None at all. Just saying."

I smile at him.

"I seem to have missed some commotion," he says. "I was out walking Toots and saw the ambulance. Is everything okay?"

I quickly nod. "Yes. A resident's blood sugar dropped. She's going to be fine."

"Melody again?" He lifts an eyebrow. "She's got to get a better handle on that."

"The flooring in her bathroom is ruined." I sigh. "I don't know how long her bathwater was running. I wonder . . . are tenants liable in cases such as this? If they damage the property?"

I don't mean to sound heartless, but our bank balance is near zero.

Ed scrunches his nose. "I think so. But Melody doesn't have any extra money. She barely manages on her monthly Social Security. Her son pays her rent. Surely insurance will cover it?"

"Probably," I muse. "Of course. I should've thought of that." I shiver and stand up. "I've got to go inside, Ed. It's the Arctic tundra out here."

He smiles. "It's good for the constitution. Toots and I try to sit out here for thirty minutes a day. You should get a heavy coat like hers."

I eye the tiny dog staring at me indignantly with her teddy-bear eyes from beneath her hood.

"I should," I agree, before I head inside.

I go straight to the office.

"Will insurance cover this?" I ask Sylvie, who is eating a doughnut.

She hesitates, with powdered sugar on her nose.

"Well, it would have."

I wait.

"If we'd paid the policy last month."

I sit weakly down. "We didn't pay it?"

"We didn't have the money. Which is the same reason your father didn't pay his life insurance. So we had to use what little reserves we had to pay for your father's burial."

My shoulders slump. "This isn't good."

She shakes her head. "No, it isn't."

"No, it isn't," another voice at the door agrees. Logan stands there, and his face is very serious.

"I'm afraid to ask," I tell him.

"I'm afraid to tell you."

"Just rip the Band-Aid off," I advise.

"This is going to be expensive. There was previous water damage to her floors, and it's rotted beneath. She can't come back to this apartment until it's fixed. The floor could collapse on top of Tom's head."

"How much?" I ask, my heart frozen.

"Well, the entire flooring needs to be redone, the tile, the floor joists, the subfloor. While it's open, we really need to replace the copper piping under there. There's also black mold in there that needs to be treated. That came from the untreated water damage. It's currently unsafe."

My stomach sinks.

"We can put her in 405 temporarily," Sylvie says. "It's vacant."

"That's just a temporary fix," I say. "We have a problem."

"Yes, we do," she agrees. "But we'll think of something. Your father always did."

"How had he dealt with this constantly and I never knew

about it?" I muse out loud. My dad was a hero, and I never knew it.

"He was just that way," Sylvie says.

"I can certainly add the labor charges to your tab, and you can pay whenever," Logan says. "But you'll need several thousand for the materials. I'll price it out and get you the estimate today."

I exhale, and I'm pretty sure my vision blurs.

I've literally never had the fate of someone else's home resting on my shoulders before. It's a pressure that I can't say I like.

"We should also address the fact that Melody could've died," I say. "I think we really need a nurse here."

"We're not a medical facility," Sylvie tells me. "That requires licensing and all kinds of red tape."

"Well, we're going to have to think of something," I answer. "We can't have people dying because we aren't equipped to deal with their health issues."

"Why, Ms. Julliard," Logan says lightly, "are you recommending that you get involved in your tenants' personal business? I'm pretty sure you told me once that it was none of yours."

"Well, I maintain that it's not good business to do so," I say snippily. "But maybe . . . it's unavoidable for a good human being."

Logan smiles knowingly.

"Don't say it," I warn him.

"Say what?" His eyes twinkle. "That your icy New York heart

has thawed a little?" He pretends to zip his lips closed. "I'd never," he declares.

I roll my eyes. "You just did."

He grins.

He reaches into his back pocket and hands me a paper.

"I found that on the internet last night," he tells me. "I thought . . . maybe it's something you could do. You know, for money. And to follow your dreams."

He winks and heads out the door.

I examine the paper.

His printer is clearly running out of ink, because it's faded, but I get the gist.

Fashionista is partnering with *Vogue* in a contest for US fashion designers. The winner gets $300,000 dollars. The two runners-up each get $100,000 and free exposure.

I suck in a breath. Could I do this?

Could I really?

Lillianna's words flash in front of me. *You'll never work in this industry again.*

I stick my chin out. She can try and block me. But she's not *God*.

I examine the paper again and tell Sylvie about it.

"The entry deadline is in a week," I read. "And the finalists will show down in a catwalk contest on Christmas Eve."

"Can you do it?" Sylvie asks simply.

I don't know.

But I picture the design I've started upstairs, the one featuring the Christmas dress from Ellie. Maybe I can.

A fluttering starts in my belly, a jumble of delicate butterflies.

"Yes," I say firmly. "Yes, I can."

"You know," Sylvie says. "It's interesting that Logan used what little free time he has to research this for you."

She stares at me and her eyes are knowing.

"What?" I demand, when she keeps waiting for a response. "What do you want me to say?"

"That it's interesting," she answers.

I stare at the paper and imagine Logan hunched over a computer, his calloused fingers tapping on the keys, hunting for things in the fashion world, a world I'm sure he doesn't even understand.

He did that for me.

"Yes," I finally acknowledge. "It's interesting."

Sylvie smiles, and the butterflies in my belly break free and fly toward my heart, which flutters along with their wings.

"It's very interesting indeed," she says.

CHAPTER TEN

$\mathcal{I}$ spend the evening researching the contest.

Last year, it had been won by a groundbreaking fledgling designer who specialized in sustainable fabrics. The year before, by an ethnically diverse fashion house that employs underprivileged women in Uganda to create the accompanying jewelry line.

I sit back in my seat, blowing my hair off my forehead.

How can I compete with that?

I stare at the Christmas dress hanging on my closet door.

"You don't," I mutter. "You focus on the task at hand."

It was something my father taught me. To focus on the task at hand, and not borrow problems that haven't happened yet.

"The world needs to slow down. It needs more simplicity, more quality," I say aloud. "It needs to return to a simpler time. A better time, arguably."

I start creating a pitch deck, rattling off my thoughts.

There comes a time when we need to stop reinventing the wheel simply to reinvent the wheel, I write. Generations ago, women invested in a few quality pieces rather than a closet full of mass-produced, ill-fitting items. Clothing was well taken care of and well worn. It was glamorous, it was utilitarian, it was flattering. Why not return to that era? Let's return to quality. Let's return to the celebration of femininity. Let's get back to class.

I lay my laptop aside and cross the room. I slide the dress on, feeling the soft, thick fabric envelop my body, like a well-worn, well-loved glove.

I turn this way and that in the mirror, admiring the way it hangs just so, the way it showcases my assets, but modestly. I've never felt more lovely than I do in this dress.

Still wearing the dress, I pick up my sketchbook and start drawing another design, then another. Beautiful dresses with beautiful lines, inspired by this one. Each one could've been worn in the '20s, the '30s, the '40s . . . and every decade between then and now. They're timeless and graceful.

On impulse, I grab my sketchbook and head for Ellie's apartment.

She answers the door on my third knock, and she's in a warm robe.

"Meg!" she exclaims. "Is everything all right?"

I check my watch. It's only nine P.M.

"You weren't in bed, were you?" I ask.

"Oh, no. I was just making a cup of cocoa. Would you like one?"

"Always," I answer. "I was hoping to get your input on these sketches, too."

"Come in," she replies. "Sit down, and I'll bring out some cocoa in a moment." She heads for the kitchen, then turns. "You are absolutely lovely in that dress, Meg," she tells me. Her eyes shine softly. "It fits you like it was made for you."

She continues on her way, and I curl up on her sofa. Her fireplace is roaring, and it feels so cozy in here.

When she comes back with a couple of steaming mugs on a tray, she pauses once again. "You remind me of me when I was young," she says. "So sweet, so full of hope and promise."

She sets the tray down, and the scent of hot chocolate wafts in my direction. I inhale it as I take the mug.

"Were you a hottie, too?" I ask glibly. She laughs.

"I can't lie. I was a dish." She presses her lips together primly, but they twitch as she tries not to laugh. Finally, we crack up together, and she puts her hand on my arm.

"I needed that," she finally says. "A good laugh is medicine for the soul." She glances at my sketchbook. "What do you have there?"

I hand it to her, and I'm a bit self-conscious. Maybe they're not as good as I thought. Maybe it's a dumb idea. Maybe I really don't have what it takes. *Why am I so self-confident when I suckkkkk??*

Ellie's eyes light up, though, and she runs her finger over the pages.

"Oh, my goodness, Meg, these are absolutely amazing."

"Really?" I ask, holding my breath. "Truly?"

"Completely," she assures me. "You would use quality fabric, I assume?" She lifts an eyebrow. "Similar to what you're wearing?"

I run the fabric of the Christmas dress between my fingers, and I swear, I feel a weird tingling jolt of electricity, something I can't quite explain. It feels strange to acknowledge it, so I don't.

"Yes, of course," I tell her instead. Because, obviously, I'm just being silly. "This fabric is amazing. High quality, graceful."

"You'll have to hunt far and wide for it, I'm afraid," she says, sighing. "They don't make things like they used to."

"That's for sure. But that's what I want to change."

I take a sip of hot cocoa, and Ellie turns to me. "I've started researching this building. It's got quite a history, Meg."

From her mantel, sparkling Christmas ornaments twinkle. I eye them. "Were those there earlier? I thought you weren't going to decorate?"

She smiles. "I needed a little Christmas cheer."

"I'm sorry to interrupt," I tell her. "What did you discover?"

"Did you know that Chicago was an antislavery hub in the Civil War?" she asks me.

I shake my head. "No, I did not. I mean, I knew it was a Union state."

"It was. But it was more than that. While Illinois didn't allow African Americans full citizen rights, they could operate businesses in Chicago. This building, my dear, was rented and operated by an escaped slave, Mr. Tobias Jones. And can you guess what he did with it?"

I stare at her blankly. "A hotel?"

"You're close!" she says. "He did rent rooms on the upper floors, but the bottom floor was a tavern. And in the basement . . . he had secret passageways dug."

"The Underground Railroad!" I exclaim. "Really??"

She nods. "Really. This building is quite a piece of history. Not only was it part of the Underground Railroad, but it also served to hide already freed slaves. Apparently, during that time, even if a former slave had a certificate of freedom, a lot of abduction was happening. If someone felt in danger, they could come here, and Tobias would hide them. Then later, during Prohibition, those same tunnels were used to smuggle in whiskey. Not such a noble cause, of course, but still historically interesting."

"I can't believe it," I say slowly. "My dad must not have known that."

"It's a very historically significant building," she says. "It won't be hard to get it acknowledged by historical societies. Its history has been forgotten, but you can bring it back to life, and preserve it."

"That's going to take money." I sigh. "And I don't have it. I don't even know if I have the thousand dollars to enter the Fashionista contest."

Ellie lifts an eyebrow again, and as she drinks the rest of her cocoa, I tell her about it.

When I'm finished, she sits back in her chair.

"My, oh, my, Meg," she breathes. "You sure have brought life back to this place."

I laugh. "By what? Being incredibly inept?"

She rolls her eyes and shakes her head. "No. By breathing fresh ideas into it." She gets up and brings back her checkbook. I watch as she starts to write a check, then it occurs to me what she's doing.

"Ellie, no," I protest. "I'm not going to take your money. I'll get it another way."

She doesn't even look up.

"It's a thousand dollars," she says dismissively. "I usually donate to good causes this time of year anyway. And this is a good cause."

She tears the check out and hands it to me.

"It's your entry fee. Enter, then win." She nods. "Let's bring this place back to life."

"But I haven't even focused on what I should do with it," I tell her. "It's so overwhelming."

"Meg, dear. Really? You can't see it?" Ellie gets up, walks to the window, and looks out over the Christmas lights sparkling below us. "You will renovate this building, make it safer for the tenants. It can be a bona fide retirement community. And in the basement, you'll have your headquarters for your fashion line, and maybe even a small museum on the other side. Maybe a working speakeasy, too."

"You've certainly got aspirations," I tell her, awed.

"I love goals to work toward," she says, shrugging. "You'll have grant money to work with, too. Although it will take time to apply and receive any grants. So it's important that you win this contest. You can do it."

"I can *try.*"

"There is no try. There is only do." I stare at her and she laughs. "My daughter made me watch *Star Wars* with her over Zoom."

I laugh at the idea of prim and proper Ellie watching Chewbacca and shake my head. "You are truly surprising, Miss Ellie."

She preens. "Thank you. But it's not entirely selfless. If this becomes a retirement community, Betsy can stop arguing that I need to move."

She gets up and literally starts unpacking.

"Ellie, I don't know if I can do any of this. Don't jump the gun," I warn her.

Ellie gives me a frank look. "Meg, there's something that your father told me many, many times about you. When you want something, you get it. So, go on . . . *get it.*"

She turns her back and starts lifting things out of boxes.

I close my gaping mouth and hesitantly walk toward the door.

"But . . ." I turn.

"No buts," she answers, without even looking up. "This is happening."

I'm in a daze as I walk up the stairs to my apartment. How had I suddenly gone from a struggling building owner to a prospective business mogul in ten minutes?

I pass Sylvie on the stairs. She's carrying an armload of red stockings and she's wearing an elf cap.

"Should I ask?" I say, almost grimacing.

"Don't be a scrooge, Meghan," she answers. "Every year, I hang stockings by each door. Then the tenants slip candy and little gifts into them for their neighbors. It's fun."

"That's nice," I admit to her.

She smirks. "You're going to need to get more into the spirit, or you'll get coal in yours. I'll see you in the morning. I left some paperwork on the desk for you to review."

I nod and continue back to my apartment.

When I get there, I find a stocking hanging next to my door. It says Meg on it in green sparkly glue. There's a small bump in the toe, so I reach in, and pull out a Hershey's kiss. I unwrap it and pop it into my mouth.

I can see myself getting into this particular custom.

I curl up on the couch and call Cassie.

I tell her about my plan to enter the Fashionista contest, and while she's excited, she answers in hushed tones.

"Where are you?" I ask, my eyes narrowing. "Are you still at work?"

"No," she whispers. "I'm on a date."

"With whom?" I ask pointedly, but without actually caring.

"With Drake," she says honestly. "Meg, thank you so much. He and I are really clicking. He wants to be the successful breadwinner, and I want to be married to one. How cool is that? And we both want two point five kids."

"You do know that you can't actually have point five of a kid, right?" I ask.

I can practically hear her rolling her eyes.

"Don't be salty," she says. "I'm so excited. And you said this was okay."

"It is," I assure her. "One thousand percent okay."

"Listen," she murmurs quickly. "I have to go, but tomorrow morning, I'll give Erin Rieman at *Vogue* a call on your behalf. The entry deadline was Thanksgiving, but I think I can probably talk her into it."

"What? Their website says the deadline is next week."

"They changed it," she answers.

"I don't want to get you into trouble with Dragon Lady," I say hesitantly.

"Don't worry about it. They don't like her any more than we do. And I owe you."

She hangs up, and I stare out at the Christmas lights in the city from my balcony.

It's odd to me, but I really don't care if Cassie dates Drake, although it surprises me that she likes him so much. He always seemed a bit droidlike to me.

"To each their own," I mutter to myself. I prefer warmer men,

men with eyes that twinkle, men who are at home in every situation they find themselves in . . . men like Logan.

My heart quickens a bit at the mere thought of him.

Those blue eyes.

"Lord have mercy," I whisper. The butterflies flip my belly over and over. "Shut up, ovaries," I mutter toward my belly. "I don't need that complication right now."

But what if he wasn't a complication?

"Of course he would be," I say aloud. "Men always are."

But Logan isn't like the rest.

I know that.

It fascinates me.

That's why, when he calls the next morning and asks me to help him Christmas shop for his nieces, I say yes.

CHAPTER ELEVEN

I shouldn't be here," I tell him as we walk through the bustling crowds on the Magnificent Mile. Although, as I glance at his off-white turtleneck and gray peacoat, and the way he wears both as though they were tailored just for him, I know that's a lie. I shouldn't be anywhere *but here*.

"It's Saturday," he reminds me. "You've got to have some time off."

"I can't. I've got so much to do. I've still got to find a contractor who will help me smash in the wall in the basement and find Ernest Hemingway's signature on the bar . . . if it exists."

"I can help with that," he assures me as he holds open the door to a toy store, and I enter.

"Are you sure?" I glance at him. "I don't want to take advantage of you."

"Is that on the table?" he asks with a grin. "Taking advantage of me, I mean."

I laugh, and those dang butterflies start swarming again.

"I want to help," he tells me. Then he stops and turns in a helpless circle. "But first, please help me. I don't know what I'm doing here. I'm out of my depth."

"Things aren't the same since FAO Schwarz left," I tell him. "But we'll still find something awesome. How old are the girls?"

"Eight and ten," he answers, and then he tells me all about them: their favorite color is pink (both of them) and they play soccer and with Barbies.

"You know what would make you the best uncle in the world?" I ask him.

"Please tell me. That's why you're here."

"A Barbie DreamHouse. Jo and I had one when we were that age. We loved that thing."

"Sold!" he says, and we turn to find the Barbie aisle. "Do you want to talk about your sister? I can't imagine losing mine. She's a pain in my neck, but I love her."

My heart twinges, because it always does at the mention of Jo. But I can't blame him. I'm the one who brought her up.

"No, thanks. Not today. I loved her. And she's gone. I miss her every day." I glance down the aisle. "Hey, look."

I point toward the Barbie house display, and Logan emits a low whistle.

"Does it come assembled?" he asks hopefully. I burst out laughing.

"No. But isn't that part of the wonder of Christmas? You get to spend hours putting it together and using all the curse words you know."

He chuckles. "Only if you'll help me."

My head snaps back. He's asking me out again already? But then again, maybe this isn't a date. Maybe I'm mistaken.

He sees my hesitation.

"You don't have to," he reassures me. "I'm sure I can manage without your tool prowess."

"Bite your tongue. I can handle a Phillips head with the best of them. That's the one with the screwy head, right?"

He says dryly, "Yes. I can see your skill."

I have to admit, it's hilarious seeing this manly man in a sea of Barbie pink, especially when he doesn't even flinch.

We wrestle the giant box off the shelf, and I talk him into getting the matching pink car.

"You're going to be the fun uncle," I promise him.

"I'd better be. I'm their only uncle."

As he pays for the toys, a group of costumed elves sing Christmas carols to our left. I catch Logan humming along with them.

"You love Christmas, don't you?" I ask him with a smile.

He shrugs. "What other time of year do we all pause for a minute and show our families how much we love them?"

For some reason, amid the Christmas carols, the snow, and the twinkling lights on the trees lining the street, that comment is a stake through my heart. Because I don't have any family left.

Logan notices, and freezes, right in the middle of the rush of people.

"Oh my god. I'm so sorry, Meg. I wasn't thinking."

I shake my head. "It's okay. Truly. I need to wrap my head around the fact that I'm an orphan now."

My throat is tight, and I feel pathetic, and I know I *sound* pitiful, but I still can't help the desolate feeling that wraps around my heart.

"You're not alone, Meg," Logan says quietly, and his blue eyes drill into mine with a fiery intensity. "You've got everyone at Parkview in your corner. And you've got me."

He's so serious, so sincere, that I almost allow myself to believe it.

But he's just being kind, because they're all acquaintances, not family. They're not stuck with me, like a family would be. They're connected to me through the building. I literally pay Logan, and if I sold the Parkview, they'd all be gone . . . the ribbon connecting us snipped.

It's a very lonely feeling, and somehow, in the middle of the holiday throng of people, I feel like I'm standing all alone.

Logan wraps one arm around my shoulder, and with the other, he somehow manages to half carry, half drag the giant toy package. Part of it drags on the sidewalk, and he pretends not to notice.

"Oh, my goodness. You're going to ruin it," I tell him, laughing. "You won't be the fun uncle then; I can tell you." I slip out from under his warm arm and pick up half of the box. We carry it like that, in tandem, until we get to Logan's truck.

I miss the warmth of his arm, and the intimate way it felt. I could smell his aftershave, musky and woodsy. And more than that, I felt safe.

It was a really good feeling.

After he stows the packages in the back seat of the crew cab, he turns to me.

"Now what?"

I lift my brows.

"Aren't we done?"

"Shopping for my nieces? Yes. Getting you into the Christmas spirit? No."

He has such a boyish look on his handsome face that I actually laugh.

"I doubt there's anything you can do," I warn him.

"Challenge accepted," he announces, grabbing my arm.

"It wasn't a challenge," I tell him quickly. "Seriously. I've got work to do."

He ignores me. "It'll still be there when we get back. First . . . we skate."

"Skate?" I stare at him. "No. Ice and I . . . we don't get along."

He ignores me again. "I've got you," he promises. Then he pulls me along with him until we reach Maggie Daley Park. Since I have to try very hard not to slip and fall on the sidewalk, I don't have high hopes for the ice-skating rink.

I'm still grumbling as I lace up my skates.

"I didn't wear the right socks for this," I mutter.

He rolls his eyes.

"I also haven't skated since I was twelve. Maybe I should get one of those push thingies," I tell him.

"The walkers on tennis balls?" He looks at someone using one. "Um, no."

"You're not secure enough in your manhood to be seen with something like that?"

"I'm very secure in it," he tells me. "Which is why . . . I can hold you up."

"What if I fall?" I ask, staring up at him. He extends his hand to help me off the bench.

"Then I'll catch you."

"What if I break a hip?"

"You're not geriatric," he reminds me, although in this moment, I'm not convinced. I wobble my way to the rink opening, and my legs feel like twigs getting ready to snap.

"This isn't going to end well," I warn him. I don't want to tell him that the last time I skated, I'd broken my left arm. I had to wear a cast for eight weeks, and even though Brian Amrine, the cutest boy in seventh grade, had signed it, it wasn't worth it.

He pulls me onto the ice without a care in the world.

The cold air nips at my cheeks as we start our slow glide around the oval. Logan looks at me.

"See? You're doing great."

"Don't let go," I tell him. He gives me an amused look but keeps his arm firmly linked in mine.

"You gotta admit," he says, eyeing the festivities around us . . . the lights, the music, the laughter, the steaming mugs from onlookers on the sides. "*This* is Christmas spirit."

A man in a Santa hat bumps me, and I cling to Logan, temporarily losing my balance. He's like a tree, solid and tall, and doesn't falter.

"Yeah, it is."

"You know Sylvie started planning the Christmas party again, right?" he asks me. My ankles wobble, and I right myself.

"She did?"

"Oh, yes. I already have my invitation. Verbal invitation," he corrects.

"But the . . ." I trail off and picture a calendar in my head. Nope, there's no way around it. "The Fashionista contest . . ."

He eyes me. "Well, if anyone can do both, it's you."

I wince. "Have I ever mentioned that I have a tendency to bite off more than I can chew?"

He laughs. "I have faith in you. "

"I wanted to throw a party," I tell him. "Before I knew about the contest. But never fear. If my friend Cass can get my entry accepted, I'll figure it out. There's always a way."

"There's the spirit."

He grabs my hand and twirls me away from him, in an effort to do a lighthearted spin. He apparently forgot I'm a novice skater. The tip of my blade stutters on the ice, and I go tumbling. In my panic, I instinctively grab at Logan, and he tumbles down with me.

It happens in a blur, and I don't feel my backside slam onto the ice.

My head doesn't make impact, because Logan's hand is behind it, cushioning the blow.

His entire body is on top of mine, from toe to waist. For a scant second, he stares into my eyes, and the tension crackles. His hips are warm and heavy. He lifts away with his elbows.

"Are you okay?" he asks, his voice husky, moving to help me sit up.

I notice the absence of his hips immediately. My own feel cold and lonely now.

I tentatively touch the back of my head. There's no bump.

"Thank you," I tell him. "You caught me. Sort of."

"Sort of." He chuckles. "Did I smash you?"

In all the best ways.

I shake my head. "Not at all. You're very chivalrous."

We suddenly realize that we're standing in the middle of the rink, and skaters have to swerve around us. "Let's get to the side," Logan says, and he pulls me along. He tucks me almost protectively into the crook of his arm. And I like it.

I lean into him more than I need to.

He pretends not to notice.

He helps me to a bench and bends down to unlace my skates. "I can do that," I tell him.

"So can I," he says casually. "I'm the one who talked you into this."

"That is true," I agree. He lifts one skate off, then the other.

I rub my hands together to warm them, and he glances at me. "We need some hot food. Dinner?"

I nod quickly. "I get grumpy when I'm hungry. And cold."

"I hadn't noticed," he lies. I laugh.

He makes me laugh so easily. I can be myself with him, without trying to be proper, or *just so*, the way I always needed to be with Drake.

It's almost frightening the way I've so quickly warmed up to Logan. I try not to focus on it.

Instead, I focus on the matter at hand.

"Where should we go?" I ask him as we walk out of the park.

"How about Macy's? The Walnut Room is nice this time of year."

"Oh my gosh, my mom used to take Jo and me to see the tree in there. We'd have 'tea' on a Sunday afternoon around Christmas," I tell him. "But we can't get in there without a reservation. Not this time of year."

"Don't worry about that," he tells me as he hails a taxi.

I narrow my eyes. "It's almost like this was planned," I tell him as he opens the yellow door for me, and I climb in.

He grins. "Well, you were so kind to help me, and I knew I'd need to feed you. It's a small price to pay."

"But you only asked me last night," I say slowly.

"Let it go, Meg," he suggests. "Let's just enjoy it."

He's right. Why ruin the moment wondering how he'd managed to get a last-minute reservation? For all I know, he knows someone.

IT DOESN'T TAKE us long to get there, and we step out onto the sidewalk amid the glittering lights. As evening falls, the lights are even more beautiful.

"I sense the Christmas spirit," Logan says as he holds the door open for me. I roll my eyes.

"Your spirit detector is off," I answer. "I'm just appreciating the decorations."

"Which is all part of it," he replies. "Christmas spirit is an entire package of different elements."

"Now you're making it sound like science," I tell him. "My least favorite subject."

He gives his name to the girl at the podium, and we wait.

"I can see that about you," he agrees. "It's too much like math. You're more creative. Artsy."

"You say that like it's a bad thing," I tell him, as I pick up my menu once we're seated. In front of us, on the table, a candle flickers.

"Not at all," he says. "I'm happy for it. People like you make the world a beautiful place."

I smile. I like that thinking.

I start to examine the menu, but the giant glimmering tree is distracting.

"Now, *that's* beautiful," I say of the forty-five-foot Great Tree hanging from the ceiling instead of sitting on the floor. Each ornament shimmers, perfectly placed.

"It really is," Logan agrees. "Does it look like you remember?"

"Exactly like," I tell him. "My sister and I used to love coming here. My mom would let us pick out one small toy, even though Christmas was coming."

"That's awesome," he says. "If I asked for anything, even a toothbrush, this time of year, my mom would say, okay, but it'll have to be part of your Christmas."

We both reach for our waters. Our fingers touch. I yank my hand away. He clears his throat and takes a drink.

"My mom died when I was little, though. So I haven't really been back since then. Thank you for having me." I glance at him. "Why *did* you ask me here today?" I ask him bluntly as I set my glass down.

He lifts an eyebrow, and I ignore the five o'clock shadow that lingers on his jaw. It's so manly, and my ovaries twinge.

"Because I need your help."

I stare at him pointedly. He stares back.

Finally, he sighs.

"Because I knew that Christmas this year would be hard for you. I didn't want you to feel alone."

"That's very sweet of you," I admit. "But you don't need to save me."

"How very modern of you," he answers. "But it wasn't about 'saving.' It was about . . . I just like you. Can't someone do something without an ulterior motive?"

"Not usually," I tell him.

"Well, in this case, I have no ulterior motive. And many people don't. That's a depressing way to look at things."

"Maybe I've been in the city too long," I concede.

"Many would consider Chicago a city, too," he answers wryly. I laugh.

"Touché."

"Can you tell me more about the hidden bar in your basement?" he asks, changing the subject. "Are you thinking it's behind that main brick wall? That's a support wall."

"I think it's behind that," I tell him, as the waiter appears. "So maybe it's not a support wall."

Logan doesn't even hesitate. "We'll take two chicken pot pies, and then we'll split a Frango ice cream pie for dessert."

I stare at him, amused.

"Was that okay?" he asks as the waiter walks away.

"That's exactly what I used to get with Jo and my mom," I tell him.

"It's what they're known for." He shrugs. But still, it's almost like he knows how special it is to me, although there's no way he could. There's no one left who knows my secrets.

"You're very intuitive," I decide.

"My sister would beg to differ. She says that it takes reality to slap me alongside the head before I see it."

"I think I might really like your sister," I tell him with a grin. He spends the next few minutes telling me about her, and how they'd grown close after his dad died several years back, how they're best friends. "We both take care of my mom now," he tells me.

"You split the burden," I say.

He frowns a bit and shakes his head. "My mom isn't a burden. She's our mom. That's what families do."

Once again, I feel a pang. That wasn't what I'd done with my dad.

Once again, Logan notices.

"Your dad didn't need to be taken care of," he tells me. "He was very healthy and capable."

"Right up until he wasn't," I agree.

"It happened in an instant," Logan says. "There was no way to foresee that. It's part of life, Meg. Sadly. But you can rest easy knowing that he knew you loved him."

"How do I know that, though?" I hear the vulnerability in my voice and it annoys me, but once words are spoken, they can't be unsaid.

Logan looks at me. "Meg, I know you like to picture yourself as a no-nonsense city girl. And that's fine. Part of you is exactly that. But part of you is a warm, inviting person, and your dad absolutely knew how much you loved him. It shone from him every time he spoke about you. He was bursting with pride about every single thing you did. He knew you'd come home to visit when you were ready. He told me so."

"Did he sound sad that I hadn't come yet?" I'm almost afraid to ask.

"No. He sounded understanding. He knew exactly why the Parkview made you feel pain. And he knew that you would face it when you could."

"You sure know a lot for the handyman," I say, and I didn't mean it as abruptly as it came out. Logan almost flinches.

"I was more than a handyman to your father," he tells me. "I was his friend. And if you'll let me, I'd like to be yours, too."

His friend.

I consider that as my glass of wine arrives and I take a sip.

I don't know if that will be enough for me. One look at Logan's kind eyes and I'm almost certain of that.

"Well, we'll see how it shakes out, shall we?" I hold my glass out, and he clinks his scotch glass with mine.

"Here's to whatever comes our way," he says. "Merry Christmas!"

"Merry Christmas," I echo, and I take a long drink, and let it slide down my throat and warm my belly.

WHEN WE'RE DONE with our meal, Logan insists on paying the check, and after he drives me home, he gets out and walks me to the door of the building.

"Have a good night, Meggie," he says. It's my father's nickname for me, but I don't tell him that. It feels nice to have some-one use it.

"You, too, Logan."

He stares at me briefly, and I wonder ... is he going to kiss me? I exhale, and wait, but he doesn't.

He just smiles.

"I'll see you tomorrow. We'll start on that basement."

With a wave, he climbs back into his truck, and my stomach muscles relax as he drives away.

No kiss.

A perfect gentleman.

Something about that makes me smile all the way to my apartment. Although, if I'm honest with myself, I know that I really wanted him to kiss me silly.

When I climb into bed, I keep thinking of his mischievous smile.

It's almost midnight when he texts me.

> I had an amazing time tonight. When can I see you again?

I smile and fall asleep with my phone hugged to my chest.

CHAPTER TWELVE

$\mathscr{I}$ wake up to a good-morning text from Logan.

> Hey, did I mention I had a great time last night? ☺

Butterflies shoot through my belly again, and I smile. One thing about Logan, you never have to wonder where you stand. He doesn't play games. I'm never going to see him waiting for three days, wondering if it's too soon to call. It's nice.

You might've mentioned it, I answer. Which is good, because I had a great time, too.

He sends me the two-girls-holding-hands emoji, and I burst out laughing.

You get an A for effort, I tell him, not sure if he knows what the emoji actually means.

Speaking of effort, I hope you're dressed. I'm arriving in four minutes.

Don't worry, I have coffee.

I don't even answer. I leap out of bed, throw on a sweater and leggings, and yank a brush through my hair, before I try to arrange it in a bun on top of my head.

I barely manage to look presentable before there's a rap on the door.

I try not to appear out of breath from my efforts as I answer it.

"Oh, hey," I greet him casually, as though I'd been up for hours. "You're out and about early."

He grins. "I leave the house at five A.M." He offers me a cup of coffee.

"You're a god," I tell him.

"Remember that," he answers and reaches into his work coat. He pulls out the tiniest kitten I've seen in a while. It has its eyes open, and it's still only weeks old.

"I found this little guy on my way here," he tells me. "It was in the snow and it wouldn't have lasted long."

"Oh my gosh. Come in," I tell him, and I reach for the kitten. His white fur is soft, and he's shivering. "Is it a boy?"

"I can't tell yet," Logan answers, handing him to me carefully with his gloved hand. "His parts are still too small."

He closes the door behind him, and I cradle the tiny cat. It shivers against my chest, and I instantly fall in love.

"You tricked me," I accuse him, all the while grabbing a blanket from the couch and wrapping it around the tiny body in my hands. Logan grins.

"I thought maybe you might want it," he answers. "It could be a building mascot for Parkview West. An emotional support cat for your tenants?" He lifts an eyebrow, and I shake my head.

"You're despicable for playing on my soft spot," I tell him, but with a smile.

"You have one?? Good to know." He nods, and I slap at his arm. "Ow, ow. Don't hurt me," he pleads, and I roll my eyes. "Maybe you could name him Snowball," he suggests.

I stare at him. "That's so cliché."

"Snowflake? I mean, I did find him in the snow."

"Everyone who has a white cat names it Snowball or Snowflake." I examine the tiny blue-eyed kitten. "I think . . . Winter White, in memory of my favorite coat. Chicago ruined it, so it's only poetic justice that Chicago gives me something cute in its place. Hello, Winter White," I tell the kitten, kissing his cute pink nose.

"That's . . . a mouthful," Logan says. "But fitting, I guess?"

"Winter for short."

"I like it."

"You have no choice. You have delivered a stray cat to me."

"An *adorable* stray cat," he clarifies. "A helpless little kitten who needs your help or it will die."

"You can stop now," I tell him. "I already said yes."

"I'm just making sure you don't change your mind," he replies.

"I'll have to go out and get him some supplies," I tell him. "I don't have anything for a cat."

"I can go with you," he offers. "The least I can do is pay for it."

"That's not necessary," I answer. "Really."

"I insist," he replies. "Besides, I want another excuse to spend time with you."

He looks at me with those eyes, and my knees go weak. *How can I say no to that?*

"Maybe I can get Sylvie to look after him while we're gone."

"I'm sure she will."

"Did you stop and see her on the way up?" I ask knowingly. He nods.

"Of course. She liked the name Snowball, too."

"Neither of you have any imagination."

"Don't tell her that," Logan cautions, as I grab my purse and we head out the door.

"Don't worry. I'll never get on her bad side again."

I cradle the kitten on the way down the stairs, and Logan's hand hovers near my elbow, a protective, gentlemanly gesture that I love.

I could get used to this.

His cologne makes my ovaries tingle, because it smells just like he should smell. Outdoorsy, manly. It's *so* him.

When we enter the office, Sylvie scoops Winter up in her arms and cradles him inside her sweater immediately.

"Poor little baby," she croons. "It's a wonder you didn't die in the cold."

"I know," Logan says. "There was no sign of a mama cat anywhere. Just him . . . all alone."

He eyes me pointedly, and I roll my eyes again. "Seriously. I'm not going to change my mind. I have a new cat."

He grins in satisfaction. "He can be your guard cat," he suggests. "He'll protect you when you're alone."

"Now you're going overboard. He weighs a pound, at the most."

"Don't stomp on his aspirations," Logan tells me.

"You're crazy."

"I think you like it," he says, his lips ever so close to my ear. Goose bumps form along my spine. Heck yes, I like it.

"Let's go," I say instead of embarrassing myself. "He needs food."

Sylvie doesn't even look up when we leave. She just cradles Winter and sings him "White Christmas."

"You're wily," I tell him as we step onto the sidewalk.

"But I'm honest about it," he replies as we walk down the street. "There's a small pet store close by."

"You already googled it, I assume?"

"Yep."

"Of course you did."

As we walk, he finds my gloved hand and clasps it within his own, holding it as we make our way down the sidewalk.

A thrill shoots up my arm from his touch, even though two layers of gloves separate our fingers.

He guides me around a huge slush puddle. "Watch that," he warns, pointing at it.

Is this man perfect?

I'm starting to think so.

We find the pet store, and the bell jingles over the door as we enter.

"We've gone shopping twice in as many days," he tells me as we head toward the cat supplies. "I think that's a sign."

"A sign of what?"

"I dunno. It must mean something, though."

He grabs a case of tiny canned kitten food, along with a little set of bowls. "We'll need cat litter," he mumbles, thinking aloud.

"Speaking of, I hate cleaning cat boxes."

"But do you love kitten cuddles?" he asks hopefully.

I stare at him.

"Look. There's a cute pink box. Would you like that one?"

"I'm sure if Winter turns out to be a boy, he'll be secure in his masculinity. I'll raise him right," I tell him. He laughs and grabs the pink tray.

I choose a small bag of litter.

"I think we're set," I tell him, but he's already grabbing a bunch of kitten toys.

"We don't want him to get bored," he tells me. He points, with a full hand, toward a little plush cat bed that looks like Santa's sleigh. "Grab that, too."

We head toward the register with all our stuff, and he pulls out his wallet.

The cashier smiles. "New pet?" she asks. I nod.

"Well, judging by all this, you'll be great kitten parents," she decides.

"Oh! We're not—" I start to say, but Logan interrupts.

"Thank you! We're going to try our best."

As we walk out, I eye him. "She thought we were together."

"Aren't we?" he asks.

I stare at him.

"We haven't even had our first kiss," I tell him, feeling a little breathless.

He literally drops his bags on the sidewalk, and pulls me to him, into the gentlest embrace I've ever felt. The irony is that his arms are so strong, I can feel the corded muscles around me. His lips are so soft as he presses them to mine, and his mouth tastes like peppermint.

We kiss for a full minute in the middle of Christmas shoppers.

When he finally pulls away, he grins at me.

"Now we have."

He gathers his bags, and I'm speechless.

"I've wanted to do that since the first day I met you," he tells me.

I'm still speechless, and he chuckles.

"Is that all I have to do to get you to stop talking?"

"I thought you liked it when I talked," I grouse. He grins.

"I do."

We make our way through the snow and people to the Parkview. We find Sylvie working at her desk, with Winter sleeping on her bosom. She's careful not to disturb him as she greets us.

"I see the baby is taking a nap," I say, but she shushes me.

"He just went to sleep," she says, her finger to her lips. "He's had a rough night, I'm sure. Poor little guy, all alone."

"He's not alone now," I whisper. "He'll be fine."

Sylvie notices the cat bed in Logan's hand. "I hope you're not planning on making him sleep on the floor," she tells me. "He's too small. He'll get cold."

"He'll sleep with me," I promise her. "This is just for the office."

Logan takes my cue and sets the bed atop the desk, where Winter can sleep, and we can keep an eye on him. Sylvie beams. "I'll have him try it out when he wakes up," she whispers. "Thank you."

Logan smiles and winks at me. Once again, he's managed to further endear himself to Sylvie. Now, though, it doesn't annoy me.

"We have one more quick errand to run," he whispers to me, and I feel ridiculous that we're whispering because of a cat. We walk out into the hall.

"Come with me," he tells me, pulling me along.

"Where are we going?" I ask, not entirely happy that we seem to be headed out into the cold.

"You'll see."

We spill back out onto the sidewalk and head down the street. Logan pauses to put some money in the red bucket, where the bell ringer thanks him warmly.

"Thank you for the coffee the other day," he tells me, remembering. I smile.

"I'll bring you some more later," I promise.

He grins and rings his bell with even more vigor.

A FEW MINUTES later, and I'm standing in front of a Christmas Tree stand.

I look at Logan.

"We already have a tree in the lobby," I tell him. "It's artificial. And it's not the best, but still."

"It's not for the lobby," he says. "It's for your apartment. I noticed you don't have one. You have ornaments in a box, but no tree to put them on."

I swallow. "That's because . . . my dad always insisted on a live tree."

"I figured. So . . . here we are. Choose whichever one you want."

For a moment, it feels almost traitorous to pick out a tree without my father. But then, I know as sure as I'm breathing that he wouldn't want me to feel lonely. He wouldn't want me to sit in an undecorated apartment. He loved Christmas. He'd want me to still love it, too.

"Okay." I sigh. "Let's do this."

We enter the fenced-in area filled with trees and Christmas music, and I actually find myself singing to "Jingle Bell Rock" as I hunt for the perfect tree.

"I like this one," I say, biting my lip as I examine a tiny tree. "But I'm not sure."

I wrap my red scarf around it to mark it, and I continue on, making sure to look at them all.

I examine a four-foot beautiful, fragrant blue spruce, but my heart is with the other one. The five-foot balsam fir that is perfectly symmetrical and satisfies my inner OCD.

I go back to it and reclaim my scarf.

Next to me, Logan says, "So this one? Nice choice."

He calls for the clerk, who comes running in a Santa hat.

Logan insists on paying for it and won't take no for an answer. Finally, I acquiesce.

"Okay. Thank you," I tell him, smiling.

"I like making you smile," he admits. I smile again, but this time, my cheeks blush a little. My chest gets a bit warm, too.

Logan carries the tree all the way back down to the Parkview, and then up to my apartment. While he's setting it up, I run back down to get Winter. Sylvie gives him to me grudgingly.

"He's so good," she tells me. "He's such a snuggler."

I cuddle him in the elevator all the way back up to my apartment, and when I enter, I'm surprised to find that Logan is already stringing lights on the tree.

"They were in the box," he tells me. "I hope it's okay."

"Of course," I tell him immediately. "Thank you."

"I can hear Winter purring from here," he observes, watching the kitten curled into my neck. "He likes you."

"He's a kitten. He likes everyone." But still, I feel immense satisfaction that he does, in fact, seem to like me.

I pull a soft blanket from the back of the couch and swirl it into a makeshift nest, then place the kitten inside. He watches lazily as I get up and join Logan at the tree.

Logan digs through the box and pulls out a golden tin star with an old school picture on it.

"How old were you in this?'

I smile. "That's not me. That's my sister, Jo, when she was maybe . . . I dunno. Eight?"

He hangs it on the front of the tree and searches for another.

This time, he does emerge with my picture, pasted onto a green-construction-paper tree, hanging with a red pipe-cleaner hook.

Before he can ask, I tell him, "I was in first grade. I'd cut my own bangs. My mother was furious."

Logan laughs and positions it carefully on a branch.

There's a popsicle manger with a paper baby Jesus in it that Jo and I had made together, and Logan notices that a popsicle stick is loose. "Do you have any glue?" he asks.

"Check the drawer by the sink," I tell him. "It's my dad's junk drawer."

While he does that, I hang other ornaments, one by one, until Logan returns with the mended manger.

"This is quite the craftsmanship," he remarks as he hangs it. "I'm not sure you need me for that wall in the basement, after all." I laugh.

"It was mostly Jo," I tell him. "She was the careful one. She was patient and took her time. I was more of a 'let's do a half-assed job so we can go eat cookies' kind of kid."

"What?" Logan feigns astonishment. "That seems so unlike you."

"Hush," I answer, reaching around him to hang a silver bell. "I have good traits, too. I forced her out of her comfort zone and into doing things she wanted."

"That also seems like you," he agrees. "What are some things you talked her into doing?"

"Oh, we put on some talent shows, for our parents and a few tenants," I remember with a smile. "We choreographed some pretty jammin' dances."

Logan barks out a laugh. "I can see it now," he says. "Can you show me a little? Of your moves, I mean?"

"You wish." I turn up my nose.

"Come onnnn," he wheedles. "I wanna see."

"You can't handle this," I tell him, gesturing at my body. "Trust me."

"Try me," he begs.

I eye him. "Fine. But don't say I didn't warn you."

I think for a second, then cue up "Bad" by Michael Jackson on my phone. As it plays, I dance to the first chorus.

Logan cackles. "You've turned this masterpiece into . . ." I glance at him. "A better masterpiece," he finishes. "I can just picture you and your sister synchronizing your dance moves to this."

"You would've liked her," I tell him, as I take a breather. "Everyone did."

"I've heard that," he says, "she was a lovely girl."

"She would've laughed at that description," I answer. "But it's true. She was."

I sit on the couch next to Winter and pet his sleeping body. "She would've loved Winter."

Logan sits next to me, his arm on the back of the couch. He smells like cedar. "What about me? What would she have thought of me?"

"Are you fishing for compliments?" I ask him, settling into his arm and looking into his blue eyes.

"Yes," he says, unabashedly. I give him a look.

"She would've said you were hot," I tell him. "Keep in mind, she was a teenager. So she'd have said you were hot, and funny." I peer at him. "And that you have great cheekbones."

"Wow. She was a very wise girl," Logan approves. I fight the urge to trace those cheekbones with my finger, and the way Logan is staring at my mouth makes me think he's fighting the urge of a few other things.

"She would probably have wondered if you were a good kisser," I tell him quietly.

"What would you have said?" he asks, and his voice is a bit husky now.

"I would've said that I can't remember. That you'd need to show me again, so that I can make a better judgment."

"I thought you'd never ask." He leans into me, pulling me close as he kisses me senseless. His hands are on my back, the warmth from his fingers leaching into me, and mine tangle in his hair, pulling him close, close, closer.

My heart beats erratically, thundering in my chest, and when he finally pulls away, I'm dazed.

"Well?" he manages to say, looking a bit disheveled himself.

"Um." I pause. "I think you should show me again. Just so I can be sure."

He pulls me close again, grinning against my lips.

Several minutes later, my toes are tingling. "I would tell her that you are amazing," I admit to him. "In more ways than one."

"Good." He winks. "That's exactly what I was going for." He stands up. "I should get going before Sylvie notices that I'm still here and I get a stern phone call."

I laugh, but because he's not wrong.

"We have to get up early tomorrow anyway," he says as we pause at the door. "We've got to start tearing down the wall in the basement and getting this show on the road."

"I'll supply the coffee and the muscle power," I tell him.

"Okay, Tiny Thunder," he answers, poking at my measly bicep, before he kisses me one last time, distracting me entirely.

After I close the door behind him, I float around the apartment, getting ready for bed. With the tree and its lights, it's brighter in here, happier.

As Winter and I curl into bed, and as he stares up at me with his little blue kitten eyes and his tiny pink nose, I realize something.

In bringing me this kitten, Logan made it so I'm not alone.

In fact, in thinking more about it, I'm willing to bet that was his plan all along.

I fall asleep with a smile on my face, and a purring kitten on my chest.

CHAPTER THIRTEEN

$\mathcal{I}$'m not fully awake as I clutch my oversize coffee mug and listen to Sylvie drone on about the Christmas party, all while she strokes Winter.

"I'm hanging lights in the courtyard," she says, as he prances in front of her on the desk. "It will be beautiful."

"I know I'm still half asleep," I tell her. "But won't it be too cold for anyone to want to hang out in the courtyard?"

She rolls her eyes, her pen paused on her list. "Someone might want to go out and get some fresh air," she says patiently. "Besides, we can see the courtyard from the ballroom."

"You mean, the conference room," I correct.

"It's used as a conference room now, but it was once the ballroom," she says huffily. "And if you ask me, it's a much better use of the space. We never host meetings in there."

"Not yet," I tell her, sipping my coffee. "But maybe someday."

She harrumphs again, unconvinced. "We should renovate it and rent it out for fancy functions, like quinceañeras and weddings," she says. I take another drink of coffee.

"How was your evening with Mr. Scott?" she asks, changing the subject and trying not to appear nosy. My heart smiles because mentioning him makes me think of his good-morning text this morning. Good morning, Tiny Thunder.

I take a long draw of coffee. "It was lovely. He's a very, very nice man."

"And not hard to look at it," she points out, staring at my mouth. She'd noticed the happy look on my face.

I laugh. "No, definitely not."

"If I were forty years younger, I'd give you a run for your money," she announces, the pom-pom on her Santa hat bouncing. "Make no mistake."

"Well, I'm glad you aren't. I don't know if I could win that competition."

"Stop flattering me." She pauses. "No, keep it up. I like it."

"Sylvie, you're amazing, and you know it. Hey"—I decide it's time to move the conversation away from Logan—"have you had any luck finding the Red Alibi research?"

She drops her gaze. "No. I can't believe I've lost it."

"It's okay." I'm not surprised at all. She seems to lose *everything*. "It's got to be here somewhere."

I turn my attention to my laptop, pulling up my email.

I skim my in-box and pause when I come across a familiar name.

Erin Rieman. From *Vogue*. I click it open immediately.

> Hello Meghan!
>
> I was pleased to hear that you've broken free from Lillianna's grasp, and even more pleased to tell you that I was able to get you into our Fashionista contest. You must be in NYC for the show at 2:00 P.M. I assume that won't be a problem. ☺ I'll have the show coordinator send you the details.
>
> All my best,
> Erin

"Holy cow," I breathe. "She did it."

Sylvie looks up at me. "Did what?"

"I'm officially entered into the Fashionista contest."

Sylvie beams. "That's so nice. You'd better get to work."

"There's a catch, Sylvie." I tell her about the contest being at the same time as the building's Christmas party.

"Hmm. That's a quandary," she answers. "I guess I can handle things here."

She's secretly pleased by the challenge, and I know it. I text Logan and tell him the news, before I pull up airlines.

"I'll try to get back in time to make an appearance," I tell her, as I scroll through flights. "The show is in the afternoon and should only take a few hours. There's a seven P.M. flight, which only takes an hour and a half to reach O'Hare. Theoretically, I can be here by ten, taking traffic from the airport into account."

"That will be fine," she exclaims. "Everyone usually stays until eleven or so anyway, so it will be perfect."

"Thank you for doing this," I tell her. "Very much."

She glows. "It's my pleasure. It's a tradition here. And in fact, your dad used to give me complete control over it."

I stare at her. "*Complete* control?"

She flinches. "Well, maybe he had a *little* input," she amends. I laugh.

I can't even be annoyed. One of Sylvie's endearing traits is her gift for exaggeration.

"That sounds more accurate," I agree. She smirks.

Her shirt has an outline of Santa on it and says I DID IT FOR THE COOKIES.

"How many Christmas shirts do you have?" I ask curiously. She grins.

"I have one for every day between December first and Christmas," she says proudly. "I've been collecting them for years."

"That is the Sylvie-est thing I've ever heard," I reply, but it does make me laugh. "I love your enthusiasm for Christmas. You'll never get coal in *your* stocking."

She busies herself at my father's desk. "It used to be my son's favorite time of the year," she says quietly.

My head snaps up. "I'm sorry," I tell her. "I didn't realize you have a son. I thought you didn't have a family."

As soon as the words are out, I realize how abrupt it sounded, and I'm appalled. "I mean . . ."

She waves her hand. "I know what you meant," she says. "No offense taken."

"What is your son's name?" I ask. "Where does he live now?"

She studies her hands. "His name was Robert Jr., and we called him Bobby."

Was.

Called.

"Oh, no." I breathe. Good lord, can I not say anything right to this woman?

"He and my husband were killed in a car crash years ago," she tells me. "Bobby was just six."

All the air whooshes out of my lungs, and a weight settles in my stomach.

"Sylvie," I manage to say. "I didn't know. I'm so sorry."

I don't know what else to say. She blinks.

"It was a long time ago," she finally replies. "Like your mom. So you probably understand. I've grown accustomed to it, but I miss them. Bobby loved Christmas so much that if I don't throw myself into loving it, too, then missing him just overwhelms me."

I think of how, when I first arrived, she'd had Bing Crosby playing in the office, and how she sets up a hot cocoa stand, complete with candy canes to hang on the cups. The stockings she hangs beside everyone's door. Her daily Christmas shirts. Her Christmas light necklace, her Christmas bulb earrings. All of it.

To keep her son's memory alive, all while not drowning in the sorrow of it.

I'm appalled that I was ever annoyed by her.

"You're an amazing mother," I say, somehow keeping my voice level. "Bobby would be so proud of you."

"I'm not a mother anymore," she says, her forehead wrinkling. "You can't be a mother when your child is gone, Meg."

"Oh, yes, you can," I insist. "You're a mother forever. Look at how you mother all of us here. Being a mother is something you become, and once you do, it doesn't just go away. No matter what, Sylvie."

In an uncharacteristic display of emotion, I put my hand on hers, and she doesn't pull away. We sit together for a few minutes, in silence. I see now why my dad liked her, why he'd allowed her to "help."

In this moment, this very moment, I vow to do the same.

"You can have complete control over the Christmas party," I finally say. "Whatever you want to do."

Her face lights up.

"Really?"

I nod. "Really. Just don't get *too* crazy."

She beams. "Meghan, this will be the best Christmas party you've ever attended. I think I'll make it fancy . . ." She trails off and starts making notes on a notepad, and I get the sense that she's already forgotten that I'm here.

When Joe Riordan stops by a few minutes later, it's a welcome diversion from looking at bills.

"Meg," he greets me with a friendly grin. "I found the clippings."

He holds up a yellowed banker's box, and I ogle it.

"That looks like more than a few clippings," I point out.

He grins again. "Sylvie gave me some research a few years back, and I forgot to return it to her."

Her head snaps up. "That's where it was! *See, Meg?* I knew it was here somewhere." She's as proud as punch that she wasn't the one who actually lost it, and Joe is oblivious about causing any concern with the missing research.

"Let's go spread it out in the conference room," I suggest. He's happy to oblige and escorts me through the halls. When we step through the heavy doors, he looks around.

"I don't think I've ever been in here," he says, eyeing the wood paneled walls and tiled floor. "It looks like a ballroom."

I sigh. "It *is* a ballroom. Didn't you attend the Christmas party last year? Sylvie said it was in here."

"I had pneumonia last year," he answers, setting the box on the table and opening the flaps. "Every year before that, different residents took turns hosting it in their homes."

"What a great idea," I answer, my hands already digging into the files. We spread them out on the long mahogany table, and I marvel at all the information at our fingertips.

"Wow," I breathe finally. "There's so much here."

"This place has some history," Joe agrees. He turns in a slow circle and looks up at the vaulted ceiling. "I wonder what this room has seen? If these walls could talk, what would they say?"

"They'd say . . . *spend a lot of money to restore me*," I intone solemnly. Joe chuckles.

"It's going to be a project, for sure," he agrees. "But a worthy one. Picture it, Meg. When you're finished, this place will be just as beautiful as she was in her youth!"

"That's the plan," I reply. "You can't imagine how helpful his research is, Joe. Thank you so much for finding it. I'm going to give it to Ellie today so she can start the applications for historical grants. She's helping me out with this."

"She's a good woman," Joe tells me. "One of my favorites in the building."

I eye him, wondering if he's got a crush on her.

"Not like that," he adds, seeming to read my thoughts. "I just like her. She's very calm and soothing."

"She is," I agree.

"She was a very respected lawyer in her day," he tells me. "I think she has quite a story."

"It seems like everyone here does," I answer. "Want to tell me yours?"

He laughs. "Mine is the least interesting of all. But someday, when you're bored, I'll tell you all about my time as a British spy."

My head snaps back, and he lets out a hoot. "Kidding. I was a junior high science teacher."

I shake my head at him. "You know, nothing would surprise

me with you. You could tell me that you were a ninja, and I'd believe it."

His faded eyes sparkle, and he stands up.

"If I can do anything else to help, let me know," he tells me as he leaves me to the silence in the ballroom.

I sift through a few more files, and then sit back, staring idly at the grand walls.

I can't help but wonder about Joe's question. *If these walls could talk, what would they say?*

I'M SORTING THROUGH the research still, an hour later, when Ellie softly pads into the room. She looks up at the grand domed ceiling, and then spins around.

"This was known as the Crystal Ballroom back in the Parkview's glory days," Ellie says softly. "Because of those." She points up at the four grand chandeliers hanging above us.

I look at them, at the many droplets of crystal, flowing from tiered stack to tiered stack.

"Those are original," I say needlessly. Ellie nods.

"As are the mahogany walls," she adds. The walls are wainscoted in mahogany, in elaborate carved wood, halfway up the wall. Royal blue satin wallpaper, faded now, rises to the high ceiling, until the heavily carved trim at the top meets it.

"If I might say so, this room is more than a conference room," Ellie tells me. "You're underutilizing it. It's too large, for one thing."

"Now you sound like Sylvie," I tell her.

"Well, it's true. This room was beautiful," she tells me, and the way she says it, so tenderly, gives me pause. "The chandeliers were the perfect shade of warm white, flattering to everyone. There used to be a Christmas tree in here during this time of year; it must've been twenty feet tall, at least." She points to the area where it stood, her eyes moist.

I stare at her.

"Ellie, did you see it back then?"

She blinks.

"This was where Francesca hosted the Christmas party," she tells me quietly. "I was standing in the middle with Frankie, in front of everyone, when it all fell apart. I ran out those doors over there, while everyone watched." She gestures to the side double doors, and my heart leaps into my throat.

"It happened here? At the Parkview? Why didn't you tell me?" I manage to squeak.

"I don't know." She sighs. "I guess . . . it seems sad, really, if you think about it. I was humiliated here, had my heart broken here, yet here I am. Living here."

"That's not sad," I tell her. "But why did you do it? Why did you return here, out of every place in the city?"

She shrugs. "I don't know, to be honest. To feel close to him, maybe. I don't know if he's living or dead. All these years, I haven't known. But to know that he did walk in this room on that night, it makes me feel like I'm with him almost."

That *is* sad.

But I don't say so.

I swallow the lump in my throat. "I'll restore this to a ball-room," I tell her. "You're right. It's too special to be a meeting room or conference center."

She smiles beatifically. "Thank you, Meghan," she says softly. "I'll hunt for the wallpaper manufacturer, to see if I can still get this print."

Ellie changed the subject so deftly, that I almost didn't notice, and then when I do, I let it go. Because it's clear she doesn't want to talk about her long-ago romance any further.

"Thank you," I say instead. "Surely we can have it replicated if they don't have it."

"Surely so," she agrees.

She takes a seat at the table, and I sit back down next to her. She pulls out a paper and pen.

"Anyway, I came down to get your Social Security number, Meg. For some of the applications that I'm doing for the historical societies. I've actually made a contact here at the Chicago Historical Society. She's the assistant to the director, and she's been an enormous help. I think she understands the significance of this place, and so I want to get the application to her while it's still fresh in her mind. Do you feel comfortable giving it to me?"

"Of course," I tell her. "I trust you." I rattle it off and she writes it down.

"Thank you, dear. I'll also need a photo of your driver's license."

"That's up in my purse. In my apartment. I'll run get it, and then email it to you."

She writes her email down and hands it to me, then takes another look at the room. "I haven't been in here in years. It smells just the same. We really should do something with it. It's too beautiful to fade away."

"Okay, Ellie. I agree. We will."

She smiles at me, and I walk with her up the stairs.

As I leave her on her floor, I promise Ellie that I'll email my license in a few minutes, then continue up the stairs.

In my apartment, as I dig through my purse for my wallet, I hear a light scratching noise.

I pause and listen.

Nothing. Silence.

I shake my head and fish out my wallet, but as I open it, I hear the scratching again.

This time, it continues. I lay the wallet down and follow the faint noise. As I get closer to the bedroom closet, it gets louder. When I open the closet doors, it's even louder, and it becomes apparent that it's coming from the attic crawl space door.

This can't be good.

I drag over the chair from next to the bed and stand on it, shoving with all my strength on the crawl space door above my head.

Several things happen at once in the next few seconds.

The attic door gives way.

The chair I'm standing on tips over.

And as I fall, something gray, furry, and squeaking falls onto my head.

The next few moments are a blur as I shriek, jump to my feet, shake my hair to make sure a creature isn't in it, and then leap onto the bed just in time to see a tail disappear underneath.

A long, scaly tail.

Oh, heck no.

I pull my phone out of my back pocket and dial the first number I can think of.

Logan's.

I shriek into the receiver, something about *I need help, come right now, oh my god.*

I run around in a circle on the bed, and as I do, I drop my phone and it hits the edge of the nightstand and tumbles to the floor.

It's the rat's phone now, I decide, seeing that it is just at the edge of being under the bed.

"Logan, if you can hear me, come quick," I yell toward it.

Logan arrives literally not more than two minutes later and bursts through the door, his face drawn.

"We have rats," I shriek, and he stops still.

"Rats?" His eyes start to crinkle at the corners.

"Don't laugh," I warn him.

"I thought you were in danger," he tells me. "I was in the basement, and I broke land-speed records getting up here. Because I thought you were being robbed or something."

His mouth curves, and he's not mad.

He's amused.

"But you have a rat," he says, as though he's convincing himself.

"It's under the bed," I tell him frantically. "Please, please, get it."

He eyes me. "My big, fancy New York City girl is afraid of a rat?"

I focus on a different part of that sentence than he intended. *His girl?*

My stomach warms, and my shoulders relax.

"It fell into my hair," I tell him in my defense, and my scalp is still crawling.

He laughs and drops onto his hands and knees.

"Um, it's not under here now," he tells me.

"What?" I screech.

"It must've run somewhere else. Maybe into a wall or something."

"*The rats are in the walls?*" My voice is now breaking the sonic sound barrier, I'm sure.

"Calm down," he tells me, getting to his feet. "Where did it come from?"

I point to the attic crawl space, and he crawls up on the chair to take a look.

I can only see him from the waist down, as the attic has swallowed his upper half.

"I have good news and I have bad news," he tells me, his voice muffled. He climbs back down with a big box in his hands.

"I'm afraid to ask," I tell him.

He sets the dusty box on the floor next to the bed. "You do have rats," he confirms. "I see signs of them up there."

I take a long shaky breath.

"And the good news?"

He turns the box around and gestures at the side. It says *Building Memorabilia* in faded blue marker.

"Oh my gosh," I whisper and climb off the bed, having already forgotten the rat. I sit next to the box and pull it open.

Stacks of photos are inside.

"Oh my gosh," I say again, digging my hands into the box. Black-and-white photos, sepia photos, old color photos. The photos seem to span decades. "Jackpot." I glance up at him. "You're my hero."

"You should thank the rat," he suggests as he sits down next to me. "What have we got?"

We sift through the photos, which look to range from the 1900s to the 1980s. "My dad bought the place in the early eighties," I tell Logan. "This must be from the previous owner."

The photos tell a story of this building in its heyday. The colors are glorious, the floors are sparkling. People wear everything from glitzy twenties garb to drab work clothing from the Depression, and everything in between and since.

"Check this out," Logan says, handing me a photo.

A young couple poses in front of a grand, decorated Christmas tree in the ballroom. He's handsome and flushed, and she's ... wearing my Christmas dress.

I peer closer and recognize the face from Ellie's youth.

"It's Ellie," I exclaim. I look closer. She's missing her right earring. "And the earring was already lost when this photo was taken." In the background, the large clock that is embedded in the wall reads eight o'clock. "She lost the earring early in the evening."

"I have no idea what you're talking about," Logan tells me. "But look at this picture. I'm no expert, but isn't this the same dress?"

I snatch the photo from his hands to examine it.

Sure enough. Another pretty young woman from what looks to be at least twenty years earlier poses in the dress. This couple is on the rooftop, leaning against the railing, amid the rooftop garden when it was in all its glory. This woman was a bit curvier than Ellie, but the dress still fits her like a glove.

I remember Ellie's words: *I'm sure it'll fit you perfectly. It has a way of doing that.*

On the back, there is a paragraph in old-fashioned handwriting.

Jessica and Raymond on their engagement, 1946. Raymond surprised Jessica, returning home from the war as soon as he could and came to meet her with an engagement ring. She said yes.

"Oh, my goodness. That sounds like such a grand gesture," I say, my eyes practically welling up. "The arrangements he must've had to make to surprise her like that. I bet he pulled his mother in on it, and she helped. It must be incredible to have somcone love you like that."

"You've never had anyone surprise you?" Logan says doubtfully. I shake my head.

"Not like that. No big gestures at all, really."

"That's a shame," Logan says. "You deserve the grandest of all gestures."

I pause, trying to decide if he's teasing me, but the only thing in his eyes is sincerity. He means it. I clear my throat because I don't know what to say.

"I should get these to Ellie," I tell him, breaking the moment.

"No worries. I'll just . . . call an exterminator," he answers.

I lean up and kiss him on the cheek. "Like I said, you're my hero."

He beams, and I rush away.

CHAPTER FOURTEEN

"Oh, my goodness," Ellie says, clutching one picture to her heart while she examines the earlier one. "That is indeed the same dress. I told you there was something special about it."

She looks at the other one and traces Frankie's face with her finger. "Isn't he handsome? I told you."

I agree. "Yes, he's very handsome."

And so boyishly young. No wonder he made such a mistake. He was just a kid, younger than I am now, and lord knows, I make plenty of mistakes.

"You have no idea how much this means to me," she tells me, cradling the picture.

"I think I do," I answer softly.

"And the other photos you found," she adds, looking at me. "They'll be invaluable to our applications, Meg. This was a gold mine."

"That's what I said, too!"

"Can I look through the other photos later today?" she asks me. I nod.

"I'll bring them down to you. One of them confirms that the old speakeasy was named the Red Alibi. It's in the background of the photo."

"Oh, my," she breathes. "This is incredible."

I LEAVE HER hugging the photo, while I return to the office to ask Sylvie about the rooftop garden from the photo.

She isn't there, however. Tom Rutherford is in her place, sitting in the office chair and playing with Winter.

"Hey, Meg," he greets me. "I'm kitten-sitting while Sylvie visits the cemetery."

I watch the tiny kitten bat at Tom's hand. "I see you like my new partner in crime."

"He's beautiful," Tom says. "I love his blue eyes. You can see he's going to be a character."

"Just like someone else I know," I tease him. He grins.

"If you're gonna be alive, you might as well be feisty," he tells me. "That's my motto."

"You live up to it well," I tell him with a smile.

"Have you heard from Melody?" he asks.

"Sylvie did. She caught a little pneumonia in the hospital, but she's doing much better. She'll be back here soon, and she'll stay in apartment 405 until hers is fixed."

"When will *that* be?" Tom asks.

"I'm working on it." I sigh. "I'm working on it."

"I got the invitation to the Christmas party," he tells me. "Save me a dance, missy."

"Of course," I reply.

"Let me know if you ever need a kitten sitter," he says, getting up to leave. "I kinda like him." He winks and ducks out the door.

"I kinda like you, too," I croon at Winter, picking him up. He bats at my nose with his little razor-tipped paws. "Let's get you some treats."

I carry him up to my bedroom and put him on the floor. "If you see a rat, and I don't care if it outweighs you, you get it," I instruct. "That's your job as guard cat."

He stares at me for a minute, before he starts chasing a piece of fluff on the floor.

He's so cute that I have to video-chat with Cassie to show her.

It takes her a minute to answer, and in the meantime, Winter disappears under the chair, so I'm on my hands and knees trying to locate him when Cassie picks up, and sadly, the camera is buried in my cleavage.

She clears her throat. "The girls are looking good tonight, Meg."

I laugh and haul my kitten out.

"Look at this face," I tell her, as I sit up.

I look at the screen, and Drake and Cassie stare back at me.

Oh, no.

They're in a restaurant, heavily decorated for Christmas, with a candle on their table.

"Ummm, hi," I say brightly, praying to God that Drake didn't see my boobs. "I didn't know you had a date tonight. I wouldn't have interrupted."

"Nonsense," Drake says easily, taking a drink of his gin and tonic. "You're never an interruption, is she, Cass?"

He has an arm looped easily over the back of her chair, and she leans into it.

"Of course not," she says, but I feel like her smile is a bit stiff.

"I just wanted to introduce you to Winter White," I tell her weakly, holding up my kitten. He stares indignantly at her, outraged by being held in the air, and Cassie peers into the screen.

"He's adorable!" she squeaks, reaching out to touch the screen. "I just want to kiss him."

"Don't get any ideas," Drake tells her with a wry smile. "I'm allergic."

Of course he is.

Cassie rolls her eyes. "I'm going to need a note from your doctor," she says. I snicker at that.

He takes another drink, knocking the rest of it back.

"I love your kitten," Cassie tells me. "I'll have to come soon and visit him. When Dragon Lady lets me out, I mean."

"Is she still on a rampage?" I ask, cringing.

"Oh, yes. And don't think for one second that she's forgotten about you. She hasn't."

"Well, at least she won't be at the contest. She'd never forgo her Christmas Eve. She'll send a junior blogger to cover it, I'm sure."

Cassie hesitates. "Never rule anything out with her," she remarks sagely. "She has a piece of coal where her heart should be. I doubt Christmas is even a blip on her radar."

"Bah."

"I think the term you're wanting is bah humbug," Drake offers.

I glare.

He smiles.

He seems perfectly happy with Cassie, which is good, but he doesn't seem like he misses me at all. I don't miss him, either, but it still bugs me because am I so unmissable? So forgettable?

"You guys, get back to your date. I'll talk to you later."

I hang up and stare at Winter.

"I'm forgettable, Kitten. How did that happen?"

He swipes at my face, barely missing.

"Hey, I need both eyes." I set him down and pick up a fishing pole toy with a crinkly fish on the end. He leaps at that for a while, trying to catch the fish. Finally, he gives in and curls up on the couch, falling fast asleep.

I sigh and slump into the couch.

I can't explain the depression I suddenly feel at the thought that I could be so quickly forgotten. Didn't I make an impact in Drake's life at all?

I mean, he wasn't my soul mate, but he did make an impact. If anything, he showed me what I *don't* want in a partner.

I've got to get some air. The walls suddenly feel like they're closing in on me. I eye Winter, who is happily sleeping, and I decide to go out.

I pull on snow boots, a heavy coat, a fuzzy hat and gloves, and head out the door.

I IMMEDIATELY REALIZE the error in my thinking.

Walking around the happy Christmas-laden Chicago streets alone does not help with the depressed feeling.

My toes feel like frozen lumps, regardless of the boots, so I stop in at the bar down the street and order a spiked hot cider. I hold my face over it, letting the steam warm me up, before I toss half of it down my throat like I'm a sorority girl on spring break. I quickly follow with the other half, then signal for another.

The bartender comes over.

"What's wrong?" he asks. "Are you on the naughty list this year?"

"Who knows?" I answer, waiting for him to pour. "I didn't think so. But maybe I am."

"I'm going to bring you some water. This stuff is potent. You only need one."

I watch in surprise as he walks away.

I decide to text Logan, which might be a bad idea, but it totally makes sense in the moment.

Do you think I'm on the naughty list this year?

Three bubbles immediately pop up.

I'm not sure how to answer this. Are you flirting?

I send him a crying-laughing emoji. I'd like to think that when I flirt, you'll know it.
Fair enough, he replies. So, you're not flirting.
He sends a sad face.
I smile.

Do you want me to flirt?

Three bubbles.

Hmm. You're a beautiful, smart, funny woman. I'd definitely not hate it if you flirted with me. What are you doing, anyway?

I take a quick selfie of myself sitting at the bar and send it.

You're at the bar alone? Unacceptable. Are you up for a good time?

I send a string of crying-laughing emojis. ARE YOU FLIRT-ING WITH ME??

He answers immediately. Yes. But I realize now how that sounded.

Crying-laughing face.

Three bubbles. Then another message from him.

> I have plans this evening, but I'd love for you to join me if you think you can handle it.

Sounds intriguing, I answer. Will it be dangerous?

Potentially, he replies. You still game?

1000%, I answer.

> I'll be there to pick you up in twenty minutes.

"Looks like your night is improving," the bartender says, glancing at me. "You're smiling now."

I beam. It *is* improving. Something about Logan makes my heart smile and all my troubles fade away.

Drake might not notice my absence, but Logan certainly notices my *presence*, and I think that's the most important thing.

"My night is definitely on the upswing," I agree. Logan arrives a few minutes later.

He eyes me.

"You good?" he asks dubiously, maybe because I'm sitting half crooked on the barstool, or maybe because my cheeks are flushed and hot.

"I'm always good," I declare. "Always. Every time."

"Oh, man." He pays my bill, amid my protests. "Maybe I should take you home instead?"

"Absolutely not," I protest. "I'm just a little teeny bit tipsy. I'll be fine."

"You're fine enough to come sleighing with my mother, sister, and nieces?" he asks solemnly as I clutch his elbow for balance.

I grin up at him, then start singing "Jingle Bells."

"Dashing through the snow . . . In a one-horse open sleigh . . ." My voice is all over the place, and I don't care.

"I'm gonna regret this," he says knowingly. "Can I get a cup of coffee to go?" he asks the bartender.

Two seconds later, he thrusts the cup into my hands and helps me to the truck.

"Drink that," he instructs after we both climb in. "We're going to have fun, but only if you don't pass out."

"Oh my gosh. I told you. I'm just tipsy. I had one cider."

He gives me side-eye but doesn't say anything.

"I've never been on a sleigh ride," I tell him as he navigates the city traffic. "Where is it?"

"Oh, about an hour away. My mom runs an event every year—for the two weeks before Christmas. She's done it ever since I was little. To make extra money."

"She has horses?" I ask. He nods.

"Yes. It used to be my job to take care of them. Not a lot of fun in the winter. But worth it in the summer."

"I can't wait to pet a horse," I tell him, rubbing my numb nose.

Logan looks unsure, and I can't blame him.

"I'll be fine. We have an hour's drive."

"That's true," he agrees. "Drink up." He motions to the coffee, and I tip up the cup.

The radio is playing Christmas carols and I sing along to "Rockin' Around the Christmas Tree."

After a minute or two, Logan starts singing, too, and before I know it, we're both dancing in the truck.

"I like this," I tell him when the song ends. "I haven't liked Christmas for years. And *especially* this year. But I like this. Tonight."

I smile at him, and his eyes are so beautiful.

I tell him that.

He grins. "I like this too. Even though you're drunk." I glare and he corrects himself. "I'm sorry. *Tipsy.*"

The warmth from the heater, the rhythmic hum of the tires on the road, and the soothing Christmas carols actually make me sleepy after a little bit.

"I'm just gonna rest my eyes for a sec," I tell him. He smiles and reaches over, pulling my hand into his. I fall asleep with his warm, strong fingers encircling my own.

WHEN I WAKE, we're pulling into a winter wonderland.

I sit up in my seat and look at the amazing Christmas lights, the freshly fallen snow, and the quaint wooden signs that point toward the entrance of the attraction.

Logan drives down the long drive, and I look around.

"We're out in the country," I observe.

"Yup."

He pulls into a parking spot, a grassy area marked with painted signs, then helps me out of the truck. He pulls my stocking cap down farther on my ears.

"I'm glad you're bundled up," he says, pulling me by the hand along the lit trail. Twinkling white lights guide us to a cute shed decorated to look like Santa's workshop. There are oversize fake gifts stacked outside, and an empty Santa's sleigh, with gifts spilling out the back.

"It's for people to take their picture in," Logan says, noticing my gaze. "Do you want a picture?"

"Maybe later," I tell him. "I'm sober now, by the way."

He smiles, then winks. "Good to know."

We walk into the shed, which is bustling with holiday cheer. Guests of the attraction gather around a hot cider stand.

"Cider?" a girl in an elf hat asks me. I cringe, and Logan laughs.

"Maybe later, Janie," he tells her.

"Is that your sister?" I whisper. He shakes his head.

"No. Janie has worked here for years. Monica is here already, outside in line. Taylor and Kaylie are with her. And of course, my mom is always here." He pulls me outside, where a line is formed around quaint, oversize candy cane line markers.

A pretty redheaded woman waves, and we join her.

"Hey, bro," she greets him, while her daughters attack him in bear hugs.

He rubs his knuckles on one girl's head, while he squeezes the other.

"You two staying in trouble? Keeping your mom on her toes?" he asks seriously. They both nod. "Good girls."

Monica rolls her eyes, then looks at me. "You must be Meg?"

He's talked about me?

My belly flip-flops.

"Yes," I hold out my hand, but she bypasses it and hugs me instead.

"It's really good to meet you," she says with a grin. "Tonight, I will share with you my lifelong knowledge of how to get under my brother's skin."

"Yay!" I crow. "Just what I wanted to know!"

"We're going to be friends," she tells me knowingly.

"*Best* friends," I confirm.

Logan looks appropriately frightened, but he plays with the girls like he's not paying attention.

When we get to the front of the line, his mother, a curly-haired woman with a friendly smile, greets us.

She hugs Logan tight, but curiously eyes me over his shoulder. After introductions, she waves for another sleigh.

"Girls, your uncle and Meg are riding alone," she tells Kaylie and Taylor. They protest, but she holds up a hand. "No, you can see them when y'all get back."

I climb into the sleigh, and Logan covers us up with a heavy fur throw.

The driver flicks the reins, and the horse takes off at a trot, with the bells on his harness jingling.

"Ohhhhh. *This* is what jingle bells means," I say, and I can see the driver's lip twitch.

Logan pats my leg. "It's okay. How were you supposed to know?"

"There are tons of songs I don't realize the meaning of until years after," I offer, thinking I'm defending myself, but I'm doing anything but. Both Logan and the driver smile now, and I pretend not to notice.

I'm quickly absorbed into the scenery, however. All along the ride, there are cute signs, beautiful trees lit up with lights, and of course, the stars are beautiful in the dark, vast sky.

I lean back and just stare.

Logan leans back with me.

"It's not something we get to see in the city often," he says.

I shake my head. "Definitely not."

"I'm glad you came," he tells me, holding my hand.

"I'm glad you asked," I answer. He looks into my eyes, and his seem as dark as the sky.

I've noticed that the more serious he is, the darker his eyes appear. He brushes his gloved hand against my cheek.

"Are you warm enough?" he asks, pulling me closer to his side. I nod.

"I'm perfect."

We stay snuggled together for the rest of the ride, and afterward, I get to pet Chestnut's nose before he has to pull another visitor.

The girls leap out of their sleigh and run for Logan. At the same time, Maryanne, his mom, bustles toward us. "Logan, dear, can you run to the house and get more hot cocoa mix? We're out in the shop."

I start to follow, but Monica grabs my elbow. "Have you seen the reindeer?"

I freeze and slowly turn to her. "You. Have. Reindeer?"

The girls giggle and pull me in the other direction, and Monica follows.

They lead me to a pen where two majestic reindeer munch on hay and apple slices.

"Reindeer," Monica says, gesturing with her arm. "At your service."

The girls, obviously well acquainted with them, climb into the pen to pet them, while Monica and I lean again the fence.

"Are they named Dancer and Prancer?" I ask hopefully.

"Barbara and Jeanette." Monica winces. "My mom's old sorority sisters."

I laugh.

"I'm glad you're here," Monica says, as we watch the girls. "I haven't seen my brother look so happy in ages."

I glance at her. "Really? He always seems happy to me."

"That's because when you see him, *you're* around," she assures me. "He had a rough year last year and then earlier this year, and I think it took him some time to recover."

"From breaking up with his ex?" I ask, completely interested now. "He hasn't said anything about it."

She nods. "He doesn't talk about it. That's his way of handling it. Talia was . . . let's just say . . . a handful. He's so much better off without her, and I can see on his face how happy you make him."

"We've only just started getting to know each other," I tell her. "He's got plenty of time to decide I'm too crazy for him."

"I know crazy, and you are not it," she answers.

"Some would beg to differ," I tell her.

"Logan has a very good heart," she says, watching her daughters. "He seems like things roll off his back, and sometimes, that's true. But more often than not, things affect him more than he shows."

"That sounds cryptic."

She smiles. "Not really. He just always tries to be the strong one. He's always had to be for our family, and I think he sees it as his role in life."

"He's a fixer," I agree. "It's sweet."

"He's sweet," Monica affirms. "And I like you. I really do. But if you turn my brother inside-out the way Talia did . . ." Her voice trails off, and she looks at me pointedly.

"I won't," I promise her quickly. "I'd never."

She smiles a bit wickedly now. "I didn't think so," she says. "I just had to point out that I'm obligated to kill you if you do."

"Of course."

I'm slightly unnerved now, how this pretty, sweet-looking woman had threatened me so quickly, while still maintaining an air of Christmas cheer. But then I decide she has every right. Logan *is* special, and those around him should protect him, just like he tries to protect everyone else.

"You have nothing to fear from me," I reassure her. "He and I are just getting to know each other, and my hands are full with the condo that my father left me. I swear, I'm not a threat."

"I believe you," she says. And then Logan appears at my elbow.

"Do you want a reindeer ride?" he asks, one eyebrow raised.

"Absolutely not," I tell him. "I value my life. And my dignity."

He laughs, and Monica grins, and for the first time, in a very long time, I feel like I belong.

For the next hour, Logan plays with his nieces while I chat with his mother and sister, and I feel more comfortable and relaxed than I have in a very long time.

CHAPTER FIFTEEN

$\mathcal{I}$'m in the office, sketching a dress with Winter at my feet, when Ellie comes rushing in the next morning.

"Meg, I have the best news," she says, as she sits down. "Someone from the Chicago Historical Society is coming to our Christmas party to evaluate the property."

"Oh my gosh." I turn to her. "You're a miracle worker!"

She beams. "It didn't take much. After presenting them with the research and the photos, they're eager to see it. I told you, that assistant I've been talking with is very eager, and very passionate."

"I appreciate you so much," I tell her.

She eyes my sketch pad. "May I?"

I nod, so she picks it up and examines it.

"Meg, this is truly amazing. It's like . . . you took the Christmas dress, and you're replicating it in the best possible ways."

I almost preen under her praise. Ellie has this way about her that makes you want to please her, and when you do, you feel so accomplished.

"I'm glad you like it," I tell her. "You're the reason I'm inspired. If you hadn't given me the dress, I'd be churning out the same ideas that everyone else is."

She pulls out the two pictures Logan and I had found of the dress.

"It's just amazing. This dress, I mean. I always knew there was something about it, but it turns out, it's more special than I ever knew."

"I feel magical every time I try it on," I admit. "It's like I don't want to take it off. I feel like good things will happen to me if I wear it."

She shrugs. "Not always, though," she says quietly. "I was wearing it *that* night. But maybe that was an anomaly."

"Let's hope." I look at the second picture, of the other couple. "Did you notice how much curvier she is than you were? And the dress looks like it fits her perfectly."

"Tailoring, I guess," Ellie says uncertainly.

"You yourself said the dress has a way of fitting," I point out to her. "There is no evidence of that dress having been altered."

"Well, I guess it's just magic," Ellie says emphatically. She's flippant, but I know she's also half serious.

"I'm not going to question it," I tell her.

"Good idea. Some things just can't be explained." She wiggles her fingers at Winter. "Can I take Winter for the afternoon?"

"Absolutely," I tell her. She beams and tucks the kitten into her arms. He hangs limply over her arm, accustomed already to being handed around and spoiled.

"I'll be upstairs if you need me," she says.

"I'll be downstairs," I answer.

"With Mr. Scott?" she asks knowingly. I blush.

"He's coming to take a look at that brick wall," I tell her. "I'm going to supervise."

"I don't blame you," she says as she leaves. "I'd look at him, too."

I blush again, but she's not around to see it.

When Sylvie comes in a little bit later, my cheeks are still pink.

"Are you okay?" she asks, handing me a cup of cocoa. "You seem flushed."

"I'm fine."

"Where's Winter?" Sylvie asks, disappointed he's not here.

"Ellie took him for the afternoon. Is Melody settled into 405?"

Sylvie nods. "Yes. And she's being very understanding about the delay in fixing her condo."

I swallow hard. "That's good. She's very sweet."

"Well, you and Tom did save her life." Sylvie shrugs.

"Hopefully, it won't be long," I say and hold my folded hands up to the sky.

"It won't," she says. "I was thinking, Meg. I have some savings. I'd love to let you use it. Kind of like . . . a loan until you get some cash flow."

I stare at her. "Sylvie, I can't do that."

She stares back at me, unflinching. "Why? I want to. I've been saving my money for years. I never go overboard on anything . . . I save for a rainy day. This is a rainy day if I've ever seen one."

I sigh. "Sylvie, you are so sweet to offer, but truly, we're going to come through on this. We'll get grants."

"But those grants will be to restore historically significant parts of the building," she argues. "Not to fix Melody Hansen's condo. Listen, just let me advance you the money for it. You can pay me when your fashion line explodes."

"And what if it doesn't?" I lift an eyebrow.

"It won't with that attitude," she lectures. "Have faith. It will."

"Hopefully, you're right."

"I'm definitely right. Now take my money. Although it doesn't come without conditions."

Curious now, I lean forward. "And what are they?"

"I want to help. I want to be your assistant."

"You already are," I tell her.

"I mean *officially*," she answers. "You don't have to pay me, but I'd like to be your official assistant. I want business cards."

"Done," I tell her. "And you don't need to loan me money for that."

"Too late," she answers, pulling a check out of her pocket. "I wrote this last night. No more arguments. I'm investing in you, dear. Your father believed in you, and so do I."

My eyes tear up as I take it, and she pretends not to see.

"I do call dibs on the cat tomorrow morning, though," she

says, as she turns away. If I didn't know better, I'd think she was tearing up, too. "I got him some special treats. Salmon flavored. They're his favorite."

"I should get him an appointment book," I say wryly. She smiles.

"It might not be a bad idea. Joe told me he wants a turn, as well."

I shake my head, but I'm honestly happy everyone else is enjoying Winter as much as I am.

"I'm going to hang this up for him," she says, holding up a miniature stocking with his name on it. "Right outside of the office. I guarantee he'll probably get more gifts than you and I put together."

"I don't doubt that a bit."

"I'm surprised you're not downstairs with Mr. Scott," she tells me.

"He's not here yet," I answer.

"Yes, he is. I saw him heading down there when I came in."

I try not to jump up and sprint for the basement. Instead, I casually get up and stretch.

"I guess I could stretch my legs and go see how he's doing," I answer. "I'm pretty stiff."

"I bet."

I DON'T HURRY until I'm well away from the office, and out of Sylvie's sight. Once the elevator opens in the basement, I practically break my neck to find Logan.

It's not hard. He's standing in front of the main brick wall, examining it.

"I think I'll knock a small hole in it for us to crawl through," he says as I approach. "Just so we can see if anything is behind there, and if it's in decent condition. I mean, before I demolish this wall."

"Sounds good," I tell him.

He looks down at me. "Oh, and hello." His eyes soften, and he gazes at me in appreciation. "You're pretty."

"You're taking cues from my coffee cup again?" I lift an eyebrow.

"Yes, but it's still true."

He grins, and I can't help it. I step into his embrace and he kisses me ever so gently. For such a strong man, he's so gentle. I love it. It makes me feel like I'm precious cargo.

"I loved that you got along with my family," he tells me. "They liked you."

"They did?" My head snaps up, and I'm almost embarrassed at my need for their approval.

"Absolutely. I mean, it helped that you sobered up before you met them." I smack his arm lightly.

"In my defense, I had no idea earlier in the night that you were going to ask me out."

"Valid point," he concedes. He picks up a mallet. "Do you want to take a crack at this?"

He points at a spot on the wall.

"What if I break it?" I worry.

"That's the whole point," he reassures me.

"I meant, what if I break it in a wrong way?" I ask.

"There is no wrong way. Just aim right here"–he points–"and swing away."

I take the mallet. "Wait," he says, and I pause. He slides a pair of plastic safety glasses onto my face. "Safety first."

He grins, and I swing.

The mallet makes impact, and it feels like my shoulder comes out of socket.

"Oh my gosh," I say, trying again.

It bounces off yet again.

"This is harder than it looks."

"The craftsmanship in the old days was amazing," he tells me. "But we just need a hole big enough to crawl through, and I can shore that hole up to make sure the wall doesn't fall in."

That gives me pause. "The wall could fall in?"

"It won't," he promises. "I just need an opening so I can shore it up. Don't worry."

"Are you a contractor?" I narrow my eyes.

"Actually, I do have my contractor's license." He laughs. "Now is a heck of a time to ask about that. Weren't you curious before?"

I don't want to say that I thought he was "just" a handyman. That would sound awful.

I shake my head. "I knew you were competent," I say instead. "That's all I needed to know."

"Well, I do have my license, and I'm bonded and insured,"

he assures me. "I just don't want the hassle of having a big company. I do just fine the way I am right now."

I lean on the mallet. "So you don't want to own your own company?"

"I do own my own company," he answers. "I'm just the only employee. So I'm only responsible for myself. That's fine with me." He eyes me. "Are you ready to try again?"

I nod and brace myself for the stinging impact. I preemptively rub my shoulder, and he laughs.

"Do you want me to do it?"

I nod without hesitation.

He laughs again and takes the mallet.

With two swings, he breaks through the heavy brick.

With two more, he frees a hole big enough to climb through. I step forward, but he holds out his hand.

"Wait. I need to jack it up."

He pulls an industrial-size jack out from the shadows and shores up the hole.

"We can't be too careful," he tells me. We both get on our knees and peer into the other side, while Logan shines a large flashlight in.

"Holy cow," I breathe.

"You can say that again," he replies, shining his light around. The light beam reflects off the fancy gilded bronze ceiling. There are still tables situated inside, brick halfway up the walls, and faded red velvet wallpaper the rest of the way up.

"I can see why it was called the Red Alibi," I say as I carefully crawl through the hole.

Even the brick is red tinged.

"Be careful," Logan says from behind me. "Wait for me."

He crawls through and stands up, and together we assess the room.

It's in near perfect condition.

There's an arch in the back of the room, so Logan and I carefully walk toward it. We pass through, and instantly, we're in the bar. A wooden bar top stretches across the entire back, with an old mirror lining the wall behind it. The mirror, probably made with mercury, has oxidized, but I can still see my reflection in it.

"Can you believe this?" I say, spinning in a circle. There are original tables in here as well, and some still have lamps sitting on them.

"This is an amazing find," Logan says. He pulls out a chair from a table and sits at it, running his finger through the thick dust on the tabletop. "I wonder who walked through this room? Who sat at this table?"

I remember Hemingway and rush to the bar. I pull off my cardigan and use it as a rag, wiping away the dust so I can see.

I start at one end and work my way to the other. The mahogany bar is beautiful, but there is no sign of a carving from the famous author.

Until I get to the other end.

My fingers find it first, a slight indention in the wood.

I wipe frantically, and then it appears.

E. Hemingway, 1920

"Oh my gosh."

I stand still, staring at the signature, and suddenly the gravity of all this hits me, leaving me weak in the knees.

"Ernest Hemingway was here," I say limply, leaning against the bar. "Al Capone. Jack McGurn. Probably John Dillinger. And God only knows who else!"

"Well, without photos, we'll never know about that for sure, but we do know one thing." Logan comes over and examines the carving. "Hemingway was here. This is proof."

I feel woozy.

"This is incredible," I tell him. "There's literally no way we'll get turned away from the historical societies now. I almost feel like we've stumbled into King Tut's tomb!"

"Let's hope this place isn't as cursed." Logan chuckles.

"Don't even say that," I warn.

Logan paces the length of the bar. "They say there was a secret passageway in here. But I don't see one."

"Didn't all speakeasies have them?" I ask, truly curious because I don't know. "I mean, they had to have a way out if they were busted."

"I think here in Chicago, and other big cities, the crime

organizations paid off the police," Logan says. "Don't quote me on that, though. I'm not sure."

"I think I've read that, too," I agree. "Sooooo, maybe they didn't need passageways?"

That makes me disappointed. But Logan shrugs. "I don't know. You'd think they would still have them as a backup contingency."

The brick floor is incredibly even, and well-laid. "You were right about the craftsmanship from back then," I observe. "This place looks like it was just closed up and hidden yesterday."

Logan pokes around beneath the back of the bar. "Did your dad not know this was here?"

"I don't know," I admit. "With all the research that Joe and Sylvie did, it's hard to think he wasn't at least curious."

"Maybe he had his hands full," Logan says. "Maybe he just didn't have time."

His eyes widen, and he peers at something.

"Look at this," he says, stunned. He holds out an old matchbook.

The Red Alibi is sketched on the red cover.

"Wow. That seems ballsy," I say. "I mean, it's supposed to be a secret. An illegal secret. And they were brave enough to print marketing material."

Logan shrugs again. "Just another indicator that the mob was paying off the police."

"This belongs in a museum," I tell him, holding it carefully.

"I agree. What are you going to do with this? It seems like a shame if you don't restore it."

"I'll absolutely restore it," I tell him.

I turn and look at the room again, and picture how it must've been in the glory days, when it was full of jazz music and flappers and illegal booze.

"It must've been very glamorous," I point out, studying the textured wallpaper. "I don't know anything about running a bar, but goodness. It does seem like a crime to not use it in the way it was intended. Although I sure wouldn't want anyone getting drunk and ruining something."

"You could make it a working museum," Logan suggests. "Like, maybe you could have things on display, under glass, but old-fashioned drinks are available at the bar? Like gimlets and such. It wouldn't be the kind of bar where college kids go to get plastered. It would be a well-established piece of history."

"I can picture that," I tell him. "Easily."

I grab his hand. "Logan, I wouldn't trust anyone else refurbishing this place. Do you think you could do it? I mean, I know you don't like the idea of having a crew, but–"

"I'll do it," he answers immediately. "I have some trusted associates that I could hire to work with me. Just for this special project. I'd make an exception for you."

The way he looks at me is so warm, so . . . intimate, that I get weak in the knees again.

"The first thing I'll have to do is knock that wall out, and make sure it's permanently shored up and supported," he tells me. "I'll get a brick mason in here to make it look seamless."

"No, the first thing is, I have to figure out how to pay you."

"Just let me get started," he suggests. "You can pay me when you get the grants."

"Logan, you'll have to pay your crew. I have to pay you up front, like anyone else would."

"You're not anyone else," he answers. My breath catches.

"Everyone keeps trying to help me," I say, rather helplessly. "And what if I can't pull this off? What if everyone wastes their money because this all falls through? I can't let that happen to you, Logan."

"Meg, look around," he says easily. "You literally can't fail with this. The Red Alibi is still standing. People will come from all over just to see it. It's a sure thing."

"I don't know," I murmur. "Have you met me? I can make anything fail. I have failed relationships and a failed career to prove it."

Logan turns my chin so that I'm looking at him.

"Your relationship didn't work out, and you paused your career to come here. That's not failure."

"You know, when people talk about relationships that didn't work out, they literally use the term 'failed relationship.' It says right in the name that I failed," I tell him.

He rolls his eyes.

"Meg. Sometimes relationships aren't meant to be. It's better that we figure that out before they go any further and waste everyone's time."

"I don't know. I sometimes worry that I'm impossible to please," I tell him. "My ex, Drake, is successful, smart, driven. Everyone likes him. Clearly, my best friend loves him. And yet he wasn't enough for me."

"I can promise you, it isn't an issue with you," Logan answers. "You're a warm, passionate person."

I shrug. "Maybe. Maybe not. But I worry about it." I glance at him. "Why didn't it work out with you and your ex?"

His eyes instantly turn guarded. "It just didn't. She wanted different things. She wanted me to want different things, and I didn't. I like fixing things with my hands. I don't see a problem in that. She did."

"You mean, she wanted you to have a different job?"

"That, and be a different person. From the way you describe Drake, he sounds like the kind of person that Talia wanted me to be."

I'm already shaking my head. "Oh, no. That's not you."

"I know," he agrees. "And the way I am just wasn't enough for her."

"That's outrageous. The way you are is perfect," I say softly. "You're so kind, and generous, and good-hearted. You help all these people every single day, without ever expecting anything in return."

"Talia considers that weak," he says, and his voice has an edge to it now. A protective, guarded edge.

"Talia is wrong," I announce. "I don't know her, but it sounds like you are better off without her. You are amazing. Anyone would be lucky to have you in their life."

I'm lucky.

I don't say that part, because it seems presumptuous.

"Thank you for saying so," he answers quietly. "Honestly, being with someone like that takes a toll on the self-confidence. It makes you start to worry if the problem is in you, when it's not."

"Just like with Drake," I realize out loud. "It's the same thing. He is someone I'm not, and that means we'd never work."

"He sounds like quite a catch, though," Logan says, and if I didn't know better, I'd think he was feeling less-than.

"For *someone*," I agree. "For Cassie. I'm happy here."

Logan's head snaps up. "Since when? The last I knew, you were missing New York something fierce."

I shrug. "I still do. But this is home. And it's feeling more and more like home every day."

"I never thought I'd see the day," Logan teases, as he helps me crawl back through the hole.

"Me either," I agree. But as I take his outstretched hand to help me to my feet on the other side, I realize that I've never meant something more in my entire life.

CHAPTER SIXTEEN

*S*ylvie studies her list.

"Okay, so I've changed the theme of the party to the 1920s, and Logan says he'll have that opening shored up in plenty of time, so that we can tour the representative from the historical society through there on Christmas Eve." She looks up at me. "Meg, this is happening!"

We sit in the morning light, and Winter plays at our feet. I'm still basking in our discovery of the Red Alibi from yesterday. Ellie and I had stayed up late drinking spiked eggnog in celebration, and my excitement still hasn't dimmed.

"Logan had a good question yesterday." I turn to Sylvie, who is wearing a shirt that has a picture of jumbled-up Christmas lights and reads GRISWOLD FAMILY LIGHTING. "Why didn't my dad ever hunt for the Red Alibi?"

Sylvie looks at me. "He had his hands full," she reminds me.

"That's what Logan said. But still. My dad was obsessed with Scottish history, so it stands to reason that he'd have loved the history of this place, as well. Or at least would have considered it valuable."

"Your dad wasn't the same as you," Sylvie says carefully. "He was satisfied with things the way they are. He liked just taking care of the tenants, and knowing that everything was going to stay the same. He liked routine. And of course, your college was expensive."

I freeze.

I'd never considered that before. My father had insisted on paying for my college.

"How hard was that on him?" I'm almost afraid to know the answer.

"I don't know," she answers. "I really don't. But I know that he wouldn't want you to know even if it was hard on him."

"That man." I sigh. "I was so self-involved. I didn't even worry about it."

"All kids that age are self-involved," she tells me. "It's human nature."

"But here I am . . . wondering why my dad didn't do more to help this place, completely not thinking about the fact that he was focused on helping *me*."

Sylvie sighs. "It's true. But like I said, he wouldn't want you to feel guilty. He just wanted you to be happy. To pursue your passions. He told me once that you'd probably sell this place when you inherited it. But that he had faith you'd sell to someone trustworthy. Someone who would care about the tenants. I know for a fact that he didn't want you to stay here and give up your dreams."

"And you didn't tell me this when I first arrived because ... ?" I lift an eyebrow.

"Because I didn't know you well enough to have that same kind of faith in you," she admits. She pauses, then says, "Look in the center desk drawer, beneath the tray."

Confused, I pull open the drawer and lift the wooden tray up. I pull out an envelope that has my name on it.

It's my father's handwriting.

"Have you known about this all along?" I whisper.

Sylvie nods. "Yes. But I wanted to wait until you were ready to read it. I'm sorry. Don't be mad."

"I can't be mad at someone wearing a Griswold sweater," I mutter. "And I guess I can't fault your logic. I was pretty, um, *impatient* when I first arrived."

"Yes, you were," Sylvie agrees cheerfully. "But now ... well ... I'll leave you in peace to read your dad's words."

She scoops up Winter and they disappear.

I stare at the envelope in my hands, almost afraid to open it.

Not having a chance to say goodbye to my father has weighed even more heavily on me than I ever realized, and now, being faced with words that must've been written while I was being a self-centered brat scares me.

I don't want to look at the vision of me that my dad must've seen.

I take a sip of hot tea, bolstering my courage, before I slice the envelope open with the letter opener.

It's dated last year.

My eyes instantly well up seeing my dad's familiar hand-writing.

Dear Meggie,

As I sit here looking out the window at snow-covered Chicago, I'm feeling melancholy. You're eight hundred miles away in the Big Apple, and I'm here, alone, surrounded by memories.

I'm staring at the tree-topper you girls made with your mother so many years ago. You fought over what color dress the angel should have, so your mother broke the tie and chose white.

The pantry door in the apartment marks your heights, from every year until Jo died, and there it stops, and I feel terrible about that. Life seemed to stop for a while, and that wasn't fair to you. We all struggled in our own ways, but I should have protected you more. I should've focused on your pain more than my own.

In my own way, I did attempt to fix that, when you wanted to move away, and I tried so hard to make it possible. I know that money can't fix old wounds, but I do hope that going to school out of state, and then starting your career in New York has helped you. I want you to always chase your dreams, my girl. I want you to always focus on what makes you happy, and then <u>do that</u>.

I found some news out today from my cardiologist. I have congestive heart failure, and they're putting me on medication. I won't tell you this now, because I don't want you to give up everything and come home. I want you to thrive, and live.

When you find this letter, I'm sure I will be gone, and you will be sitting at my desk. Please don't sacrifice for me. That is the job of the parent, not the child. I want you to find a suitable buyer for the building, someone with a heart, and then use that money to pursue your own future.

I want you to be happy. If it is with Drake, so be it. If it is not, cut him loose. The right person will find you. Don't settle for anything less than the love that your mother and I had. A love that kept us going through bad times and good, through thick and thin.

I love you so much, my girl. I hope I'm doing the right thing in not telling you about my diagnosis. If it is not, please forgive me. I only want what is best for you, now and forever. I don't want you to worry about me. When it is time for me to go, I will do so willingly, knowing that I will soon see your mother and sister. The tenants here are family, and until I go, I will take care of them, and in turn, they take care of me, too.

Until we see you again, know that I will give your mom and Jo your love, and we will watch over you your entire life.

I love you.
Dad

P.S. I know that Sylvie might tell you she can be trusted with the building keys, but never, under any circumstances, give her the only set. SHE WILL LOSE THEM. (She means well.)

I smile through my tears and sit silently for several minutes after I finish reading, my hands shaking.

His death was not unexpected to him. He was prepared, he just didn't want me to worry. He didn't want to crush my dreams. Is that what real sacrifice is? Bearing something all alone so your loved ones don't have to?

I slump in my chair, and I don't know what to feel.

I'm not angry that he kept it from me, although I'm sad he felt he had to.

I could've handled it. But he's right. I would've come home, and then I wouldn't have landed my position at Stitch, although in hindsight, that wouldn't have mattered. Lillianna hates me now anyway.

It also makes me sad that he assumed I'd just sell this building. He said it himself, he considered the tenants here family.

And now, I do, too.

"I'm not going to sell the building, Dad," I whisper. "This is our home, and I'm going to save it. It's falling down, but we'll fix it. I'm going to pay you back for sacrificing everything for me."

I get up and go to the ballroom.

"The Crystal Ballroom," I murmur as I walk in the doors, making a mental note to have a nameplate engraved.

As I sit in one of the chairs, I picture the Red Alibi downstairs, and then I look around this room, pairing the two in my head, and visualizing how this entire building must've felt back in the day. We have to tie it all together, and bring it up to modern standards, while still honoring the era it was created in. The glamour, the glitz, the character.

I pull out my phone and search for the best interior designer for historic buildings in Chicago. I send her an email, explaining the situation.

We have to restore Parkview West to its former glory, I write, finishing the email. *Can you help?*

I press send.

For the first time since I arrived, everything seems to make sense. Everything seems to fit together. My new line will be timeless clothing, some of which could actually have been worn back when this building was in its prime. Clothing that will stretch or cling as a body changes, inspired by my sister so long ago. This building will be restored, just as I build my own line of clothing inspired by that time period.

It almost seems as if it were meant to be, puzzle pieces snapping together, almost by design.

A sense of serendipity surrounds me, so strong that it's almost tangible.

"Fate," I whisper. Is it real?

Does it exist?

I'm starting to believe it does. Without coming back here, I wouldn't have met Ellie, been inspired by her dress, or found the Red Alibi.

I also wouldn't have met Logan.

The mere thought of that makes my chest constrict.

I pick up my phone again to text him.

> Hey, what are you doing tonight?

He answers back almost immediately.

> Hopefully spending time with you.

Logan is so open, so honest. He doesn't play games and that is so, so, so refreshing.

I answer with a heart emoji.

> Just what I was hoping to hear. Besides, you have to come visit our kitten. ☺

Our.

Just the thought of that word in reference to Logan and me . . . it's comforting. It's exciting. It's everything.

I think he has my eyes, Logan answers with a winkie face.

> He definitely does. And my ears.

I send a cat-face emoji.

He sends back a crying-laughing emoji.

I'll provide the dinner, he adds. An old family recipe.

I SPEND THE rest of the day floating on a cloud, looking forward to our date. I pick up Winter from Sylvie and clean my apartment. I paint the bedroom white, which takes several hours. I make a wide berth around the attic crawlway door, just in case, although the exterminator gave me the all clear.

I'm stepping out of the shower when I hear someone at the front door. I immediately check the time.

It's only five forty. It can't be Logan.

I throw on a robe and towel-dry my hair as I answer it.

I almost drop the towel when I see who it is.

Drake Dillard stands in front of me in a three-thousand-dollar suit and a Cartier on his wrist.

"Hey, Meg," he says easily.

"Hi," I say dumbly. "Um. What are you doing here?"

"Cassie sent me," he answers. "Can I come in?"

"Sure," I say uneasily, swinging the door wide open.

He casually looks around, and I catch him staring at Winter.

"You're not really allergic, are you?" I ask. He smiles.

"No."

"Okay, good. Sic 'im, Winter!"

Winter stares at us, unmoving, and we laugh.

"He's my guard kitten," I explain. "He's still in training, but he's very vicious."

"I can see that," Drake answers, nodding his perfectly groomed head. "May I sit?"

"Of course."

He sits on the sofa, his long, lean legs crossed at the ankle, and I sit on the chair while I wait for him to tell me why he's here.

He doesn't make me wait long.

"Cassie wants me to invest in your building," he says, cutting to the chase. Winter plays with his shoelace, but Drake doesn't even glance at him. "She said you want to upgrade it into a retirement community with all the amenities, and after examining the local market, I think it's a wise investment."

I stare at him.

"You want to invest in my building," I repeat slowly. He looks so out of place in this small living room. I almost can't fathom what he's saying.

"Yes," he answers promptly. "Show me what you have so far as a business plan. I think we can make it work."

"You're assuming I want a partner," I tell him, and it sounds harsher than I meant it. "I mean, what makes you think that I do?"

It still sounds harsh, but it's a good question.

He doesn't flinch.

"I know what you made at Stitch, and Cassie has told me about the repairs this building needs. You need me, and I like good investments."

You need me.

What a Drake thing to say.

My blood starts to heat.

"I don't need you," I tell him. "I didn't ask you to come here."

"Cassie figured you'd be irritated," Drake says. "But just hear me out. I know good investments, and this is one. If you bring me on, I can make sure we both make a huge return on investment. It's called ROI, and you'll make a lot of money."

"Are you seriously mansplaining to me?" I narrow my eyes. "I know what an ROI is."

He doesn't miss a beat.

"You know that I'm good at what I do," he says. "So trust me with this. Let me make you a nice nest egg. We'll build this place up and then sell it."

"You want to sell this building?"

"Of course. You won't want the headache of running it."

He sounds so sure of himself, and I'm once again reminded of why he and I didn't work. He assumed so much about me, things that he just doesn't know.

"I do want to run it, actually," I tell him. "I don't want to sell. I want to make it better and help the residents who live here."

Drake stares at me for a moment, as though that doesn't compute.

"But there is an opportunity to make a lot of money here," he says slowly.

"I already have plans for renovating," I continue. "I don't need your help. Why can't you ever trust that I can do things on my own?"

I don't need you.

I stare at him.

He stares back.

"This puts me in a bad position," he says. "Cassie really wants me to do this. To prove that everything is water under the bridge and that she and I can work while she remains your best friend. That there's no weirdness."

"You're the one making it weird right now," I tell him. "You flew to Chicago without even calling me first. I'd have told you no over the phone."

"I know. That's why I came here instead," he answers.

"Well, you wasted a trip. Now, if you'll excuse me, I have a date to get ready for."

Drake doesn't even blink. I don't know if I wanted him to be even just a little jealous, or not. But he's not.

He stands up. "I'll be here until tomorrow. Just think about it. If you change your mind, call me."

"I won't change my mind," I assure him, as I walk him to the door.

"You know, I do feel a little itchy," he says. "Maybe I am allergic to cats."

"Then it's time for you to go."

I open the door.

Logan stands there, and his face changes from happy to shocked to suspicious in the matter of an instant. He looks unbelievably handsome and smells good in a manly, freshly showered way.

"Um. Hey, Meg," he says, a thick pizza box in his hands. "I hope you don't mind that I'm early."

"My hair is wet and my ex-boyfriend is here. Of course not," I say weakly. "Now is a perfect time."

Drake holds out his hand.

"The ex-boyfriend," he offers. Logan shakes his hand, but doesn't take his eyes off him. The difference in their appearance is striking. Logan is handsome and rugged. Drake is handsome in a very groomed, very aloof way. There is literally no doubt which look I prefer.

"Call me, Meg," Drake says before he walks away.

I stare at Logan.

"It's nothing. He just wants to invest in the Parkview."

Logan walks in and sets the pizza box down.

"I thought we were doing this together," he says slowly. I nod.

"We are."

"But Drake flew all the way here?"

"It's a long story." I sigh. "Can we eat while I tell it?"

"Absolutely. You might want to get dressed, too."

Logan is still suspicious. And I can't blame him.

"I'll be right back."

I throw some clothes on, run a comb through my wet hair, and return to find Logan putting pizza onto plates. He hands me one.

"I thought you were bringing an old family recipe?" I ask, trying to lighten the mood.

"It is. My family has been calling in dinner to Giordano's for years."

I smile. He doesn't.

"Logan, seriously. Drake is with Cassie now, and she wants everything to be okay between the three of us, with zero weirdness factor."

"Then why didn't she come with him?" he asks.

Which is a good question.

"Because her boss—my ex-boss—is a heartless dragon who hates Christmas. She won't let anyone leave."

"I'm really not trying to be suspicious or commandeering," he says. "I don't want to be controlling. It's just . . . my ex used to play all kinds of games, trying to make me jealous, and I don't want that ever again." This grabs my attention.

"You haven't mentioned much about her," I tell him. "Do you want to talk about it?"

He stares at me. "I'd rather have a root canal."

I stare back. "Well, I mean, if you feel suspicious toward me because of things *she* did, I'd like to hear about it. I'd like to understand."

Logan groans. "I don't want to give her any more real estate in my head, and I certainly don't want her in yours. She wasn't a good person, let's just say that. Deep down, she has insecurities that make her play games with everyone, trying to make her feel good about herself."

"I would never do that," I promise. "I swear to you, that's not what this is. I hate games. I can barely even stand to be in the same room with Drake now, to be honest. I told him no. This is *our* project, Logan."

He smiles now, the corners of his eyes wrinkling. "Okay. I swear, I won't bring past baggage into this relationship."

"Is this a relationship?" I ask innocently, cutting into the deep-dish pizza with a fork.

"I'd like to think so," he answers. "When I saw Drake here, I felt a flash of anger I haven't felt in years."

"You were jealous?"

"I'm ashamed to admit, but yes. You were in a robe, he was here . . . I'm sorry. It's not like me."

"Your ex worked you over," I say. "Your sister told me a little bit. Just know . . . I won't do that. I'll never, ever cheat. I'll never play games. What you see is what you get."

"I like what I see," he says, and his eyes are so sexy.

"Good," I answer. "Also, you smell good."

"Are you sure you aren't smelling the pizza?"

"Not unless it smells like a sexy lumberjack."

He grins. "I'm not a lumberjack."

"No, but you're sexy."

He grins again.

"Thank you. Are you sure you don't prefer the pretty boy?"

I sigh. "Ugh. Why are we talking about Drake again? He seems like a little boy compared to you. You're a man."

I pick up his hand. "I like your calluses . . . They show you work for a living. They show that you know how to fix things, that you're capable and strong."

Logan swallows. "You like that? You wouldn't prefer that I run a boardroom instead?"

"Absolutely not. If Drake needs a light bulb changed, he calls someone. You are a *man*," I repeat. "Dare I say . . . *my* man."

"You may dare," he answers, his blue eyes sparkling.

He dips his head and kisses me, and all thoughts of Drake fade completely away.

He pulls away, but I pull him back.

"Do that again," I breathe.

He smiles against my lips and obliges.

In the next instant, however, he yanks away and howls, grasping his leg.

Winter dangles innocently from his thigh, the kitten's razor claws digging into Logan's flesh.

I can't help but giggle while I detach him.

"Awwww, did you get him with your little furry needle mittens?"

Logan gives me side-eye. "I think he drew blood."

"Did I just say you were manly?" I ask. "Because I take it back."

He laughs and takes Winter from me. "You, little kitten, are a menace." But he nuzzles Winter's nose with his own. "A cute one, though."

"Okay, you're manly again," I decide. "You'd have to be secure in your manhood to kiss a cat."

"I'm secure in my manhood," he confirms. He kisses me again, as if to prove it. My fingers tangle in his hair.

When I get my fill, I sit back and stare at the pizza longingly.

"Dig in," he says. "I know you want to."

I do. I eat voraciously.

Logan watches me in appreciation. "I love it when a woman actually eats on a date," he tells me. "It's like . . . *we know you eat*. It's okay to do it in front of us."

I laugh. "You won't have to worry about that with me." I take another bite. "What do you want to do tonight? Want to watch the greatest movie ever filmed?"

"I'm always up for that," he tells me. "What it is?"

"*Pride and Prejudice*," I answer.

His face visibly falls. "Ummm."

"It's amazing," I tell him. "The angst between Mr. Darcy and Elizabeth is palpable."

Logan is still unconvinced.

"And if you fail to be entertained by the literary prowess, Keira Knightley is in it. And she's hot."

Now he's appeased. I elbow him.

"I'll clean this up. Can you go grab it? The DVD is next to the TV in the bedroom."

"I see this won't be the first time you've watched it recently." He winces, and I grin as I carry the plates and glasses to the kitchen. I dig around for a decent bottle of wine and pull out two clean wineglasses.

When he's still not back after I have poured the glasses and allowed them to aerate, I go looking for him.

"Surely you found it," I'm saying as I realize that my bedroom door isn't open. The other bedroom door is.

My heart seems to stop, and I walk in.

Logan is standing in the middle of the bedroom that my sister and I used to share.

He looks so odd standing among the sugary pink-and-white room, with the matching twin beds. He looks out of place and like a deer in the headlights.

"I'm sorry," he stammers when he sees my face. "I took a wrong turn."

"This was my bedroom growing up," I say needlessly. There is a picture of Jo and me together on the nightstand in between the beds. She's bald, but radiant. I was posing, trying to look happy when I wasn't. My sister was dying, and everyone knew it.

"You never changed it?" he asks, sitting gingerly on one of the beds.

I shake my head. "My parents wanted it this way. It was a shrine to her. It made moving forward a little . . . difficult."

"I bet," he says carefully. He picks up the teddy bear carefully placed on the pillows.

"That's Mr. Tibbins. Jo took him to every treatment, even though she was a teenager."

"He must've brought her comfort," Logan says.

I nod. "My gran gave him to her for Christmas when we were little. She slept with it her entire life. My mom wanted to bury it with her, but my dad wanted to keep it."

"I can understand that," Logan says gently. "Both those things."

"I didn't at the time," I answer. "They grieved in very different ways, and I couldn't understand why they couldn't just agree."

"Parenthood doesn't come with a handbook," he points out. "I'm sure they just didn't know what to do. They probably struggled with processing everything. Parents are human, too."

"I know."

I sit down on the opposite bed, the bed that was mine. "I used to lie here and watch her sleep," I confess. "I'd make sure she hadn't stopped breathing."

Being here now makes the memories, and the emotions associated with those memories, come flooding back. This is the exact reason why I've avoided coming home. I didn't want to feel any of this.

Jo's shoes sit lined up against the closet, as if she'll be back to use them soon.

Her jacket hangs on the back of the door.

"It must've been so hard to go through that," Logan says softly. He opens his arms. "Come here."

I do it without a second thought. He closes his arms around me, and I close my eyes against his hard chest.

"It still smells like her in here," I tell him. "Can you smell it?"

"No. But I don't doubt that you can."

His heart beats against my ear, steady and strong. "Grief is a powerful emotion, Meg. It's okay to feel it however you feel it. It's not linear. It can come and go. That's fine, too."

"You know this because of your dad," I realize. He nods.

"Yeah. It's not the same, I know. Your sister was so young."

"Loss is loss," I tell him. "We're never ready for it, and it's always hard."

I stare at the pretty white vanity that Jo and I had shared, lined with lip gloss. A string of photos from a photobooth captures us acting goofy, making faces, and I smile.

"She was a great sister. She never acted like I was the pain in the butt that I know I was. Was your dad a good dad?'

"He was," Logan answers. "Strong, silent. But he had good advice when I needed it. He was a great example. I hope that someday, when I have kids of my own, I'm half the father he was."

"You will be." I'm certain of that.

"He was a small plane pilot," Logan tells me. "He was a pilot in the service, and he never lost his love of flying. It's how he died."

I look up at him. "He died flying?"

Logan nods. "He was flying a small Cessna and somehow got turned around in the night. It was foggy, but he was experienced. No one knows how it happened. But I can tell you this. To this day, I don't like flying. Every time I get on a plane, the emotions just kind of overwhelm me. The memories of my dad, and how I used to sit in the cockpit with him as a boy. The sad memories outweigh the good memories in that situation. So I understand what you're going through."

"Maybe you do," I decide, because that's exactly how I feel. That I have so many good memories that should be dominant, but I've allowed my sad ones to control me.

"Maybe we should both work on focusing on the good things, our best memories. Not the sad ones," he suggests. "I'll do it if you will."

I nod slowly. "I can try."

"I have an idea," he says. "I see that the TV in here has a DVD player. How about we watch the movie in here? It might feel good to be surrounded by your sister's energy. Maybe it will make grieving for her easier, if you allow yourself to be near her."

"Exposure therapy?" I ask, trying to joke, but nothing feels funny.

"We can call it that," he tells me.

A knot swells in my throat, and I don't know how I can be so strongly affected when it's been so long. Or how Logan can be so thoughtful.

"Okay," I whisper.

"I'll go get the movie. And I won't complain one bit," he promises.

He's true to his word. We watch the entire movie in my childhood room, with my head on his chest and his arms wrapped around me. I've never felt so safe and secure, and when I drift to sleep, I don't even think about where I am.

CHAPTER SEVENTEEN

*W*hen I wake up, the sun is streaming in my face. Winter isn't curled up with me, which is unusual, and there is old-fashioned music coming from my kitchen.

I rub my eyes, and it's still there.

I pad out to look and find Logan in the kitchen, stirring scrambled eggs with Winter at his feet.

"I hope you like scrambled," he says with a smile. "It's pretty much all I know how to make."

"They're my favorite," I assure him. I feel a little self-conscious, because he saw me in a very vulnerable place last night. But he doesn't comment on it. He doesn't want me to feel uncomfortable, I realize. My heart overflows, and I grab him, gently kissing his cheek.

"Thank you for last night," I murmur.

He nods silently.

"I'm sure it wasn't the 'staying over' you were hoping for," I add, lightening the mood with a smile. He grins back.

"It's the kind of sleepover you needed," he answers. "That's all that matters."

"What's with the music?" I ask him, eyeing his iPhone playing on the counter.

"I'm getting ready for the Christmas party," he tells me. "I'm tightening up my moves."

"You can dance to jazz?" I lift an eyebrow.

"You can't?" He arches his own.

I laugh. "Um, no. I was born in this century."

"Technically, you were born last century," he points out. "Just like jazz. And before you say anything, my mother made me take lessons in junior high."

"Oh, my. You must've been a total chick magnet."

"You'd think," he says thoughtfully. "I don't know how it didn't work."

He grabs my hand.

"Watch," he says. "This is the foxtrot."

He demonstrates. "Feet together, left, right, left, together."

I try it. "This isn't hard," I say in surprise.

"Now, let's do it together. Slow, slow, quick, quick."

I stumble everywhere, and he chuckles. "It's okay. Just follow my lead."

We try again, and when I trust him to lead me through, it works. We dance in unison.

"I can foxtrot!" I say in wonder. He smiles.

"More or less."

I elbow him. "Let's try again."

We do it again and again, and when I'm finally satisfied, our eggs are cold, but we don't care. We eat them while we drink hot coffee, and don't even notice.

"I have to go to work," I say regretfully.

"Me too," he answers. "I'm working on your basement today. I've got to shore it up and get it ready for my crew." He grabs my hand and kisses it. "Can I see you again tonight?"

My heart flutters.

"Yes."

"Until then." He bows exaggeratedly. I smile and decide this is the way I want to start my days until the end of time. "I'm gonna go home, change my clothes, brush my teeth, and I'll be back." I kiss him, and he leaves.

I'M STILL HUMMING jazz when Winter and I enter the office downstairs an hour later.

"I've decided I love the party theme," I tell Sylvie as I open the door, but I soon find she isn't alone.

Drake is with her, and he looks just as out of place in this office as he did in my apartment.

Sylvie stares from him to me, and I see the wheels turning in her head.

"Hello, Meg," he greets me. "I brought you a bagel."

"I already ate," I tell him, setting Winter on Sylvie's lap. "But thank you."

"I came to see if you'd changed your mind," he says. "My flight leaves in an hour."

"He's been here for an hour already," Sylvie says. "I tried to call you, but you didn't pick up."

Shoot. I hadn't even checked my phone. That heads-up would've been nice.

"I'll take the bagel," Sylvie says. "Did you bring cream cheese?" Drake nods and hands her the bag. Sylvie's shirt today is an ugly Christmas sweater with TEAM SLEIGH embroidered on the front.

"Sylvie, would you mind taking that to the ballroom?" I ask her. "I need to speak with Drake alone."

She nods and quickly scurries out.

I turn to Drake.

"I'm not going to sell this building," I tell him firmly. "Thank you for coming, but it was unnecessary. I'm not going to change my mind."

"What should I tell Cassie?" he asks, standing up.

"The truth. You can tell her that I appreciate the gesture, and that there is zero weirdness. I'm glad the two of you are happy."

"Truly?" Drake doesn't seem sure.

"Truly."

"You're sure?"

"One thousand percent."

I'm firm, and he finally gives in.

"Okay. If you're sure."

I don't even comment. I open the office door. He steps through and turns back to me.

"I know you don't need my approval, Meg, but I'm proud of you. This isn't something I'd ever have seen for you, but your conviction is inspiring."

I stare at him dumbly.

"What?" He chuckles.

"I think that's the first compliment you've ever paid me," I tell him honestly.

"Really?" He thinks on it, and then shakes his head. "Man, I can be an ass sometimes."

I stay silent, and he laughs again.

"Meg, I wish you all the luck in the world. If there's ever something I can do for you, just call."

Before I even know it, he hugs me.

It's quick, and almost formal, but it happens.

And when we pull apart, wouldn't you know it, Logan is coming around the corner wearing his toolbelt.

Drake nods a greeting as he walks past, and Logan's eyes are frozen to mine.

"It was nothing," I reassure him. "He came to make sure I didn't change my mind. He wished me well."

"I bet he did," Logan grumbles, staring after Drake.

I turn his chin to me. "Don't," I tell him. "I swear. He's nothing to me but a memory."

Logan nods and finally smiles. "Okay. I'm sorry. Old habits die hard, but I'm trying."

I hug him and good-naturedly steer him toward the elevator. "You have a building to save," I remind him. "I'll figure out some other way to pay you than money."

I waggle my eyebrows and he laughs.

After the elevator doors close behind him, I join Sylvie in the ballroom.

She's eating the last of the bagel and making a list.

"So that was the ex," she says without looking up.

"Yes." I sit down across from her.

"He's good-looking in a dandy kind of way," she says, still not looking up.

"Don't worry, Sylvie. He doesn't hold a candle to Logan."

Now she looks up.

"Mr. Scott is in a class of his own." She sniffs. "There was never even a question."

"Of course not," I assure her. "Not even a question."

She stares at me over the top of her reading glasses. "Good. Now, take a look at this menu. I'm trying to be as authentic as possible."

We pore over it, examining each item. Imperial sweetbreads. Roast chicken. Petits fours. Stuffed mushrooms. Glazed duck.

"The drinks will be authentic, too," she says, pulling out another list. "Check this out."

The Gin Rickey. The Bee's Knees. The Southside. The Singapore Sling.

"I like these," I tell her, and she beams. "In fact, we need to keep them on the menu in the speakeasy. If we decide to actu-ally serve alcohol in it."

"I think we should," she offers. "It's what it was meant for."

"I tend to agree," I answer. "Can you look into what it takes to get a liquor license?"

She adds it to her list, but I also text Ellie and ask her to do the same thing. Just to be sure. As I'm typing, someone clears her throat from the doorway.

I LOOK UP to find a strange woman leaning against the door-jamb.

She's slender, around my age, and pregnant. She's pretty, al-though her face is a little long, and her eyes are just a little sharp.

"Excuse me," she says. "Can you tell me where Logan Scott is?"

Her arm jangles with bracelets, and gauging the size of her belly, I'd say she's at least five months pregnant. Maybe six.

"He's in the basement working," I tell her. "Can I give him a message?"

Who are you???

She sighs. "I really need to deliver the message in person. Could you possibly take me? It's important."

I try not to express my curiosity, or my dismay. Something in my heart tells me that something is wrong. "Of course. I'll show you the way."

I accompany her to the elevators, and her perfume is cloying. She's wearing far too much of it. She smells like bathroom spray.

As I poke the B button for the basement, I glance at her.

"I'm Meg."

"It's nice to meet you," she mumbles, but it's clear she doesn't care. "I'm Talia. Logan's girlfriend."

Logan's.

Girlfriend.

I stare and she rolls her eyes.

"Technically, we broke up earlier this year, but I think that will change after I speak with him."

She gestures at her belly and I almost swallow my tongue. *This can't be happening.*

"He's the father?"

"Well, I'm not here for my health," she almost snaps as the elevator comes to a stop. She wrinkles her face as the doors open. "God, what's that smell?"

"Mildew," I tell her. "I'm sorry."

I'm not sorry.

I lead her to the brick wall. From here, I can see Logan's broad shoulders swaying as he swings a hammer, making contact with the stones. I call out his name.

He turns, with a smile that dies when he sees Talia.

I have a slight moment of satisfaction, until I watch his gaze drop to her belly. He freezes.

"Talia?" he asks, confused. I can almost see the wheels turning in his head, doing the math. So . . . he's adding months as quickly as I am.

"Can we talk?" she asks him. He nods quickly and silently, setting the hammer on the floor.

"I'll just leave you to it," I mumble, rushing back to the elevator before my shock starts to show. How can this be happening? I literally just met Mr. Perfect, and now he's taken?

When the doors slide open on the main floor, Sylvie is waiting for me.

"Was that who I think it was?"

"If you mean Logan's ex, then yes," I say weakly. Then, "Do you have any chocolate?"

"In the desk," she answers. "Let's go."

She pulls me into the office and rustles around for the candy. Handing it to me, she eyes me.

"It's not what it looks like," she offers.

"Oh, I think it is," I tell her, tearing into the Hershey bar like an animal.

"She can't just . . . show up and expect him to drop everything," she says, sinking into the chair.

"She's pregnant with his child," I answer, trying to get some semblance of comfort from the candy. It doesn't work. My heart pounds and pounds.

"He won't . . ." Sylvie trails off, because she knows better.

"He's a man of honor," I say with a sigh. "He will."

She knows I'm right, and she holds out her hand. I break off a couple pieces of the chocolate and give it to her. We munch on it in unison.

"What if—"

"No," I interrupt. "It is what it is, Sylvie."

"I hate that saying," she decides. "It is what we *accept*."

"Something like this is pretty cut-and-dried," I tell her. "Besides. Since when do you care about my love life?"

She looks shocked. "Meg, I just want you to be happy. Your dad isn't here, so I thought I'd step in."

I lay my head down on my arms.

"Thanks, Sylvie," I mumble. "But nothing can be done about this."

"Mr. Scott," she answers, and it takes a minute for me to realize that she wasn't answering me, she was greeting him.

I lift my head, and he's in front of me, his eyes anguished, his face pale.

"Meg, let me explain."

"There's not a lot to be said at this point," I say painfully, and he swallows.

"I didn't know. Can you believe me?"

"It doesn't matter what I believe," I tell him stiffly, standing up and scooping up Winter. "It won't change anything."

Painfully, I brush past him. I hold my breath as I do, so I won't inhale his cologne. It would hurt my heart even more.

"Meg!" he calls from behind me, but I make a break for it, rushing for the stairs.

I just can't right now.

I'M EATING CHUNKY Monkey straight from the container when there's a knock on my door twenty minutes later.

I don't answer. Instead, I put another bite of ice cream in my mouth, then offer Winter a lick from the spoon.

"Meg," Ellie calls. "I know you're in there."

"I am not," I call back.

"Can I come in?"

"No." I chew on a chocolate chunk.

The door opens, however, because I hadn't locked it. Ellie comes in, looking chic as usual, in her gray slacks and matching cashmere turtleneck. I shove another bite of ice cream into my mouth while staring mulishly straight ahead.

Ellie sits down next to me.

"I bumped into Sylvie," she says gently. "She told me about Mr. Scott."

I don't answer. I just chew.

"Meg, Logan is a good man. I know that he would never have led you on if he had any idea about this."

I look at her, and my chest constricts.

"Ellie, I don't care what he knew or didn't know. The fact is, he's got a pregnant ex, and I know it's stupid to say this, but I think I was falling for him."

My eyes get hot, and before I can stop it, the tears start to fall.

"Do you have any idea how hard it is to meet someone who is handsome, and funny, and gentlemanly, and did I say handsome?"

I chew on ice cream and tears, and Ellie pats my leg.

"Actually, yes, I do," she says, comfortingly. "But it's not impossible, and whatever is meant to be will be."

"Oh my gosh. You didn't just say that." I stare at her. "You lost the love of your life. Please don't offer me platitudes."

She shrugs. "I lost him because I let my pride get in the way. That wasn't fate. That was my own stupidity. I gave up. I was rather trusting that you wouldn't do the same."

"I shouldn't give up? Do you know Logan at all? If she's pregnant, and she obviously is, then he will do the right thing. He's so old-school that I bet he'll marry her."

I throw myself into the couch cushions dramatically.

"You know, this is an era where a child can be coparented very well by two parents who aren't together," she tells me. "He doesn't need to marry her."

"It's such a complication," I groan.

"Were you expecting life to be without complications?" She raises a perfectly manicured eyebrow.

"Stop speaking logic to me," I mutter. "I have no idea if he still loves her, or if this changes everything. I want to mourn."

She sighs. "Well, if you've set your mind to that, I guess I can't change it. Should I tell you instead about my progress? Sylvie took me to the research Joe found, and I've started compiling applications to historical societies. I'm going to send one today to that contact in the local society I mentioned to you. And you know the representative is coming to see the property. This ball is rolling, Meg."

"Thank you," I tell her. I still feel sullen, but at least that aspect of my life is moving somewhere good. "I appreciate you."

She smiles. "How are the designs for the contest coming?"

I don't say anything.

"Meg, I know everything seems upside down right now, but this is your dream. You should keep at it. Put your pain aside, and focus on making this happen."

"Like you did?" I ask, staring into her eyes. "You became an attorney after Frankie left you. Did you pour yourself into that curriculum so you'd stop thinking about him?"

She's quiet now, and I wonder if I've gone too far.

"Yes," she finally answers. "I did. And no. It never stopped me from missing him. But it did give me a huge sense of self-worth and accomplishment. Your dreams shouldn't be attached to a man, Meg."

"They're not," I assure her. "And I'm sorry if I sounded harsh. I'm just upset. I treasure you, Ellie. I would never hurt your feelings on purpose."

"I know." She pats my leg. "Now go wash your face, dear. Then get up, and get going."

I exhale, then nod. "You're right. Of course you're right."

"I usually am," she announces, and I laugh. "What? It's the benefit of having lived for over seventy years. I'm wise."

I roll my eyes, and she stands up. "Chin up, darling."

I nod. "Chin up."

She leaves, and I stick the ice cream back into the freezer. "You live to see another day," I tell it, as I put my spoon in the sink and wash my hands.

I take Ellie's advice and splash water on my face, too. It can't hurt. The cold water almost serves as a reset, because it makes me focus my attention on the iciness of the water, not the fact that Logan's ex is pregnant, and *here*.

When I return to the living room to check on Winter, my phone has four unread messages. All from Logan.

Please talk to me.

Please call.

Listen, I know it seems bad.

But I think I'm falling for you.

My heart leaps into my throat as I type out a response.

Is your girlfriend still pregnant?

He answers immediately.

My EX-girlfriend. And yes.

A tear escapes from my eye as I reply one last time.

I know you well enough to know that you are an honorable man. You'll do what is right, and I love that about you. But that leaves me in a place I don't want to be. Alone. Again. Goodbye, Logan.

Wait!! He replies immediately. Did you just say I love you?

I ignore the text and set my phone down, because even though I haven't even admitted it to myself yet, and it hasn't even been that long, I know that I do. I love him.

I stay holed up in my apartment for the rest of the day and at bedtime, I fall asleep crying into Winter's white fur.

CHAPTER EIGHTEEN

The first thing I do when I wake up the next morning is call Cassie and tell her.

She's rightfully outraged and rails for a good, long while. I wait her out by tossing a ball across the floor for Winter. He chases it, his tiny tail twitching. Then he crouches behind the sofa leg, wiggling his butt as he stalks it. I manage to laugh at his antics, despite my heart pain.

"What are you going to do?" Cassie finally asks when she settles down.

"There's nothing *to* do," I answer. "Literally. He's going to have a baby with someone else."

"But he's falling in love with *you*," she protests.

"It's all unfortunate timing," I agree. "But clearly, he's got enough on his plate without adding me to the mix."

"Don't give up before it's even begun," she says with a groan. "Promise me."

"It's not begun," I tell her. "It's over. It's finished. What do you not understand about that?"

"What does he say about it?"

I'm silent, so she answers for me.

"He said that he knew it looked bad, but that he was falling for you."

"I've gotta go," I tell her. "I can't right now. I've got to work on . . . you know, work."

"How's that coming?" she asks, allowing me to change the subject. "Are you going to be ready for the Fashionista show?"

"Yes. I'm not worried about that. I'm more worried about this building, and holding it together until then. If I can win that contest, it'll all be blue skies and clear sailing after. But from now until then, I've got leaky pipes, an apartment where the bathroom ceiling is ready to fall in from water damage, an elevator that is limping along on its last legs . . . The list goes on and on."

Cassie is quiet. "Man, you really did inherit a lot of responsibility," she finally says.

"Yeah. I know."

"I wish you would've let Drake help."

"I don't need his help," I snap, then immediately feel bad. "I'm sorry. But I don't need his help."

"Okay," she answers. "Well, then, I want you to focus on

sewing the most perfect pieces you can for this show. Everything hinges on it, Meg."

"No pressure though," I mutter, and we hang up.

I scoop up Winter and feed him his breakfast before we head downstairs. The fire is blazing welcomingly as we walk through the lobby into the office.

Sylvie has a picture of my father framed on my desk, and she beams when I notice.

"He'd be so proud of you," she tells me, and her 180-degree opinion shift of me is hard to miss. I don't question it, though. I need all the positive vibes I can get right now.

"I haven't done anything yet," I remind her, pouring a cup of coffee as she takes Winter from my arms.

"But you're attacking this!" she tells me. "You will do something. Also, Logan is working in the basement."

She looks away quickly, like she's afraid to see my reaction. My eyes well up.

I sigh, trying to hide the fact that I'm secretly having a panic attack. "Why? I should hire someone. It seems like the right thing to do."

She arches an eyebrow. "With what money? Don't look a gift horse in the mouth. You don't have to see him."

"I feel like it'll be impossible to avoid him forever," I point out.

"You can do it," she tells me. "I've been avoiding Mr. Mack in 212 for two years. It can be done, trust me."

"What's wrong with Mr. Mack?" I ask curiously. She shakes her head.

"He can't keep his hands to himself," she whispers, as though it's a sin to even talk about. I smile.

"Well, you're a dish, Sylvie," I tell her. She glares at me.

"My looks have nothing to do with his inability to control himself," she tells me primly. "He pinched my tush in the hall. *In broad daylight.*"

"You're right. That's egregious," I agree. She levels a gaze at me. "It'll be hard to avoid someone who has volunteered to work on this building," I continue. "You can hide from Mr. Mack. I can't hide from Logan."

"I didn't suggest hiding," she clarifies. "I said avoid. There's a difference."

"I don't see the difference, but I'll take your word for it."

Winter bats a little crocheted ball across the floor. Sylvie flushes. "I made him a couple toys last night," she tells me. I follow her gaze and find a small mountain of crocheted delights for him in his bed.

"A few," I agree with a smile. Logan had been right all along. Sylvie hides a heart of pure gold behind her gruff bark.

Today, she's wearing a shirt that says OH, SNAP! It has a picture of a gingerbread man with a leg broken off. I hide my smile.

"I'm going to go talk to Mr. Scott," she announces. "This situation just won't do. You deserve more than this. And so does he."

"You will not," I tell her sharply. She freezes in place.

"He should do what he thinks is right," I tell her. "His decision should have nothing to do with me."

"He loves you. Any fool can see that."

My heart seems to break in my chest.

"It doesn't matter," I tell her. "There's another life in the balance. An innocent little baby who needs its father."

Sylvie sighs and sits down. "This fabric came for you," she says, handing me an opened box. Cranberry-red knit gleams from the top of the stack, tiny golden threads shimmering through the weave. The same fabric, but in black, is beneath.

"You should probably get to sewing," she tells me. "I'll have lunch sent to you. The table in the ballroom is free. I already put sewing supplies in there for you."

"Thank you," I say limply. "You're awesome, Sylvie."

"You're welcome," she answers. "Go get busy. It'll distract you. Tom Rutherford is scheduled to watch Winter this morning."

"Did you actually create an appointment book?" I ask, eyeing a small powder-blue book on her desk. She smiles sweetly.

"That cat is beloved."

I carry the box of fabric in, and then run upstairs to grab the Christmas dress and my sketchbook.

I hang the dress on the wall in the ballroom, within my line of sight. It is, after all, my inspiration for this entire line.

I measure and cut, measure and cut. I consult my sketches, do some math in my head, and measure and cut once again. I pin the fabric, and lay it out in the appropriate order.

Every move I make is haunted by the pain in my heart.

The knowledge that the man of my dreams was right in my fingers and can't be with me is gutting.

I numb the pain by focusing on sewing straight lines. I hunch over the machine, and I'm not even sure where Sylvie found it, nor do I care. It gets the job done.

Sew, check the line, sew.

Straighten, sew, straighten.

I develop a rhythm, and before I know it, I'm holding up the finished cranberry dress. It's beautiful, and soft, and shimmery. It's everything I wanted it to be.

I glance at the door, then pull off my clothes and step into the dress.

The fabric clings to me, yet conceals.

It's elegant, yet sexy.

It's perfect, yet . . . the shoulders don't fit right.

I touch them, feeling the way the seam is too lumpy, somehow.

I cross over to the Christmas dress, running my hands over its shoulders. I turn it wrong side out and examine how the shoulders were sewn. As I do, my fingers feel something sharp, something out of place. I hold it into the light, and it is there that I see a sapphire earring.

My breath stops.

My heart stops.

The beautiful, fragile jewel is wedged in among the threads, accidentally lost so long ago. The impact that this tiny piece of jewelry played on someone's life is heavy, particularly as I see where it has been this entire time.

It had been lost, yet not lost. It was here.

Just beneath Ellie's nose.

Hidden.

I carefully untangle it from the thread, and then race up the steps to Ellie's apartment. I bang on the door, and she answers quickly, confused.

"Meg, what in the world?"

I hold out the earring, completely out of breath from running up the stairs.

"Look ... what ... I ... found."

Her eyes widen, and she goes white.

"Where?" she says simply, taking it from my hand.

"In the seam of the dress," I tell her, following her into the apartment. "It was inside the dress. It was there all along. Did you put the earrings on before the dress, by chance?"

Ellie thinks about it. "I think so," she finally says. "I was wearing a robe while I got ready, and Francesca came in with the earrings. I put them on immediately. It made her so happy."

"And then, when you pulled the dress over your head, the earring came out, wedged in the dress, and no one noticed," I say. "The mystery is solved, Ellie. You're cleared!"

Her lovely face is drawn now, and she sits down.

"Not really," she answers. "They'll never know. To them, I'll always be guilty."

She holds the earring in her hand, clutching it for dear life. I kneel by her chair, cupping her hand with mine.

"But I know. And you know. It's simply not true, and never was."

"But, darling, that was never the problem. I always knew I

was innocent, but it was a situation that I couldn't control. A situation that changed the course of my life, and there wasn't a thing I could do about it."

"But . . . maybe you could've," I finally say. "You never looked back. You never tried to contact him. What if you had, and he had cooled down, and he realized that he knew your heart, and he knew that you'd never do such a thing? That would've changed your life, too."

"I couldn't take the risk," she says. "I was too humiliated. I simply couldn't have borne it to hear him say out loud that he'd changed his mind."

"Was an entire life wondering about what *could've been* any better?" I ask her simply.

She looks stricken. "No."

I wait, and she exhales, her slender shoulders slumping into the chair. "No, it wasn't." She turns to me abruptly, gripping my hands hard. "Don't be me," she says fervently. "Meggie, don't be me."

I stare at her, into her sincere eyes.

"This isn't a parallel," I tell her. "That wasn't what I was trying to say."

"Whether you were trying to or not, it's the truth. You cannot give up on this without speaking to Logan. You HAVE to see what the situation is, not what you think it might be. Give him a chance, Meg."

"I don't know," I say weakly. "I can't handle it if he says it's over."

"If you don't speak with him, it will most certainly be over. Listen to me. I lived that. Hearing him say the words won't kill you, Meg. Living with regret will."

I swallow hard and square my shoulders.

"You're right. I'm stronger than this. I'll talk to him."

She smiles, a gentle, wise smile that is laced with sadness. "Thank you," she says softly. "Thank you."

She looks at me, at the new dress I've sewn.

"Meg, this dress is stunning," she says. "You are beautiful in it."

"Thank you," I answer, picking at the shoulders. "It's not right yet, but it will be."

"Yes," she agrees. "It will be."

"I'll talk to Logan at some point," I tell her again. "I just don't know when. My heart hurts, Ellie."

"I know, sweet girl," she answers. "Trust me, I know."

I leave her holding the earring, and I return to the ballroom.

I SPEND THE rest of the day fixing the dress, and getting the shoulders right. By five o'clock, it's perfect, and hanging on a hanger next to the original dress.

"Woooo-eeee," Tom exclaims, coming in. "Did you make that? It's a beauty."

"Thank you," I answer. "I'm entering it into a contest."

"Yes, Sylvie told me," he replies. "You'll win."

"Thank you for the vote of confidence."

"It's just the truth. Hey, little lady, I have an issue. As you know, there's a garden on the rooftop. Years back, there was an irrigation system put into all the planters . . . They line the edge of the roof. And I just went to check on the evergreens to see if any of them have grown holly that I could give Sylvie for the party, and I noticed that the watering system has a leak. It's been freezing all over the roof."

"Oh, no. That can't be good."

Yet another thing that needs fixing.

"I know. Can you come take a look? I'll show you." I follow him, and when we're in the hall, he pauses by the office. "You need to grab a coat. It's forty degrees."

"Forty? That's a warm front for a Chicago winter." I try to joke, but it falls flat because my heart isn't in it. I grab my coat and pull it on in the elevator.

We get out on the top floor and wind our way through the hall to the rooftop entrance. As we step out into the cold, Tom looks around.

"Did you know this was created as a way that the original guests could enjoy a garden in the middle of the city? It was fancy, and during the summers, they'd have tea parties and whatnot up here."

I follow his gaze. "I suppose it was pretty," I tell him. Although it's hard to imagine right now, because the whole thing is covered with snow.

"Watch your step," he says, as he guides me to the far side of the roof. "It's over here."

He points at the ground. "See the ice?"

I sigh. "Sadly, yes. Has it leaked into the building yet?"

"I don't know," he answers. "That's why Sylvie called Mr. Scott. He's meeting us here."

My eyes snap up and meet Tom's, and there is something there, something more than a man wanting to fix a roof issue.

"Tom, did you set this up?" I ask him slowly.

He fidgets, clearly uncomfortable.

"Ellie called Sylvie and they arranged it. They pulled me into it. I couldn't say no."

"Well, you could've." I sigh.

"But I didn't. And look, right on time."

I follow his gaze to find Logan stepping onto the rooftop.

"I'll just let the two of you examine this problem," Tom says, as he makes his way to the door. When he closes it, there is a suspicious click.

"Did he . . . he didn't," I exclaim.

Logan hurries to the door and pulls on it.

It doesn't budge.

"He locked it," Logan confirms.

I must look as outraged as I feel because he rushes to defend himself.

"I had nothing to do with this," he promises. "It's freezing out here. I wouldn't."

My phone buzzes with a text.

It's Sylvie.

Let me know when the two of you have talked. I'll come let you out.

I grit my teeth.

"No, it wasn't you," I tell him. I'm shivering already, and I don't like being ganged up on.

"Um, there's a space heater over here," Logan says, poking around next to the edge. "It's already plugged in and everything."

"Sylvie." I sigh again.

He chuckles as he turns on the heater. "You have to give her credit."

"For what? Interfering?"

But she has a good heart, and I know it.

I turn to Logan.

"Logan, it feels like my heart is breaking."

His face instantly sobers, and he reaches for me, but I pull away.

"No, don't. I can't say what I want to say if you touch me." I take a deep breath.

"I don't know what happened with Talia. I don't know when you were last with her, or when she got pregnant, but I do know that you are a very, very good man. That's how I know what you're going to do."

Logan waits, his blue eyes almost smoldering. "And what is that?"

"You'll do the right thing." I edge closer to the heater, rubbing my arms, trying to make my teeth stop chattering.

"What do you consider the right thing to be?" he asks, moving closer to me. He reaches out and rubs my arms, warming them up.

"You'll get back together with Talia so that your baby will have both parents," I tell him. "A great family life, just like you had growing up."

"I don't have to be together with Talia in order to be a father," Logan says firmly. "I know, for a fact, that when parents are unhappy at home, it affects the children. I saw it firsthand with Monica and the girls. Before she finally got divorced, they all suffered. It wasn't good. The girls are happier now than they ever were before."

A spark of something . . . hope, maybe, ignites in my belly.

"You really feel that way?"

He nods. "Of course. Talia and I aren't meant to be, Meg."

He rubs my arms again. "But I think you and I are. I certainly want to find out."

I see my breath in the air as I exhale.

"I don't know if I can do that," I say, trying to force my heart to not break. "I don't know if I can come between a family."

He stares at me. "Meg, we aren't a family. She's my ex-girlfriend. Someone who is deviant, and mean, and someone I don't want to be with. She's not the person I would've chosen to have a child with, but I'll have to make the best out of the situation and be the best father I can be. But I won't be with

Talia. Not now, not ever. Whatever happens between us, that isn't changing."

I can't feel my legs, and I'm not sure if it's because of the cold or from relief.

"Are you sure?"

He nods. "One thousand percent," he replies, using my favorite phrase.

I smile, and for the first time since earlier in the day, it feels like I can breathe again.

He pulls me closer, and I absorb his warmth, his strength.

"Do you feel better?" he asks, whispering into my ear.

"I do."

"Good. Can you call Sylvie and ask her to let us out now?"

I laugh into his chest and pull out my phone.

CHAPTER NINETEEN

*T*he days leading up to Christmas Eve are a flurry of activity, and each day, I find myself sucked further and further into the Christmas spirit. The tenants of Parkview West make it impossible not to be, and the excitement of uncovering the Red Alibi is just icing on the cake.

That's how I find myself allowing Sylvie to plant a red Santa hat on my head on December twenty-third, as we stand in the basement together and survey the opening, which Logan and his team have cut out, shored up, and are in the process of re-bricking.

"It's going to look like it originally did," I say, astonished.

The white ball of the Santa hat jauntily bounces every time I move, but I don't even care.

"Mr. Scott promised it would," Sylvie reminds me. "He's

never fallen short of his word before, and I seriously doubt he'll start now, with you."

"Are you talking about his work ethic, or is this a pointed reminder that I can trust him in every way?"

Sylvie has the gall to look dramatically innocent. "I don't know what you're talking about," she says. "I was just stating a fact. Take it however you want."

"Your loyalty is admirable," I tell her with a smile as we walk into the front room of the Red Alibi.

"That extends to you, too," she tells me. "I mean it. You're my family, Meg."

"And you're mine," I answer.

I run my finger along a newly dusted table, one of the originals still here in the bar when we found it. "I think we should have pieces of glass cut to overlay on top of these," I tell her. "To protect them. They're historic, after all."

Sylvie pulls out her ever-present list. "I agree."

Her shirt today says MY OTHER CAR IS A SLEIGH and has a picture of Santa tossing presents out over the side of his. For extra flair, she's also wearing a lighted Christmas bulb necklace, which shines brightly in red, green, blue, and orange.

"You know, even if they hadn't gotten the electrical working down here again, it would've been okay. Your necklace could've lit the way."

She stares at me. "It's called Christmas cheer, Meg. You should try it."

"I'm wearing a Santa hat," I answer. "Don't push it."

But my belly is warm with happiness, and my face has a perma-grin. There hasn't been any awful news about Talia all week, and Logan has been perfect, as usual.

I doubt anything could dampen my spirits now.

"Are you ready for tomorrow night?" Sylvie asks as she walks behind the polished bar. She digs beneath it and counts the packs of napkins. "I hope the embossed napkins are ready today," she mutters. "They told me they'd try. I'd rather use those than these plain white ones."

"As ready as I'll ever be," I answer. "The dresses are ready to go, they've assigned a couple models to me, and my plane tickets are printed out."

"Ellie confirmed that the historical society representative will be arriving at nine o'clock tomorrow night. Do you think you can make it by then?"

"That'll be cutting it close, but I'll do my best." I twirl in the middle of the room. "Sylvie, did you ever, in your wildest dreams, think we'd be renovating a bar?"

She laughs and tucks her list into her pocket.

"Never," she confirms. "But I like it. It's going to be perfect."

"I agree," I say happily. "I really think it is! Let's go look at what you've done to the ballroom. I haven't been in there in a few days."

"You've been working so hard on the dresses," Sylvie agrees, as we step into the elevator. "I don't know that I've seen you taking breaks for lunch or dinner."

"Maybe not, but the dresses sure look good," I answer. "Even if I do say so myself."

When we open the grand doors to the ballroom, we find Ellie sitting at one of the tables. Sylvie had had the conference room table carried out and replaced with round tables covered in red-linen tablecloths lining the edges of the walls for people to use during the party.

"This is beautiful, Sylvie," Ellie tells her, gazing at the garland, and the holly, and even the mistletoe hanging to the side of one door. "This truly makes me remember what it was like back in the old days."

She sighs happily and stares around in wonder, and I impulsively hug Sylvie.

"You're amazing," I tell her. "Did you use actual holly from the rooftop?"

She nods. "Yes. I wanted everything to be as authentic as possible."

"Well, it wouldn't be possible without you funding it," I tell her. "I'll be grateful forever. And I swear, I'll pay you back."

"When you can." She waves me off, unconcerned. "I'll be enjoying the party, too, so it's not like I don't get something out of it."

"Maybe Mr. Mack will save you a dance," I tease her, and she glares.

"It's not too late to put a stop payment on that check," she warns, and I laugh.

"Of course it is. I already cashed it, and I've paid Logan's crew. That money is long gone, Syl."

She purses her lips, but I see them twitching. My sense of humor has grown on her.

"Well, we're a great team," Ellie tells us. "Sylvie, you have carried off this party beautifully. Meg, you and Logan have quite literally found a piece of history and are restoring it, and I have contributed in a small way by bringing the historical society on board. This has been an amazing exercise in teamwork, and I'm proud of you all."

"We couldn't have done it without you, Ellie," I tell her, giving her a hug. "In fact, you also inspired my new dress line. So if I hadn't met you, none of this would be happening."

She smiles brightly.

"And I spoke with Betsy. She's willing to stop hounding me about moving until we wait and see what the new building will be like."

"That's amazing news!" I clasp my hands. "Everything is coming together!"

Sylvie's eyes are misty. "Do you regret coming here now?" she asks, and the look on her face causes me to mist up. I shake my head no, and soon the three of us are huddled into a hug.

"Um, is everything okay?"

Logan stands nearby, two cups of coffee in his hands, and a concerned look on his face.

I smile and pull away.

"Yes. We're just counting blessings."

"Well, I brought coffee for two of the prettiest girls in Chicago," he says, handing the cups to Ellie and Sylvie. I smile, because I know that coffee had been for us, but boy, it sure does make the other women happy.

It's no wonder Logan has the tenants wrapped around his calloused fingers.

"We're finishing the wall today," he tells me. "So it should be dry for tomorrow night. Is everything else ready?"

I nod. "Thanks to these two superstars."

"Okay, okay, now you're just flattering us," Ellie says.

"But you can keep going," Sylvie suggests.

Logan grins at them and pulls me away, into the office, where Winter is sleeping in his sleigh bed.

"I dreamed about this last night," he tells me.

"About what?" I ask.

"This," he says against my lips, kissing me soundly. My arms wrap around his neck, pulling him close. Lord, I could stay in his arms forever. "You always smell so good," I tell him. He grins.

"Do you want to model your dresses for me tonight?" he asks. "I'd love to see them."

"I think that would make me nervous," I answer. "Speaking of nervous . . . have you spoken with Talia?"

A pall instantly falls onto the office. "Nice segue," Logan says ruefully.

I shrug. "It was the best I could do."

He shakes his head. "No. I've left her several messages. But ever since I told her that we would have to be very effective co-parents who are not together, I haven't heard a word."

"You don't think she'd try to cut you out of the baby's life, do you?" I ask instantly, my forehead wrinkled. "That would be awful."

"It would definitely be something she'd try to do," Logan answers. "She's not a nice person, Meg. But I'll do what I have to do. If we have to fight in court, so be it. That child will need a good influence to balance out Talia's."

"She can't be that bad," I answer. "I mean, you loved her at some point."

Logan stares at me. "I did. But little by little, her true nature came out, and she's just a very selfish, spoiled brat, who always expects to get her way. She really doesn't care about anyone else. Not in the slightest."

"Oh, man. She's not going to be a good mother," I say, which is an understatement.

"I worry about that," Logan answers. "I mean, they say motherhood changes people. Maybe it will work on her."

"We'll pray for that," I reply.

"Anyway. I've gotta get downstairs. I'll call you when it's ready for you to come see." Logan plants a kiss on my forehead and ducks back out the door.

I turn around and Winter is stretching. He's got a red plaid Christmas ribbon tied around his neck in a bow.

"Sylvie," I mutter, shaking my head. I leave it on, though, because it looks cute.

I sit at the desk and go through all the receipts from the recent work on the basement, and when a deliveryman from the caterer comes, I direct him to the kitchenette near the ballroom.

The flurry of people has been constant this week, so I don't think twice when there is another light knock on the door.

"Come in," I say, without looking up.

"Do you have a second?" a woman's voice asks. My head snaps up *because I know that voice.*

Talia stands in the doorway, her hand cupping her belly.

Yeah, rub it in.

"Of course. Logan is working downstairs, if you're looking for him," I say pointedly, yet still slightly civil.

"I know. I don't need to talk to Logan. I need to talk with you. But I don't want to do it here. Can you meet me for lunch?"

I hesitate. "Um. I don't think that's a good idea. This is really between you and Logan."

"No, it really isn't," she says. "You're involved now. I think we both know that in every relationship, the woman calls all the shots."

"Ummmm. Not in healthy relationships," I answer. "Relationships are supposed to be based on compromise and respect."

She rolls her eyes. "Maybe in a perfect world. Anyway, can you come for lunch?"

"When?"

"Now."

Of course. She doesn't want me to tell Logan first.

But something about the confident way she's looking at me, like she thinks she can call all the shots, and I'll just be another person to manipulate, annoys me, and I stand up.

"Yes. I'll come. I don't have long, though."

I grab my purse, and we leave the building. She hails a cab and tells the driver, "Macy's."

"Macy's? I thought you wanted lunch?"

"They have a restaurant," she says, patronizing me.

"I'm aware," I answer coolly. But it's impossible to get in this time of year.

The short ride is awkward and quiet, and I don't give her the satisfaction of asking questions. When we arrive, she greets the maître d' with a kiss on the cheek.

"Martin," she says, as warmly as I've ever heard her. "Thank you for working us in."

"Always, ma cherie," he answers in a heavy accent. "You know I adore you."

As he leads us to a little table, she tells me, "He's a close family friend. He actually got Logan and I reservations to eat here this month—he put it in the books this time last year. We'd broken up earlier this year, of course, so we didn't use them. But still. It was the thought that counted."

Holy crap. Logan brought me instead.

I knew it was impossible to get reservations so last minute in December. Bile rises in my throat and I swallow.

After the waiter comes, Talia orders a glass of wine. "Are you supposed to have that?" I ask.

"The doctor says one is fine."

I've never heard that, but of course, I've never been pregnant. So I have to let that slide.

"What are we doing here?" I ask her, when the waiter leaves to retrieve our drinks.

"I'd like to speak with you woman to woman," she says simply.

I stare at her, not saying a word.

"Listen, I know you probably have a very unflattering idea of me," she says, pulling her cloth napkin onto her lap. "But I think surely we can agree that in a breakup, there are two sides to the story. You've only heard Logan's."

"Logan is a gentleman," I remind her. "He hasn't said too much about it."

"If I know his sister, I'm sure *she* has," Talia answers. I don't reply. "That's what I thought. Anyway, I'd like for you to hear my side."

I start to stand up. "This lunch is over," I tell her. "I don't need to hear yours."

She places a hand on my arm. "Please wait. Don't you want to know all sides to the story so that you can decide for yourself?"

"Decide what?" I ask, my eyes narrowed.

"Who is right."

"There isn't always someone in the right," I answer, sitting back down. "Sometimes, there are just bad situations."

"Logan and I dated for several years. Did you know that?"

She stares at me, almost defiantly, and I don't respond.

"I met his family, and he met mine."

"So? I dated my ex for two years, and I met his family, and yet we still weren't right for each other *at all*."

"But did your ex propose? With his mother's ring? Was your wedding planned?"

This gives me pause, and I look at her suspiciously. Monica and Logan both told me she's a manipulator.

"You're lying."

She pushes a ring box across the table.

"See for yourself."

It's a vintage box. And inside, I reluctantly find a vintage ring.

"You didn't give this back when you broke up?" I ask.

She lifts a shoulder. "He gave it to me. It's mine. And I knew that we'd end up using it. We're meant to be together."

"You weren't good to him," I tell her. "He ended things for a reason."

She shakes her head. "I got annoyed with him when he worked all the time. I wanted to see him more."

I was the same way with Drake. His job had always come first. But that's not how Logan has been with me, and I tell her so.

"Just wait," she says knowingly. "It'll happen."

The waiter takes our food order, and when he's gone, I look Talia square in the eyes.

"What exactly do you want from me?"

"I want you to break up with Logan. I want you to tell him that he's wrong about me, and that he should give us another chance, for the sake of our child."

She cups her belly again, and I want to throw my water glass at her.

"That's not my place," I tell her.

"It's absolutely your place. You're the only one who can. One thing about Logan is that he is ridiculously loyal. He feels like he owes it to you to stay with you, because you've started a relationship. He's quick to judge when someone makes a bad decision. He just needs a nudge to realize that I deserve a second chance. And that since he was with me so long, I'm the one who deserves his loyalty."

"You sound deranged," I tell her, but honestly, she makes a little bit of sense. She was with him a long time, and I've only been with him for weeks.

The idea of stepping into this on her behalf makes me feel physically ill, though.

"I can see you care about him," she says, studying my face. "Of course you do. He's such a good guy. But I don't think he'll fulfill you in the long run. You need something more. You need someone who aspires to be more."

"That's the furthest thing from my mind," I tell her. "I love him just the way he is."

"You left this place to do big things," she says, and my eyes widen. "Yes, I did some research," she adds. "I know you left. I know that you're working on your career."

"That's not creepy at all," I mutter.

"It's not a secret," she says in defense. "You literally have a fashion blog. Good call on your latest red lipstick pick. I, too, prefer cranberry to cherry."

"Don't," I warn her. "Don't try to make me think we're alike. We're not."

"No, we're not. I've realized that my life is here with Logan. I'm okay with that, I'm great with that, actually. My fatal flaw is that it took me too long to realize it. I just need a second chance. Our family needs this second chance."

Her eyes are pleading, and I almost can't look away.

I stand up. "Just think about it," she pleads.

I pull out a couple twenties, drop them at my place setting, and walk away.

CHAPTER TWENTY

$\mathcal{I}$ stick to myself the rest of the afternoon.

I curl up with Winter in my apartment, watch chick flicks, and try not to think about anything that Talia had said.

But it's always there, in the back of my mind.

I want to discuss it with Ellie or Sylvie, but I know what they'll say. They'll say to stay with Logan because he makes me happy.

They'll want the right thing for *me*, but what if being with Talia is the right thing in the long run for *Logan*? What if she really has changed? What if their baby really does need both parents?

"I hate this feeling," I tell Winter. "You need to give me some advice."

He licks his paw.

I text Cassie instead.

Do you have a minute to talk?

She answers five minutes later. It's December 23rd. The January issue isn't ready. Dragon Lady's hair is on fire. Is it important?

I'll just text it, I tell her. You can reply when you can.

So I tell her all about it in a novel-length text. All of it. Every single thing I can think of.

I've barely finished and sent it when my phone is ringing.

"What are you thinking?" she hisses. I can hear horns and traffic in the background, so she's walked out into the cold to call me. "Are. You. Insane?"

"She seemed so sincere," I tell my best friend. "I mean, I know she messed up in the past, and I don't really trust her, but you didn't see her face. I think she's scared. I mean, I would be. She's pregnant and alone."

"Because of her own actions," Cassie reminds me. "She was horrible to Logan. His sister told you all about it. You need to listen."

"Maybe Monica is just being protective," I suggest, trying to play the devil's advocate. "We all make mistakes."

"Do not be a martyr with this," she says. "You are not going to fall on your sword so that she can get the guy. The guy is yours. You deserve him, and you're perfect for each other."

"You've never met him," I remind her.

"But you've told me all about him, and I love him already."

"Cassie, focus," I tell her. "I need you to be unbiased right now. Look at this with a completely clear lens, and tell me what you think."

She doesn't hesitate. "I think she had her chance, and she blew it. Now it's your turn."

"Even though there's a child involved?"

"You already spoke to him about that, and he's confident that they'll be better coparents if they're not together. Why are you second-guessing him? He should know better than both of us combined."

She has a point.

"Maybe I'll just ask him to think on it again, very hard. I want to give him all the time in the world to make the best choice. I don't want him to resent me later," I tell her. "That would be awful."

"He's not going to resent you," Cassie says, and someone honks almost directly into the phone. "Listen, I almost got run down in the street. I've gotta go. Just do the right thing for yourself, Meg. It's also the best thing for Logan."

She hangs up, and I'm left alone with my nagging doubt.

Logan is set to come over shortly, so I pack my little bag for the show. I'm taking the Christmas dress to wear, since it was my inspiration. With any luck, I'll be accepting an award in it. I also take makeup to freshen up after the flight to New York City. I do everything I can to distract myself from thinking about the situation at hand.

I've literally lost everyone else in my life.

I don't know what I'll do if I lose Logan.

Stop thinking about it, I tell myself. I cuddle Winter, I plump the cushions on the couch, I take a shower.

I'm applying perfume when Logan knocks on the door.

I swallow hard, square my shoulders, then answer it.

"Do you want to come see the Red Alibi?" he asks me in greeting, his face aglow from excitement. "It looks *so good*. You're going to be so happy."

He grabs my hand, and I see the exact moment he realizes something is wrong.

His entire face tenses.

"What is it?"

"I had a visitor today," I tell him as I sit on the couch. He sits next to me, his shoulders tense. "I'd like to talk to you about it."

I tell him all about the lunch, and every word that Talia said, and how she'd looked sincere, and maybe even a little sad.

The entire time, he gives me the respect of listening without interrupting, even when his mouth tightens and horror fills his eyes.

When I'm finished, he's silent for a moment.

"I thought we'd already been through this," he says limply. His hands are clasped between his strong knees, and he looks helpless. So much so that I feel incredibly guilty.

"Yes," I answer. "But what if you were wrong? What if she's telling me the truth?"

"She never is," Logan tells me firmly. "Listen, she's a master at lying. I don't blame you for doubting everything after speaking with her, but do you trust me?"

"Of course." My answer is immediate.

"Do you know me to be someone who is fair and gives other people the benefit of the doubt?"

"Yes."

"Then why would you question my judgment on something so important?" he asks. "Please believe me. I want what is best for this child. I will do everything in my power to give it a good life. But not with Talia."

I sigh, and the pit in my stomach tightens.

"I hope that's the case," I tell him. "But truthfully, I won't feel right unless you take some time to really truly consider this. Put your feelings aside and look at it with an unbiased lens. Can you do that for me?"

"I don't need to," he protests, but I interrupt him.

"Logan, please. Do this for me," I urge. "If you make a rash decision now, and regret it later, I never want you to resent me. That would kill me."

"I don't make rash decisions."

"So you carefully considered the idea of using your and Talia's Christmas reservation at the Walnut Room on me?"

Logan freezes. "It doesn't sound great when you say it like that. But the reservations were already there. She and I had been broken up for months. I wanted to go with you."

My heart clenches uncomfortably.

"That was a beautiful night," I tell him. "I just hated hearing from Talia that it was intended for her."

"It was never intended for her," he tells me vehemently. "She would never have had as much fun ice skating as you and I did. She isn't a good sport. She hates everything I love. *We are not suitable for each other.*"

"She says she's changed. That she knows now what she gave up, and that it was a mistake."

Logan stares at me, and his blue eyes glitter harshly.

"Meg, please."

"Just think about it," I tell him. "I'm going to New York tomorrow, and then I'll be back, and we can discuss it. After you think about it carefully. Weigh all the options. Be fair to yourself, Logan. Think it through."

I stand up, and it's clear that I want him to leave.

"I hate that you don't think I know my own heart," he says, as he pauses at the door. "I know my heart. It lies *with you.*"

That's all it takes to make my eyes well up, and I practically shove him out the door. I lean against it after I close it, and the dam breaks. I cry and cry, and I slide to the floor. Winter comes over and rubs against me, almost like he knows how sad I am.

I glance at the picture of my mom and dad on the fireplace. "You guys, tell me what to do," I plead. "I want to be a good person. I want to make the right choice. But I love him."

I love him.

With all my heart.

After I cry until I'm weak and spent, I sit up and take a deep breath. I'm restless. I need air. I need to get out of here.

I give Winter a treat and grab my coat.

I SOON FIND myself on the Chicago streets, lost in the Christmas shopping crowds.

The cold air freezes my cheeks and ears, but I don't notice.

I don't notice the people jostling my arms and bumping into me. I don't notice their cheer, or their impatience.

They just want to find gifts for their loved ones.

It's that time of year.

I buy a hot chocolate and sit on a park bench, ignoring the way it freezes my legs. It's like I can't feel anything.

I think about how far I've come since coming here, how I've grown from being self-absorbed and impatient into someone wanting the best for all the people in my building, and in fact, I'm willing to sacrifice my own relationship for the good of other people.

"That's growth if I ever saw it," I mutter.

But growth won't keep you warm at night, my inner voice says. *You're self-sabotaging. You deserve this. Stop fighting it.*

I shake my head to clear my thoughts. I stand up and glance both ways down the street. Big box stores adorn the street, but those don't call to me.

A tiny antique shop does.

Its faded sign hangs jauntily. OLD DAYS ANTIQUES.

A warm yellow lamp shines in the winter, almost like a beacon.

I start walking.

When I open the door, a bell jangles, and an elderly man comes out from the back. Old music drifts softly from the back room. I envision an old wooden radio.

"Hello, there," he says kindly. "How can I help you?"

"I'm just browsing," I tell him.

He nods. "Feel free! Just let me know if you need anything. My name is Walt."

"I will."

He gives me space, which I appreciate, and I browse through the relics on the shelves. This shop has everything from beautiful vintage jewelry, to furniture, to old books and knick-knacks.

I run my hands over faded satin ribbons, pick up old antique dolls, and look into blemished mirrors.

Walt sits at a desk, whittling something, and I look up. "I'm renovating an old building," I tell him. "I'd love to include authentic things from the 1920s."

His face lights up. "I have a couple light fixtures from that era," he tells me. "Is that what you're thinking?"

"I don't know yet," I tell him. "But I'd love to see them."

I'd love anything that distracts me from the pain in my heart.

He shows them to me, and I do love them. They're twin fixtures, beautifully twined vines, a semiflush mount, and crystal droplets hanging from the leaves.

"These are exquisite," I tell him. "I'll take them both."

"I love that they're going to an era-appropriate home," he

tells me happily. "That warms this old man's heart. I'll wrap them up for you."

"Thank you. I'm just gonna . . . keep looking."

He pauses. "Pardon me if this is out of line, but you seem pretty sad, young lady."

His face is kind and something about him just makes me feel like I can open up.

"I guess I am," I admit.

"Troubles of the heart?" he guesses.

"Is there any other kind?"

He chuckles. "None worth having, I guess. Come over. I'll pour you a brandy, and then you can tell me all about it."

He gestures toward a green velvet chair in the window, next to the lamp. "Take a seat, I'll be right back."

I get comfortable, and soon he joins me.

"I like sitting here," he tells me, handing me a crystal lowball glass. "I get a good view of the people."

He gestures toward the hustle and bustle of the sidewalk, and it is a stark difference from the calmness in this store.

"All those people are lucky," I remark, watching a mother pull along her two little children. She's tired and cranky, but surely she's happy. Her children are beautiful. I wonder if they have both parents. Probably so.

I flinch.

"We don't know their stories," Walt says. "You never know what is happening behind the masks people wear."

"That's true," I agree. "Maybe it's like social media, where everyone only posts their highlights. They never talk about their heartache."

"Heartache is hard to hear about," he says thoughtfully. "But I'm willing to listen."

I smile. "You're very kind, Walt."

He shrugs. "I've just had enough of my own to recognize it in others," he says.

"It seems that everyone has," I say softly. "Literally everyone I know has a sad story to tell."

"Everyone has had heartache," he points out. "It's what we do with it that counts. Life isn't all peaks. Sometimes, it's valleys."

"Very true," I agree. "You're very insightful."

"Again, it's just the product of decades of living." His faded eyes twinkle, and I can see that he used to be dashing. He's got that air about him, that energy. He was handsome, and he knew it. And now, he's aging, and wise.

"So what's your trouble?" he asks gently, lifting his glass to his lips.

I sigh. "I don't really think I want to talk about it, honestly. It doesn't seem to help."

"I've been there," he says. "The best thing to do is listen to your gut. It won't fail you."

"Maybe my gut is confused, though," I answer.

He smiles gently. "That's the hard part. You have to sort out what it's trying to tell you. The main thing is, don't ignore it.

That led to the biggest mistake of my life. And that's the way it is for everyone. If you ignore your instincts, you'll regret it. Every time."

I think on that. From the very first time I'd met Talia, she'd made my hackles rise. Was that my gut telling me something? Or was that just me, being on guard around Logan's ex?

"Listen, here's the best advice I can give you," Walt says, leaning forward. "Real love is hard to come by. The kind that consumes you and makes you feel all the emotions on the spectrum. When you find it, hold on to it."

"And listen to my gut," I add.

He smiles. "Yes. Always listen to your gut. I didn't, and I've paid for it."

"Do you want to talk about it?" I ask.

He shakes his head. "No. I know what I did wrong."

I nod, completely understanding. "Well, if you ever change your mind, I'm here."

"You haven't told me your name, young lady."

"It's Meg," I tell him. "And I'm going to make a habit of coming in here and seeing what 'new' old items you get in every week."

He beams now. "I'd like that, Meg." He touches my shoulder, then takes my empty glass from me as he hands me a pocket watch I had been looking at. "And please keep the watch. It's my gift to you. Merry Christmas."

Walt goes in the back and gets the large bag that holds

the two light fixtures, and as I walk home with them, I think about how nice it is to meet a kind stranger, someone who simply wants to sit and talk. Someone who would give a gift to a stranger, just to make their day better.

It's the kind of person I want to be.

In fact, he inspires me.

I'm keyed up with nervous energy anyway, so I decide to use it in a constructive way.

I STAY UP late making Ellie a dress. It's the least I can do since she gave hers to me.

It's on my list of things to do, anyway . . . to make sure that I have pieces in my line that will change to fit a woman's needs as she ages. Something modest, elegant, and still absolutely beautiful.

I have enough cranberry material left for a second dress, so I carefully cut and sew a dress for my dear friend. I have to guess on the size, but it's a special skill I have. I can literally look at anyone on the street and accurately guess. I'm right nine times out of ten.

It's two in the morning when it's finally finished, and I hold it up in the light.

Ellie will look stunning in it.

I dig through my closet and find a garment box, and carefully fold it, and then tie a bow around it.

I write a quick note: *Ellie, for all the ways you've inspired me, thank you. Love, Meg*

I tiptoe down to Ellie's door and set it down, adjusting the bow so it lies just right. By the time I return to my apartment, wash my face, and fall into bed, it's two thirty. Morning will come quickly, but lucky for me, I'm exhausted enough to overcome my nerves and finally fall asleep.

CHAPTER TWENTY-ONE

L ord, morning *does* come quickly.

When my alarm goes off at five A.M., I wake up feeling like a red-eyed zombie. When I swing my legs out of bed, the first thing I think of is how much my heart hurts because I'd turned Logan away.

And the second thing I think of is how scared I am about the contest.

Everyone's fate in this building rests upon me now, and that is a scary, scary thing.

I've never done anything of this magnitude before, and I don't know why I thought I could do it now. But I square my shoulders and decide to push forward.

"Just go through the motions," I instruct myself. "Fake it till you make it."

I shower, brush my teeth, do my hair and makeup, and feed

Winter his breakfast. I dress in fancy city clothes, and then I grab my kitten, my purse, and my bag and head downstairs.

"Sylvie is keeping you today," I tell Winter. "Please be good. Don't get into her tinsel again. It's not good for you."

Winter's eyes are barely slits, as though even he is outraged by this inhumane hour.

"I know," I tell him. "But I've got a long day today, and it starts early. So suck it up. Sylvie is meeting us downstairs."

I feel badly about that, asking Sylvie to get up at this god-awful hour.

But as I round the last flight of stairs, I see the most incredible thing.

Sylvie, Tom, Ellie, Joe, Melody, and dozens of other residents line the main hall. Many of them are holding signs that say GOOD LUCK or YOU CAN DO IT!

My throat tightens, and I stop in my tracks.

The looks on their faces are priceless. They believe in me. They're behind me. My family isn't here, but these wonderful people are.

The only one missing is Logan, but I try to put that out of my mind. I'd asked him for space while he seriously considers the situation. He's simply doing what I asked. I should be appreciative, not sad.

"You guys are all wonderful," I announce, handing Winter to Sylvie and wrapping an arm around Ellie. "Truly. You make me feel so loved."

"I think it's safe to say that you *are*," Ed tells me. He's holding

Tootsie in one arm, and she's wearing a white faux fur coat. "You are loved. We know you can do this."

"You're so talented," Sylvie says. "You're going to crush this." Her sweatshirt today has a snowman on it and says JUST CHILL.

"Bring it on home," Ellie tells me. "We believe in you."

"Thank you," I whisper, unable to form any other words. This display of support is overwhelming, and I already feel emotionally fragile. "You guys . . ."

"We know, dear," Ellie says. "Now, go. Win that contest."

I nod, blinking back my tears, and I yank up the handle of my carry-on.

"Wait." I pause, turning back to Ellie. "Did you find the box?"

She nods. "I haven't opened it yet. But I'm sure I'm going to love whatever is inside."

"Good. I really hope you do." I lift my chin and march out to the curb to hail a cab to the airport. I don't look back, or I know I'll full on sob.

While I'm waiting in O'Hare, I text Cassie.

> On my way to you. Are you coming?

She doesn't answer until I'm boarding my plane.

> Lillianna assigned the show to me. I'm interviewing the winner! We having dinner after?

When I get to my seat, I reply.

Can't! I have to get back to the Christmas party at the Parkview. The historical society is coming to evaluate our building.

On Christmas Eve???

Says the woman also working on Christmas Eve, I answer.

Good point, she replies. Ok. I'll see you at the show. Please win—It'd set Dragon Lady's hair on fire. Have a safe flight!

I intend to, I answer, before slipping my phone into my purse and buckling my seat belt.

The plane takes off uneventfully, and I think back to Logan telling me about his dad's plane crash. Of all the times to think about it, I choose now. While I'm on a plane. Because of course I do.

He must've been so scared. Or maybe it happened too fast.

Either way, I understand why Logan doesn't like flying now. He must think about it every single time he's on a plane. It freshens those old sad memories.

And here I am, thinking about Logan again, after I promised myself I wouldn't today.

"Today is about this show," I reprimand myself quietly.

"Excuse me?" The flight attendant in the aisle looks at me. "Can I get you something?"

"Um. Just a strong coffee, if you have it."

She brings me a cup of strong brown water that is supposed to be coffee, but isn't. I drink it anyway.

The lady next to me sleeps the entire way, and the flight is short. We touch down at LaGuardia an hour and a half later.

I grab my bag and bolt from the plane.

The air smells different here, like rushing and impatience, like hot dogs and happiness, like high fashion and smog. I love it.

Yet at the same time, it doesn't feel like home anymore.

It's an odd feeling, something I contemplate as I hail another cab. I fight the urge to spray my perfume in the back of this one, because I don't fancy arriving at the show smelling like a hamster cage.

By some miracle, the drive to Tribeca only takes half an hour.

I tip the driver and stand in front of Spring Studios.

I'd wanted to come to Fashion Week here this year, but of course, I'd had to quit Stitch, and it wouldn't have been likely anyway. Only senior employees score tickets to that. It's an elite affair, and I was low on the totem pole.

So standing here now, even if it's for a different event, feels significant and huge.

And I feel small.

Why did I think I could do this?

I fight the urge to spin around and run away.

It's only the memory of the faces that had lined the hallway this morning, so filled with confidence in me, that gives me pause.

They think I can do it.

I *can* do it.

My designs should speak for themselves.

They're good.

I take a deep breath in, then out.

"Breathe in confidence, breathe out fear," I tell myself. I do it a few times before I gather the courage to enter the building, pulling my bag behind me.

A WOMAN AT a table greets me, gives me my credentials to wear around my neck, and thrusts a map of which station is mine backstage.

It feels surreal as I poke around, watching the models dress, all tall and lanky and sophisticated.

When I find mine, 6E, two of those beautiful women wait for me in robes. They lounge in folding chairs, and somehow make it look comfortable.

"Hello," I greet them. "I'm Meg Julliard. Are you here for me?"

They nod. "We're just waiting for you to clothe us," one tells me. Her voice is cool. I'd forgotten that about this whole scene. Everyone is too cool for school. And even if they aren't, they pretend to be.

I unzip my bag and kneel over it, rifling through.

I hand the girl nearest me the cranberry dress, and the other the black.

"I have one change of clothes for each of you," I tell them, handing one a gold dress, and one a black with silver threads laced through it. "As you can see, they're soft and easy to get on and off. So it won't take long to change."

They purposely seem bored and sit back down, holding the dresses.

"You have to go to a team leader meeting of some sort," one of them tells me. "Someone came around talking about it a minute ago."

I nod and set off to find someone in charge.

Hunt for someone with a clipboard.

I do one better and find someone with a clipboard and an earpiece.

"Yes?" she snaps at me, as I approach.

"I'm showing my line today, and I need to know where to go for the team leader meeting."

"You're late," she snaps.

"I'm not," I protest. "I'm right on time."

She ignores me, looks at my credentials, and consults her list. "Room 1B."

She stalks away before I can ask for directions.

As I look, I pull out my phone, hoping to find a good-luck text from Logan.

There isn't one.

There are several from Cassie, though.

> I'm working on something for you today.

> Keep your chin up, everything is going to be ok.

Those are intriguing enough, but then . . . she texts one last one.

> OMG, Lillianna is coming, too! I just found out.

I read this one just as I find the door to room 1B and open it.

Lillianna Cox's face is the first one I see inside.

She makes eye contact with me immediately, and her red lipstick curves into a not-so-friendly smile.

Actually, it's anything *but* friendly.

The woman speaking pauses to allow me to come in, and I quickly find a seat at the back.

"As I was saying, we are fortunate enough to have Lillianna Cox herself here today from Stitch. I don't need to tell you how influential Stitch is for rising fashion lines, and even well-established ones. Even if your design doesn't win today, having this exposure could exponentially further your careers. Ms. Cox, would you like to say a few words?"

Dragon Lady dips her head, receiving the compliments, and stands up. Somehow, she'd managed to hide her devil horns in her hairdo and stuff her tail in her pants.

Stop, I tell myself. *You've got to play nice.*

But she won't. That much is certain as Lillianna maintains eye contact with me during most of her speech.

"Normally, I would send a junior exec to this," Lillianna says. "But I do so love to keep my finger on the pulse of rising trends, and when I found myself free today, particularly after

I found out an old . . . colleague . . . is competing, I just knew I had to make a personal appearance. Don't worry, contestants. I won't favor her. My assessments of your designs will be fair and impartial in our next issue."

Her icy glare assures me that they will be anything *but*, at least for me.

Even after she sits down, and the coordinator takes back over, explaining the schedule and what would happen, Lillianna maintains her cool stare toward me.

Message received.

Loud and clear.

"She's not a judge," I whisper to myself.

The guy next to me overhears. "She might as well be," he answers quietly. "She owns this industry."

Like I didn't know that.

I'm sunk.

I'm literally sunk before I even get started.

My chest feels suffocated with dread as I make my way out and try to get away before Lillianna can get to me.

I'm not successful.

She grabs my arm in the hallway.

"I was surprised to see your name on this list," she tells me. "Especially after I warned you what I would do to you."

Her fingernails feel like talons on my arm.

Her sleek black bob shines as she enunciates her words carefully.

Once upon a time, I'd be terrified right now. I'd be shaking in my stiletto boots.

But honestly, right now, I've so much more to worry about than this woman with an inflated ego complex.

I sigh.

"Lillianna, I'm sorry that I texted you that night. I was drunk, which is no excuse. But what I said wasn't a lie. People do call you the Dragon Lady. Look at the way you treat people! You work them to the bone, all day every day, and on every holiday. You prefer when they are afraid of you. You intimidate instead of inspire. It's sad, and I'm done with it. I've worked hard on my line. I've worked hard to be where I am. Do your worst."

I yank my arm away and stomp off.

I feel her staring at me as I do.

I doubt anyone has walked away from her in a very, very long time.

"That was either the stupidest thing I've ever seen, or the bravest," one of my models whispers to me, awestruck.

"Sometimes, you've just got to stand up for something," I tell her limply. "It was time."

"It's going to blow up in her face," the other model whispers.

"I heard that," I answer. I pull out my phone and text Cassie.

She's here. She's angry. I confronted her. My life is over.

Cassie doesn't answer.

Are you listening? She basically threatened me. My career is over!!

Cassie still doesn't answer.

Dang it.

I'm on my own.

"Places!" the woman with the clipboard calls. "It's showtime in five minutes."

I take off my clothes and pull on the Christmas dress, then realize that I've forgotten my shoes. I'll have to keep these black stiletto boots on, but oddly, they look pretty good with the dress.

"These dresses are classy," one of my models tells me. "It's nice to not have to wear nipple paint."

I stare at her. "Um. Yeah. That was the point, I guess. No nipple paint."

"You both look amazing," I tell them. "If we don't win, it won't be because of you."

"I know," the one nearest me says, as she messes with a tendril of her long hair.

"It's time to line up," I tell them. "Break a leg."

"Don't say that," the other answers. "This is how we make our money."

Clipboard Lady calls out a second time, and I rush away to find the presenter's line.

From behind the curtains, I wait with the other nervous presenters as they peddle out their designs one by one. There are things with feathers, things with sequins, things with G-strings and body paint. There's nothing else like mine.

I get a slight buoying sense of hope.

However, when the current presenter ducks back through the curtains, her face drenched in nervous sweat, I get a glimpse of Lillianna in the front row and the hope dissipates.

It feels like she can even see me with the curtains separating us.

It gives me cold chills.

Unfortunately, I don't have time to really gather myself, because it's my turn and I'm practically shoved through the curtains onto the stage.

HUNDREDS OF FACES stare at me in a sea of chairs. I gulp and stumble to my place.

"I'm Meg Julliard, and this is the Timeless line." Model number one struts through the doors and down the catwalk. "Mindy is wearing a monochromatic jersey dress that was inspired by glamorous eras of the past. Designed to wear for years to come, it can be dressed up or down and is suitable for any number of occasions. This dress is designed to be classy, durable, elegant, and, yes, timeless."

Mindy saunters into the back, and Kylie takes her place.

"Kylie is wearing a jersey boatneck, an elegant throwback to times past, when women dressed for every occasion, and every detail counted. The stitching is gold, the lines are sleek, and like every piece in my collection, it embodies class and elegance, while making the wearer feel timelessly sexy."

I take a breath and realize that my hands have stopped shaking. I glance at the front row and find that the people sitting there are paying close attention, and even Lillianna seems interested now.

I exhale. *Breathe out fear.*

When Mindy reappears, I relax and am able to more casually comment on her dress, and by the time Kylie returns, I am completely comfortable.

When they're finished, Mindy returns to join Kylie, and I walk to their sides.

"My line is inspired by two different things. One was my sister. She battled cancer many years ago, and her body changed rapidly due to her treatments. It inspired me to create fashion that can change with the woman wearing it.

"My other inspiration is the dress I'm wearing. It's a vintage piece, elegantly stitched and durably made back in a time when women invested in quality pieces. This dress is the cornerstone for my entire line. I intend to bring back simplicity, elegance, quality, and class in ways that make every woman wearing my dresses feel sexy and confident. As you can see by my choice of footwear"—I hold out a boot—"you can dress it up, dress it down, or modernize it. It's fluid and lends itself to many situations.

"If I win this contest, I will be using the prize money to

fund the start-up of my fashion line, and the offices will be located in a historic building in Chicago. If I don't win, I'll still be founding my fashion line in a historic building in Chicago. I'm that determined. I'll find a way because I really feel like the fashion world, and every woman, needs timeless pieces in her wardrobe to make her feel special. I also intend on donating a chunk of my yearly profits to cancer research. Although don't factor that into your decision. If I win, I want it to be solely on the merit of my work. Thank you all for being here today."

I grab Mindy's and Kylie's hands, and we bow before we return backstage.

I feel like collapsing as we burst back through the curtains, and several people shake my hand.

"Great job," one lady says. "Beautiful pieces."

"Thank you," I tell her, absolutely relieved that it's over.

I wait in our stall while the other competitors finish, and during the judges' deliberations, until Clipboard Lady calls for everyone to line up for the awards.

I'm so scared that I can't feel my fingers or toes.

We file out and wait while the spokesperson from *Vogue* says nice things about us all, about the fashion world, about the contest organizers. Blah, blah, blah. I try to focus on something other than the sound of my pounding heart.

"Now, let's get to the moment we're all waiting for," she says with a smile. "We have seen some amazing designs today. Groundbreaking, envelope-pushing, beautiful, and classic—you really ran the gamut today. Second runner up goes to Carter Evans's City Light line."

The crowd applauds and my knees get weaker. I'm either one step closer or one step further away, depending on how you look at it. Carter either took my spot, or I'm one place higher than he is.

"First runner up goes to Macy Lowe's Naughty Angel line. We feel your cutting-edge shapewear will innovate women's choices for shaping their bodies. Congratulations, Macy!"

Macy takes her envelope, and the crowd applauds.

I see movement in the back of the room, a person ducking and weaving through the crowded seats, and then I see my best friend's face.

Cassie.

She made it.

I could literally sigh in relief. Even if I lose, it will be nice to have someone here for moral support.

"And now, it's time for our grand prize winner. We live in a time where so many try to push the boundaries, to make things edgy for sensational reasons, to be outrageous just to be outrageous or to spur a reaction. While those fashions do have a purpose, today, we are pleased to celebrate a different kind of fashion."

Oh my gosh.

Oh my gosh.

Could it be?

She turns to me.

"Ms. Julliard, your Timeless line embodies what true fashion should be . . . enduring pieces that outlast trends, stand the test of time, and embolden any woman who wears them. With that said, our grand prize goes to Ms. Meghan Julliard. We look forward to seeing how your new line transforms the market. Congratulations!"

With limp fingers, I take the envelope.

I stand and allow the crowd to cheer for me as they rise to their feet.

Cassie claps furiously, still trying to make her way to the front.

Even Lillianna is clapping. Grudgingly, but still.

This moment is surreal. I can't believe it.

I won.

I can afford to fix the Parkview. I don't have to give up on my dreams. My fashion line will become something . . . and based on this reaction today, it will become a success.

I smile at the crowd and wave.

I'm still stunned as I walk backstage afterward, and as I sit limply in a chair, holding the envelope. I'm afraid to look inside, but with shaking fingers, I open it.

The check has more zeroes than I've ever seen.

Three hundred thousand dollars.

Made payable to me.

I'M STILL STARING at the check when Cassie bursts into our stall.

"Meg," she says, out of breath. "Congratulations!"

I look at her in confusion. "Were you running?"

"Yes. Congratulations on winning. You were amazing, but we need to go."

"Why?"

I'm not following, but her cheeks are flushed and she's clearly excited.

"You know the romantic airport scene in every chick flick ever filmed?"

Okay, now I'm more confused than ever.

She grabs my arm. "Get your stuff. You have a happily ever after to get to."

"What are you talking about?" I'm impatient now because she's not making sense.

She grabs my bag and starts shoving things into it.

"I'll explain on the way, Meg."

She pushes me through the throngs of people, and I trip over my own feet. She doesn't stop pushing until we run into Dragon Lady.

We come to a complete stop, and Lillianna turns to us. Her austere eyebrows lift.

"Congratulations, Meghan," she says. "I didn't think you had it in you."

Cassie and I are frozen.

"Regarding what you said earlier," she continues. "I'm hard on my staff because I'm hard on myself. I expect great things from them, because I expect great things from myself. That's not a negative quality."

She glances at me.

"Please let Stitch know when your line releases to the public. We'll want an exclusive. Also, don't forget this when you're the head of your own fashion house. I always call in my favors."

Words cannot express my shock, and I have to consciously not drop my mouth open. Lillianna turns her attention to Cassie.

"Have her interview on my desk by eight A.M. tomorrow morning."

She turns and walks away.

Cassie and I stare at each other before she grabs my arm and rushes me through the rest of the building until we get to the street.

She practically throws me into an SUV waiting at the curb.

As the vehicle pulls away into the street, I turn to my best friend.

"Tell me. Right now. What in the world is happening?"

Cassie takes a deep breath and looks into my eyes.

"After you told me everything about Talia, it wasn't sitting right. I did some next-level spy stuff and figured out that this is her pattern! She dates guys, fakes a pregnancy, and then gets taken care of like a sugar baby until they figure it out."

I stare at her, afraid to hope.

"She's just out for herself," Cassie continues. "Logan was just collateral damage."

My heart begins to flutter.

"Why are we hurrying to the airport?"

"Because obviously I shared this with Logan, and he tried to get a flight to your show, but couldn't get one in time. Drake booked him on a puddle jumper, and he should be arriving at the private airstrip in . . ." She looks at her watch. "Twenty minutes." She glances up at the driver. "Can you hurry?"

The car picks up the pace and I can't believe what I'm hearing.

"He hates those little planes," I tell her slowly. "His father died on one."

Her eyes widen. "I didn't know that. He must love you a *lot*, Meg."

The gravity of today hits me . . . winning the contest, hearing this news . . . and I begin to cry and laugh at the same time like a madwoman. Cassie, because she can't be near someone crying without crying herself, starts crying, and I actually feel sorry for the driver in the front seat.

"Everything's going to be okay, Meg," she tells me through her tears, hugging me.

And for the first time in a very, very long time, I know she's right.

"You're happy with Drake?" I ask through my tears. "Because you seem so, so happy. I know he and I were a mess, but you and he just seem to vibe."

Cassie nods. "He's the yin to my yang," she says, and her mascara is smeared. "Thank you for not making it weird."

"I'm just happy you're happy," I tell her honestly. "I love you."

"I love you, too."

CHAPTER TWENTY-TWO

$\mathscr{T}$he SUV's tires crunch to a stop near the tarmac of the private airstrip, and we watch a tiny Cessna roll to a stop. I clamber out of the back seat and scramble out of the vehicle. Before Cassie is even out, I'm already running toward the plane.

The steps drop down from the little plane, and soon, battered work boots emerge.

By the time he reaches the bottom, I'm propelling myself into Logan's arms like I've been launched by a cannon.

We collide and I start talking, a slew of words and phrases that I'll never be able to remember later.

"I love you. I shouldn't have hesitated. It didn't matter if she was pregnant or not. I'm behind you all the way. I trust you. I love you. I trust you."

At least, that's what I think I say, but honestly, with the tears that are flowing down my face, my words are garbled, and Logan looks a little confused.

But also happy.

His grin is a mile wide, so whatever I'm saying, he's hearing it.

His arms hold me tight, and from my periphery, I see Cassie clasping her hands to her chest and bouncing up and down. Her tears are flowing, too.

"I love you," his lips murmur next to my ear. "Please don't ever leave me again."

I shake my head. "I won't."

"I wanted to be here for your show, but there weren't any flights."

"I can't believe you got on this plane," I tell him, eyeing the tiny machine. "Are you okay?"

He nods. "I would literally cross oceans for you. Don't you know that by now?"

I start crying all over again. This time, Cassie comes over and hugs me, and Logan has two crying women on his hands. He pats both of our backs awkwardly, while the flight attendant looks on from the top of the steps, watching Logan with sympathy.

"We won!" I finally am able to tell Logan. "We won first place!"

"You won," he says. "Your talent. Your designs. You're amazing, Meg. And by the way, you look so, so beautiful!"

I feel sweaty from running and hurrying, but I'm wearing the Christmas dress. Logan pushes a stray tendril of hair from my cheek.

"You're so beautiful," he repeats, and then he dips his head and kisses me.

Cassie squeals and then looks at her watch.

"Hey, if you want to get back in time to meet with the historical society, you guys need to get back on that plane."

I freeze and look at Logan.

"We don't have to," I tell him. "I have a commercial flight booked. I'm sure there's an extra seat to buy you."

"There isn't," Cassie says. "I already checked. It's Christmas Eve, Meg. Tons of people are trying to get home for the holidays. Logan, if you want to get back with Meg, you'll have to fly on this plane. I'm sorry."

She's apologetic, but I hug her again. "Cassie, you got Logan to me. Don't ever apologize for anything again."

Logan looks down at me. "I'm ready. Let's go."

"Are you sure?" I ask him solemnly. He grins.

"I wouldn't miss this for anything."

We climb up the steps, and Cassie follows us with my bag. We all three buckle ourselves in, and I hold Logan's hand tightly.

"You're coming, too?" I ask my best friend.

"Obviously. Now that you've tamed the wild Dragon Lady, maybe she'll show some mercy."

"Don't count on it," I warn her. She laughs.

"Drake will be coming, as well."

"It was really nice of him to charter this flight," I tell her. She smiles.

"I told you he was a nice guy. Deep down."

"Well, you're perfect for each other," I answer, and I lean my head on Logan's strong arm. She's as perfect for Drake as I am for Logan. I'm glad that I've allowed myself to see it now.

As the plane rolls down the runway, Logan's fingers only slightly press into mine, the only sign that he's bothered. Once we're in the air, he relaxes, and I talk to distract him.

"Have you talked to Talia?"

"I called her," he says. "She denied it, of course, so I called her mother right after we hung up. She had no idea about any of this, and also, she told me that Talia was out partying last weekend with her sisters."

"So she was lying," I murmur. "Her belly, though . . ."

"There are tons of ways to look pregnant," Cassie points out. "Pillows, those pregnancy simulators that they have . . . tons of things."

"That's a lot of work to go to just to sell this thing," I mutter.

"Have you heard about sugar babies?" Cassie asked me. "They set out to get taken care of, and usually choose an older, well-established man to do it."

"That doesn't apply here," I tell her. "Logan is her age."

"She's altered the playbook to suit her needs," Cassie says, waving her hand. "Either way, she's not your problem anymore."

"Cassie's right," Logan tells me. "I told her mother everything, and however they choose to handle it is their business. She's not a part of our lives now."

Lord, that feels good.

"Sylvie has the building all ready to go for the party," Logan tells me. "She's really done a good job. The decorations look incredible. She feels so important now that you let her infuse the budget with some of her own money. Thank you for that."

"She does like to belong," I agree. "But she did us a huge favor. Without her investment, we couldn't have afforded to throw a fancy party—and with the historical society coming tonight, I really wanted it to look its best."

"How many are coming?" Cassie asks. "Do you need my help entertaining them?"

"No karaoke," I tell her with a grin, remembering the last time Cassie had helped entertain clients with me at Stitch. She flutters her eyes.

"No promises."

Logan laughs. "Ellie didn't say. She's been speaking with an assistant, but she doesn't know who will show up. We'll just need to be ready for whatever happens."

"Well, Sylvie ordered enough food for an army," I tell them. "So I think we're prepared."

Logan holds my hand tightly for the rest of the flight. He barely flinches when we land, although his palms get a little clammy, the only outward sign of his distress.

"Thank you for coming for me," I tell him softly as the plane taxis to a stop. "No one has ever done a grand gesture like this for me."

"I can't believe that," he answers. "You're so grand-gesturable."

"I don't think that's a word," Cassie says, and he flushes, because he didn't know she could hear. She laughs.

"You've earned my stamp of approval," she declares, as she unbuckles her seat belt and stands up. "You can marry my best friend."

My head snaps back.

"Horse, you'd better go catch up to that cart," I tell her, pointing out the open plane door. She laughs, but shakes her head knowingly.

"Mark my words," she says, as she disappears down the steps.

Logan and I find another SUV waiting for us, courtesy again of Cassie and Drake. Cassie is already settled in, and Logan throws my bag in the back, then helps me into the back seat.

"I feel a little like Cinderella on her way to the ball," I say offhandedly. I pretend to wave at the masses like a princess.

"You do look like a princess in that dress," Cassie tells me. "Or a silver-screen siren. Or maybe a flapper. I can't decide."

"You can wear one of my designs tonight, if you want," I tell her. "I have four of them in the bag."

"You have three," she corrects. "I already stole one for myself."

I laugh, because of course she did.

"Well, you earned it," I tell her.

"I know."

"Your sense of modesty is admirable," Logan tells her, chuckling.

"It's one of my best qualities," she quips back.

"I like you," he tells her.

"People usually do." She sighs dramatically. "Heavy is the head that wears the crown."

I roll my eyes now. "It's getting thick in here."

They laugh, but I love the energy between them. If we can all four get along, it will make life so much better.

"Drake will be here," Cassie tells us. "He'll just be late."

THE SUV SOON pulls up in front of the Parkview, where Sylvie has added festive white-lit trees in the inside of each window—all since this morning.

We walk in, and the lobby looks stunning.

Red poinsettias line the mantel, along with creamy white candles. Live garland is looped along the front counter, and candles flicker there as well.

A sign points to the Crystal Ballroom.

"This is impressive," Logan says. I nod.

"I have no idea how she pulled it off."

"Especially because the last time I saw her this morning, she had lost her list and was looking for it."

I laugh. "Of course she was."

"But clearly she found it," he says as we walk down the hall to the ballroom.

Sylvie stands in the open doors, and when she sees us, her face lights up.

"You're back!" she exclaims. "Ellie told us the news! You won!!!! I knew you would!"

"*We* won," I tell her. "And everything here looks so beautiful, Sylvie. I couldn't have done all this without you."

She beams and waves off the praise.

"This is the party I've always wanted to throw," she tells me. "Thank you for allowing me."

"But I thought you said my father always gave you free rein?" I tease.

She blinks. "I might have exaggerated a little."

"That's what I thought." I grin. "Well, I'm glad you had free rein this year. It's the prettiest Christmas party I've ever seen."

And that is the truth. As we step into the ballroom, I find that all the carved wooden trim has been polished, candles are everywhere, and the chandeliers gleam, casting a soft glow upon all the fancily dressed tenants. A massive Christmas tree almost reaches the ceiling. It rivals the one in the Macy's Walnut Room. Light Christmas music is being played by a small string quartet in the corner.

Sylvie.

I smile, because she had really, *really* outdone herself. I scan the room, hunting for strangers who might be from the historical society, but so far, they don't appear to be here.

A caterer in a white shirt and black tie offers me a crab cake, and I take it, realizing that I haven't eaten all day. It's so good that I chase after the server and grab two more.

"I'm very ladylike," I tell Logan.

He grins.

"It's what I love about you."

He loves me.

That knowledge makes me feel like I'm floating above the floor, my feet barely touching.

My nerves, though, are still on edge. Because even though I now have the money from the contest to invest, the building is going to take a lot of money to fully renovate, and having the historical society's stamp of approval will mean *everything* as we go forward with the Red Alibi.

The band starts playing a waltz, and Logan outstretches a hand.

"Dance with me?"

I nod. "Someone taught me once."

He grins. "I hope that guy was good."

"The best," I answer, taking his hand. He pulls me to his chest, and we dance to the soothing string notes of "I'll Be Home for Christmas."

It feels so ironic, because I am home for Christmas.

This is my home in every way.

I only wish my dad could be alive for this moment, to see me welcomed home again with open arms.

Oddly, as Logan leads me around the dance floor, I feel like maybe my dad can see.

Maybe he *is* here.

This building, with its old and storied history, truly makes a person feel like memories and people linger here, long after they're gone.

I picture my dad standing next to Sylvie right now, and he'd have that one smile on his face, the one he'd worn when I graduated college, the proud one. The one that says, *I knew you could do it.*

It's in this moment that I realize he did know I could do it.

He'd known he could leave me this legacy, and I'd honor it. He'd known that I'd grow comfortable here at home, and in fact, all those years, he was limping this place along so that I'd have a home to come back to.

My eyes well up again, as they have so many times over the last two days, and this time, it is from happiness.

Thank you, Dad, I mouth, just in case he can see me.

I picture him standing with Sylvie, nodding his head in reply.

My heart feels like it's overflowing, and when the song ends, I tell Logan that I need a drink.

We make our way to the side, and he walks away to the bar that Sylvie had set up at the far end of the room. From here, I see Logan chatting with Ed as he waits in line. Ed holds Tootsie, who is dressed in a fancy pearl collar for the occasion.

"Meg," someone says, and I turn.

Walt stands there, in a suit, with his hair nicely combed.

"Walt!" I exclaim. "How nice to see you! Do you know Sylvie? Oh, my word, I should've invited you myself!"

He smiles and pats my arm.

"No, dear. I don't know Sylvie. I'm a trustee for the Chicago Historical Society."

I think on that, and of course. It makes perfect sense. He owns an antique store, after all.

"Oh, my word! I had no idea!" I tell him. "But I've never heard of anything so fitting in my life!"

"Well, I'm an old relic," he jokes. "It only makes sense that it's my job to safeguard other old relics."

"You're not old, you're wise," I protest.

"I like that better." He winks. "I have to tell you, Meg. This Crystal Ballroom looks lovely. It reminds me of what it looked like back in the day. I can see where if you replace the wallpaper, the place would easily shine again."

"I know," I tell him. "This is the easy part, though. I want to refurbish the rest of the building to become a retirement community, with modern amenities, while retaining the historical elements that make the Parkview unique and special."

"I know you can do it," he tells me confidently. "Is it true that you've uncovered the Red Alibi?"

I nod excitedly. "It's so amazing, Walt. It was bricked up, almost completely untouched. It's literally like we can just step inside history. We've knocked that wall out, shored it up, and I can't wait to show you."

"I can't wait to see it," he answers. "It's rare for a place of historical significance like this to be left intact. I've done some digging, and it seems that the owner of the Parkview in the late 1970s was a suspicious person and was afraid the Red Alibi could house the ghosts of mobsters. To be on the safe side, she had it bricked up, hoping to keep the bad spirits inside."

"Oh, my goodness. Really?"

He nods. "It's rumored that many of the mobsters from back in Chicago's organized-crime days frequented this building.

She was afraid that bad things had happened down there and didn't want any victims to haunt her."

I flinch. "Are there stories of murders or ghosts here?"

I'm almost afraid to hear the answer, but Walt shakes his head.

"None that I can find. I think you're safe, Meg." He winks again and starts to say something else, but freezes, his eyes focused on something behind me.

I turn to find Ellie standing in the doors to the ballroom.

She looks stunning.

Tall, elegant, her white hair smoothly coiffed in a chignon at the base of her neck. She looks as stately as a retired ballerina. Every move she makes is just that graceful.

I hear Walt's breath hitch, and I can't blame him. She really looks absolutely stunning. I'd been right about that color on her, and she wears ruby earrings that hang like red droplets almost to her shoulders.

"That's my friend—" I start to say.

"Ellie," Walt says. Startled, I glance at him, and he is transfixed, his eyes almost glassy.

Ellie locates me as she scans the room, and she smiles. Then she notices Walt.

Her mouth falls open, and, as if she's in a daze, she walks straight to us.

Straight to Walt.

WALT REACHES OUT his hands, and Ellie takes them.

I step out of the way in astonishment.

"Frankie," she breathes, staring into his eyes like she's on a desert island and he's the last bit of water.

"This is Walt," I say uncertainly. "He owns an antique store."

But Walt is shaking his head.

"My name is Frances Walter Lutz," he tells me, without breaking Ellie's gaze. "I haven't been able to go by the name Frankie since this beautiful woman walked out of my life. I couldn't bear to hear it spoken from anyone's lips but hers."

A tear slips down Ellie's cheek.

"You thought I was a monster," she says, although she doesn't pull her hands from his.

"No, I didn't. I was just a kid, and I didn't know what to do. My mother was overcome with grief, and she was unreasonable, and I didn't know how to handle the situation. I've missed you every day that you've been gone. I searched for you," he says. "I couldn't find you."

"I wasn't here," she answers. "I was in Indiana. I was hiding, afraid to show my face. I couldn't stand the thought of you thinking so little of me."

"I really didn't," he protests. "I knew you'd never steal from us. I swear it."

Ellie pulls her hands away now and unclasps her little black evening purse. She reaches inside and pulls out the sapphire earring.

Walt's eyes widen.

"It turns out I did have it," she says. "Meg found it recently . . . tangled inside the seam of the dress I was wearing that night."

"*That* dress," Walt says, nodding toward me. "I'd recognize it anywhere."

"Yes, that dress. I didn't know I had the earring."

They stand still, staring into each other's eyes, a thousand thoughts passing between the two of them, about the years they'd lost, and the time they'd wasted.

But in this moment, it feels like they've never been apart.

The love they have is so palpable, I feel as though I could reach out and touch it.

"Dance with me," Walt suggests.

"Yes," she whispers.

Ellie hands me her purse, and they don't look back. They walk straight to the middle of the ballroom floor, likely in the spot where Francesca had humiliated Ellie so long ago.

A lump rises in my throat as I watch them. Walt handles her carefully, as though she is the most fragile of glass, and she stares at him as though he'll disappear.

"This is a fairy tale," I say out loud.

Cassie appears at my elbow.

"I don't know what's happening, but it seems interesting."

I tell her a shortened version of the story, and she gapes at my dress.

"That's incredible," she finally answers. "That dress is that old?"

I nod. "So you can see how I got the inspiration for my Timeless line."

"Absolutely."

When the song is over, Ellie and Walt join Cassie, Logan, and me.

"I'd love to see the Red Alibi," Walt tells me. "I mean, I want to spend every moment with this beautiful lady, but I did come here with a job to do. So I'm going to do my job, then spend every moment of the rest of my days trying to convince her to give me another chance."

From the soft smile on Ellie's face, I'm guessing that's already a done deal.

"Follow me," I tell him. I lead our group down to the basement, where Sylvie had left the lights on in the Red Alibi. She had staged it with whiskey bottles behind the bar, and glasses, napkins, and matchbooks on the tables. Indeed, it looks like we could simply start using it as a bar right this minute.

"Hemingway's signature?" Walt asks.

"Right this way." I lead him to the corner of the bar, and he bends over, examining the carving.

"This is extraordinary," he finally says as he straightens back up. Beside him, Ellie beams.

"I'll be recommending this building for funding," he tells me. "You'll be contacted by someone in the department to coordinate everything."

Ellie claps her hands in delight, and I smile more broadly than I ever have in my life.

"Thank you," I tell him. "So, so much."

Walt looks down at me. "Whoever would've thought, when you walked into my shop the other day, that we'd be standing where we are right now?"

Ellie looks at us in confusion. "You've met?"

"I didn't know who he was," I tell her, and then he explains.

"Fate has such a funny way of working out," she says when he's done.

"A very funny way," I agree, as we get into the elevator to return to the party.

When the door opens back up, Walt and Ellie are lost in each other's eyes, and they return to the ballroom floor, dancing once again.

"They're trying to make up for lost time," Logan says softly. I nod.

"This is the best day," I decide. "Ever."

Logan pulls me to him. "Ever," he agrees.

He kisses me softly, and I close my eyes, soaking in the sound of the quartet, the smell of Logan's shirt, and the feel of his hands on my back.

"I'm so happy," I tell him.

"Good," he replies. "I hope to make you that way every day for the rest of your life."

My eyes pop open.

He laughs. "Don't worry. I'm not proposing to you yet. But I will. And when I do, you'll never forget it."

I laugh, and relax.

"I can't wait," I tell him honestly. I'm surprised by the fact that I really can't wait. Logan feels right. I'm not unpleasable, like I thought I might be, once upon a time. I just needed the right person by my side.

Just like Ellie and Frankie.

I glance at them, and they're still lost in each other, oblivious to anyone else dancing around them.

"When Ellie first told me her story, I was jealous of her, that she'd had such a great love, even if she'd lost it," I tell Logan. "But I've found my great love, too."

He hugs me tightly.

"I want you in my arms," he tells me. "For the rest of the night. Let's go dance."

I nod, and he pulls me out to the darkened floor.

I press my ear to his chest and listen to his heart as we sway to the beat of the music.

We dance this waltz, we dance the foxtrot, we dance to other things that I don't even know what they are. We dance until Sylvie eventually taps the microphone and asks for everyone's attention.

She's not wearing one of her trademark Christmas sweaters tonight. Instead, she's dressed in a silver sequined A-line, with red sequined shoes, and a red headband.

"Everyone, we all know who we have to thank for being here tonight." She pauses and stares pointedly at me. I flush. "When Meg first arrived, I think we all wondered, 'How in the heck is this young girl going to take over the Parkview, and make it flourish?'"

She glances at everyone and then shrugs.

"Okay, maybe it was just me."

Everyone, including me, laughs.

"I wasn't easy on her," Sylvie tells them. "I thought she was flighty, and that she didn't care. I thought she was self-serving, and only interested in what would benefit her."

"Geez, don't hold back, Sylvie," I grumble.

"But she quickly proved me wrong. She cares about every single one of you. She's worked tirelessly to find solutions to fix our home, and it is with great respect that I thank her this evening, and to inform you all that she's accomplished something truly great. She won first place at a *Vogue* fashion contest, as well as secured funding from the Chicago Historical Society. Our home is safe. Our home will become better than ever. Her father would be so proud. Ladies and gentlemen, Meg Julliard!"

She throws open her arms, and everyone bursts in applause.

I smile, and flush, and walk into Sylvie's embrace, where she hugs me tight.

"You're a good girl, Meg Julliard," she whispers into my ear. "Can you say a few words?"

I hadn't been expecting this, and so it takes me a minute to gather myself before I clear my throat.

"You guys, I never asked to inherit this building. Sylvie is right. When I first arrived here, I was out of my depth. I had no idea what needed to be done, or how to do it, and I was lost. If it weren't for Sylvie, and Logan, and Ellie, and so many of you, goodness only knows where we would be.

"But you all showed me the real meaning of community, and family. You pitched in, even when you didn't need to, and helped me work toward a better tomorrow for all of us. I couldn't have done any of it without you, and that's the truth."

I look at the room, at each shining face, and I've never felt so happy in my life.

"When I first came here, I thought I had to give up my aspirations. I never knew that life could be so much more than I even dreamed. Because of all of you, and your support, I will be able to live my dream, and so much more.

"I will be headquartering my new fashion line right here in this very building. We're also going to reopen the historic Red Alibi speakeasy and renovate the entire building in ways that will make you more comfortable and give you fun new ways to spend your leisure time, including restoring the rooftop gardens that were once known across the city. I want to give back to you the sense of community you've given me."

Everyone claps, and I smile.

"I guess what I'm trying to say is . . . thank you for giving me a home."

I step away from the microphone and am passed from person to person as I'm hugged and congratulated.

When I'm finally back to Logan, Cassie is with him, along with Drake.

I greet my ex warmly and thank him profusely for the use of the plane.

"You're most welcome," he tells me easily, one arm looped

over Cassie's shoulders. "What you've done here is amazing, Meg. I owe you an apology. You never needed my help. You had this all along."

"Thank you," I tell him sincerely. "You have no idea how much it means to me to hear you say that."

He smiles, and Cassie drags him away to the dance floor, leaving Logan and me alone.

"I'm so proud of you," he tells me, wrapping an arm around my waist. "You're everything, Meghan. I'm lucky to have met you."

"Yes, you are." I laugh and then quickly sober up. "I'm the lucky one."

"And you just keep getting luckier and luckier." He points upward.

Mistletoe.

Sylvie.

I notice her staring at me, and she gives me a big wink, right before Logan pulls me back into his arms and kisses me soundly.

Merry Christmas to me.

EPILOGUE

Three Years Later

Ellie

The Crystal Ballroom has never looked more lovely, draped in white flowered garlands, white candles, and white tulle. The wallpaper has been restored to its original glory, and the wood has all been refinished and polished to a sheen.

Frankie and I sit in chairs with white bows and flowers on the backs, as we wait for Betsy and her new husband to appear in the doorway, having been married one hour ago at the Holy Name Cathedral.

"Thank you for not making me call you Walt," I whisper to him, enjoying the way his cheek feels against my nose, as I duck in close to him.

"You can stop thanking me," he says, grinning. "It's been three years. You should know by now that as long as you stay Mrs. Lutz, you can do anything you like."

I smile and twist my wedding band around on my finger. I feel naked without it now, so I never take it off. It's the plain gold band he'd bought so many decades ago, fully intending to slide it on my finger at our wedding. After that fateful night, he'd carried it in his pocket all these years, as a reminder of our love.

When he'd finally slid it on my finger two years ago, it was already scratched, having been carried around with his keys and coins, but to me, that made it all the more beautiful. It showed his dedication to me, his never-ending hope.

"I love you," I tell him. "I'll never get tired of saying it."

"Me either," he admits.

"I think I'll go check and see where Bets is," I tell him. "I'll be right back."

I stand up and weave through the people sitting in chairs, sipping champagne and patiently waiting.

When I step into the lobby, Sylvie stands at the desk, directing traffic in an authoritarian way, and her assistant, Joel, stands to the side with his headset on.

"Remind me later to check on Mrs. Boles," she tells him, and he makes a note. "She's been under the weather and I want to send her a gift basket."

"Yes, ma'am," Joel tells her. I see him stealthily ordering the basket quickly on his phone, already knowing that Sylvie will forget. Joel has been good for her, allowing her to stay in charge, and he never makes her feel like she forgets anything. He does everything on the sly, without wanting anyone to know.

He's a good boy. I pat his shoulder as I approach. "Good afternoon," I greet them. "Has anyone seen my daughter yet?"

"She's still changing her clothes," Sylvie tells me. "She was such a beautiful bride, Ellie. You must be so proud."

I smile. "She focused on her career for so long that she has a good idea of who she is and what she wants. Jake will be the perfect husband for her. I just know it."

"I think you're right," Sylvie answers. "And he's not hard to look at, either."

She winks, and Joel flushes.

"Have you seen Meg?" I ask. Sylvie nods.

"She's downstairs. Didn't she do an amazing job on Betsy's gown? I've never seen anything so lovely!"

I have to agree. That wedding dress was stunning, and my daughter was a pure vision in it.

"She's got so much talent," I say.

"And she's got the business to prove it," Joel says. He wasn't around when Red Alibi Fashion had begun. He didn't see the endless nights Meg had spent designing and sewing and hunting for production companies and supply chains.

He sees the success that she is now, as the CEO of a successful fashion house.

Her designs have been featured far and wide this year, on supermodels, celebrities, and in millions of households across America.

Yet still, she's just "our Meg." She's humble and sweet, like she was from the beginning.

Although there's a little more to her now, since she's six months pregnant.

"I'm going to go pop my head in," I tell them. "See you at the reception."

Sylvie nods while she takes a call at the switchboard, and I punch the down button for the elevator.

The shiny brass doors open, and I step inside. It carries me smoothly and quickly to the basement. One of the first things Meg had done with the renovation budget was have the old elevator replaced, while still staying true to the look of the original one. This one looks like it was made in the twenties, but feels as safe and quick and the one that it is, one built only three years ago.

When I step into the basement, it's not the same as it used to be, but feels like it is.

The walls and halls are made from brick. If I choose to go to the left, I'll arrive at the Red Alibi Speakeasy and Museum, which is now a popular tourist attraction and hangout for the trendy, hip crowd of Chicago. Joe Riordan, from apartment 110, is the docent. He's a history buff and loves to entertain visitors with stories of our building. He always ends his tour by guiding the group out the hidden passageway, where they emerge into the alley down the street. He never tires of the looks on the visitors' faces and always credits his "ninja skills."

I don't go to the Red Alibi today, though.

Not the bar.

Instead, I go to the right, where I find the headquarters to Red Alibi Fashion. It used to be the only location, but as the business exploded, Meg had to buy a building downtown. She still works from this location at least half of the week, now that she's pregnant.

She hasn't slowed down much, but Logan insists on her taking it at least a *little* easy.

I find them both in her office, discussing this very thing.

"Meg, I want you to start taking the weekends off," he urges her. He's rubbing her swollen feet, and she's leaning back in her chair. Her belly is the size of a tiny beachball.

"Hey, kids," I say as I walk in. "I agree with Logan, Meg. You need to rest. When Josephine is born, you won't have time to blink, much less nap."

Meg screws up her face. "Don't gang up on me. You know I have a lot to do."

"You have an assistant," Logan reminds her. "And an entire staff. You can take time off."

"I know." She sighs. "I do." She looks at me. "Why are you down here? Shouldn't you be at the reception?"

"I was just coming to find you," I tell her. "You weren't there."

"I'm sorry," she says quickly, standing up and sliding her feet into fluffy slippers. "I'm coming right now, I swear."

I smile at her, and Logan rubs the small of her back as she walks.

When we're in the elevator, Meg leans against Logan, and he wraps an arm around her. They're just the sweetest couple I've ever seen, and it's been so wonderful to watch their relationship grow.

"Betsy's dress is so beautiful," I tell Meg once again. "I love how you took elements of your own wedding dress, but still made it something that is entirely Betsy. You're so skilled."

Meg blushes. "Thanks, Ellie. Betsy is so gorgeous; it wasn't hard to get inspired."

"Did you make her dress for the reception, also?" I ask her.

Meg shakes her head. "No. I offered, but she said she had something."

"I tried to talk her into using Winter as her ring bearer," Logan says. "But Betsy wouldn't hear of it. She thought he might be too contrary."

"How rude," Meg exclaims dramatically, knowing full well that her cat is the most charmingly spoiled cat in the world. "He would've looked so handsome in a little cat tuxedo."

"What time is it?" I ask, changing the subject. "Do either of you know? I don't want to miss them coming in."

Logan pulls out a pocket watch, the one Frankie had given Meg three years ago.

The one that is inscribed with *True Love Is Timeless.*

"It's two fifteen," Logan answers. "We'd better hurry."

When we get back to the ballroom, Betsy still hasn't appeared, and I sigh a little in relief. I need to be one of the faces she sees when she steps into the room.

"Welcome back," my husband says, as I sit back down. "I missed you."

I smile. "I missed you, too."

He tucks his arm around my back, and we sit together, listening to the small quartet play softly.

I know when my daughter appears by the hush that comes over the room. I turn in my seat, and Betsy's radiant smile is the first thing I notice as she lingers in the open doors on her new husband's arm. She looks so much like me, the same figure, the same hair, the same eyes.

Her eyes meet mine, and she smiles.

I love you, I mouth.

Then, however, I freeze. Because she's wearing *the dress*.

The Christmas dress that I'd worn that fateful night with Frankie, the one that I'd given to Meg. I'd know it anywhere.

My fingers curl around Frankie's arm.

"Is that my dress?" I ask him quickly.

He studies Betsy.

"It sure looks like it," he answers. "But it can't be. Didn't Meg give it away?"

"She donated it a couple years ago," I answer. "I know she did. She and I discussed how we shouldn't keep such a special thing to ourselves, how we needed to share it."

I lean forward and tap Meg on the arm.

"You donated the dress, right?"

She nods. "Yes."

"Then how is Betsy wearing it?" I ask. "Did you make her a replica?"

Meg's eyes are wide. "No, remember? I was going to make her a dress, but she said she already had one."

Meg and I get up and make our way to the bride.

She expects us to hug her again and opens her arms. I do hug her, but then I pull away and bend close to her, examining the forest green fabric of her dress.

"This is the dress," Meg confirms.

Betsy stares at both of us like we've lost our minds.

"Where did you get this dress?" I ask her.

"Some little shop in New York," she tells me. "It was actually the weekend I met Jake. Remember? We'd been chatting online for months, and since we both had to be in New York for business at the same time, we decided to meet for dinner in person. I found this dress earlier in the day, and I wore it on our first date. It seemed only appropriate to wear it to the reception today. Why?"

She looks worried now.

"Does it look bad?"

I'm astounded, and Meg is floored. We stare at each other, and then we both shake our heads.

"No," Meg finally answers. "It's beautiful. You're beautiful."

I run the fabric of her sleeve between my fingers, as though convincing myself that it's real.

But it is. There's no mistaking it.

My fingertips practically tingle as I touch it, with an energy that I can't explain. Meg's face echoes my own sense of wonder.

"What is wrong with you two?" Betsy asks in confusion, looking at both of us.

"I'll tell you the story another day," I promise. "Today, you have a party to attend."

Betsy practically glows, and I hug her. "Enjoy this," I tell her. "This is the start of your forever."

I kiss her cheek and release her. She mingles in the crowd, as Meg and I look at each other.

"There's no explaining that," she says. "Other than . . ."

"Magic," I tell her. "Isn't that what I told you when I first gave it to you? That it fits everyone like it's magic?"

"You and Frankie, Logan and me . . . Betsy and Jake . . ." Meg muses. "That dress brings love with it."

"In some cases, it just takes longer." I laugh, staring across the room at my handsome husband.

"Well, it can't work miracles," Meg answers. "You and Frankie . . . you had an interesting story."

"Maybe it does work miracles," I tell her. "Because we *did* have an interesting story. And here we are today, together, with you and Logan, living in this magnificent building where it all began. That seems like a miracle to me."

"Just getting Betsy to agree to you staying here was a miracle," Meg mutters.

I grin. "Not really. Not after you started doing all the work that you did. But even that, all that work, was made possible by the inspiration of *that one dress.*"

We both look at Betsy wearing it, at the way it molds to her figure, at the way she looks so happy in it.

"You're right," Meg decides. "That dress works miracles."

"I'll make sure to talk Betsy into donating it somewhere," I answer. "Magic like that shouldn't be kept to ourselves."

Meg nods. "I agree. And obviously, when we need that magic to return, it does."

We both watch Betsy dance with her new husband, as he leads her across the floor.

"I think I'll go dance with my own husband," Meg decides, getting to her feet and rubbing her belly.

"And I'll go dance with mine," I tell her. We walk toward our men, and I glance down at Meg's belly.

"How are you feeling, other than being tired?"

"I feel amazing," Meg answers. "Other than being tired, having swollen feet, and having to get up twelve times in the night to use the restroom."

"It'll be worth it," I assure her. "All of it."

"It had better be," she grumbles.

"And Logan hasn't once doubted that you're really pregnant?" I ask her, feigning innocence, as I remember his manipulative ex-fiancée and her fake pregnancy.

Meg's mouth drops open before she laughs.

"Too soon, Ellie. Toooooo soon."

I laugh with her. "It's been three years," I answer. "If we can't laugh about it now, when can we? It all worked out in the end."

"That it did," she agrees.

We stand in front of our husbands now, and they hold their hands out to us, both perfect gentlemen. As the band plays on, my handsome Frankie takes me in his arms and spins me in a circle. We laugh, and dance, and laugh and dance, in the exact spot where fifty years ago, on a fateful day, I'd lost an earring, but gained a very entertaining story.

"I love you," I tell my husband, holding him tight. "I wish we hadn't lost so many years together because of our pride."

"It doesn't matter, Ellie," he says, looking into my eyes. "True love is timeless."

That it is, my friends. That, it is.

We spend the rest of the evening dancing amid Christmas lights in the room that changed our lives in so many ways, in the building that will be our home for years to come.

"Merry Christmas, Ellie," Frankie tells me softly.

"Merry Christmas, Frankie."

He kisses my cheek as the band plays on, and we dance and dance and dance.

ACKNOWLEDGMENTS

Thank you to my grandparents, who showed me true love. My grandpa bought my gran's wedding ring overseas when he was in the war and carried it in his pocket until he returned home and could propose. He'd end up carrying it in his pocket again, for forty more years, after she had to have it cut off when she was pregnant with one of their three children.

Thank you to Maria Blalock for inspiring me with her Christmas shirts. You're quite a bit younger than Sylvie (decades) but your love for Christmas was a huge inspiration for her character.

Thank you to my agent, Kevan, for always believing in my storytelling. You've been such a source of comfort over the years, and knowing you are on my team is the best feeling ever.

Thank you to my editor, Tessa, for trusting me to bring your story to life. I've never told a story in this particular situation before, and I have to say, it was so, so fun.

Thank you to my family—as always—for putting up with me while I bury myself in other worlds. This year, as I finished up this story on Christmas Eve (How apropos is that??), you waited patiently for me so we could begin our festivities. You always wait patiently for me to type *The End*, and I will never be finished saying I'm thankful for it.

Thank you to my readers. I will never tire of saying that you are the best readers on the planet, because you are.

I hope all your Christmases, and all your days, in all your years, are merry, bright, and blessed!

ABOUT THE AUTHOR

COURTNEY COLE is a *New York Times* bestselling author who loves eating her emotions for breakfast. She also loves witty banter, cashmere socks, and walking along the beach at midnight.

Speaking of midnight, she decorates for Christmas at 12:01 A.M. on November 1.

She believes that blond hair dye and red lipstick can change your life, and a well-timed smile can change the world.

To learn more about her, visit courtneycolewrites.com.